Capucine

and

Her Three Feline Philosophers

Jim Yates

Édition d'Amélie

Published by
Édition d'Amélie
Dublin, Ireland

ISBN 978-0-9555836-3-6

Also by Jim Yates

Oh! Père Lachaise
2007
The Sadness of the Little Sparrow (Play)
2012
The Catching of the Camino Wind
2019

For Kay

Contents

Capucine is dead.
Her only survivors were her three feline friends:
Océane, Cheyenne and Tutalou –
This is their tale.

We Can Take or Leave You

Cats!

You can love or hate us. We don't mind. We are either adorable pets you love with passion and devotion or vermin you can't wait to dispose of. We can also be creatures you want to groom, indulge, and spoil or want to skin alive and wring our scrawny necks and hang us out to dry, and do so with pleasure. The truth is, there are never any half measures when it comes to how humans treat us felines. We don't care either way what humans think or feel about us. You may not believe this, but we can take or leave you. It is as simple as that. I know this might surprise some of you, especially those who think the world revolves around them and they are God's gift to the universe, but you are not the centre of *our* universe – far from it. We do our own thing. Unlike most humans, we are always happy in our skins – we do not suffer hang-ups about whom or what we are and take life as it comes. So long as you feed, water and indulge us, we will be loyal to you. However, if you fall down on these vital feline necessities, we will be off in an instant to find someone who will and believe me there is a never-ending supply. As most women adore us, we will never be left in want of home or sustenance. One such woman was the lovely Capucine, who unlike most humans understood the feline mind. She was in tune with us and knew the rhythms of our being and the beating of our hearts.

We felines have a lifelong romance with ourselves, which gives us a feeling of superiority and invincibility. To be honest, there are no creatures quite like us. Try as you may, you won't find any other species remotely like us because, believe it or not, we are unique amongst all the creatures of the world.

If you don't like cats, then this tale is certainly not for you. If you do, then read on and hopefully enjoy our adventures with the lovely Capucine while reflecting on her life and the illness that drove, controlled, and finally consumed her, leaving us, her devoted pets, heartbroken and in need of tender loving care.

The Cries of Lausanne

The city of Lausanne was in shock. Could it be true? Had it really happened as many predicted, as she herself had? Was this really the demise of Lausanne's favourite adopted daughter, their fragile and vulnerable flower? After all the near misses, the threats and traumas, after all the cries for help, was this the last act of a life in turmoil, a life of pain and suffering – the end of the lovely Capucine, the beauty of Lausanne?

The news was grim. It was a violent death – a public one – an unnecessary one. It did not take long for the sad and distressing news to spread across the city, into every home, café, and place of work. There was a collective and regretful sigh as they heard the news – many would say the inevitable news. Many tears were shed for this most beautiful and tortured of souls, shed, not only for her demise or the horrific nature of her going but also for her unbearable suffering.

Those who witnessed her fall heard her cry, 'Mamma, Mamma', as she crashed to the ground from her eighth story penthouse apartment. They ran to her aid but nothing, nothing could save her. Fate had cast its die, and nothing could or would alter that. One young woman froze at the sight of the broken body at her feet. An elderly man bent down beside the victim. Gently taking her limp wrist, he felt for any vital signs of life. There was none. He stroked her face and uttered a prayer. A woman carrying her groceries stood dazed at the sight before her. The scene below shocked neighbours, drawn to their balconies by the cries. A dog nearby howled as he scented despair in the air.

On this clear March day, darkness descended, as another soul departed this world – taken before its time into the arms of the gods. A large crowd had gathered, standing around in silence, the silence finally broken by sobs and whispered prayers. The elderly man placed his rosary beads in the victim's hand as a teenage girl put her arm around the shoulder of a hysterical woman and gently directed her away from the scene. A young man stood rigid to the spot; his eyes fixed on the horror before him. He began to cry as the enormity of what confronted him began to register.

Once it became clear whom the victim was many began to cry, others stood numb with shock and disbelief. A priest made his way through the crowd and kneeling administered the last rites, followed by a decade of the rosary, with many of the crowd joining in.

Soon the medics arrived along with the police. They knew in an instant their services were not needed. All they could do was look after her dignity. One rearranged her clothing to protect her modesty and the other covered her face. They heard cries from above and looking up to the eighth floor from where the victim had fallen, noticed three sets of cat's paws dangling from the balcony, their heads protruding through the rails. Their agonizing cries and that of the dog added to the distress of the crowd as they tried to comprehend the gravity of what had happened. The crowd slowly departed with heads bowed and heavy hearts, leaving the police to carry out the formalities.

On this most beautiful of spring days, Lausanne was a city in tears.

The Sorrow of Love

In the end, humans always lose the ones they love. Try as they may it is a fate they cannot avoid. They must live with its aftermath and learn survival without the ones they love. It is hard. It is cruel; it is the way of life. They survive in their own particular way – there is no rulebook for coping with loss, pain, heartache or the loneliness and the depression it brings. If the loss is expected, because of illness or age, they can somehow, although difficult and traumatic, handle this, but when unexpected loss trespasses on their lives, well, that is a different scenario altogether. They are crushed and unstable with their world torn apart. Life has no reason or meaning. Many are inconsolable. Some lock themselves away in their despair trying to hide from the horrible reality of their loss. Some cry oceans of tears in their agony until the ducts of despair run dry. Some withdraw into themselves, become isolated from family and friends, and wither away. Others drown themselves in sorrow at the bottom of a glass, while others waste away from neglect and follow their loved ones to the hereafter. Yes, this is the reality of loss, of excruciating pain and depression – the hard reality of the human condition.

What of us felines, do we suffer the loss of loved ones as humans do? Do we feel the pain of bereavement or experience love with all its highs and lows? Do we suffer broken hearts and more still, the agonies of unrequited love? Do we experience all this? You may be surprised, but yes, we do and more, as this surreal tale will tell. We loved, lost, and suf-

6

fered broken hearts in the process, hearts that have yet to mend from our devastating loss.

**

Here is a tale of three philosophising felines, Océane, that's me, and my pals Cheyenne and Tutalou, an eclectic lot with a common cause, that cause being the care and protection of the beauty of Lausanne. We were the devoted companions of Capucine, a French model, and actress, an icon of her age, with stunning looks, poise, and class, who we dearly loved. We lived with her in the penthouse of an exclusive apartment block in that fashionable Swiss city of Lausanne that sits on the banks of Lake Geneva.

She had lived there for most of her adult life and adored the city. Everything about Lausanne appealed to her, its panoramic view of Lake Geneva, Mont Blanc, the Alps beyond, its parks, shops, restaurants, its general setting, and way of life. Capucine and Lausanne –their names roll off the tongue as though they were always destined to be together and made for each other.

She was, without doubt, a stunning woman – five foot seven of elegance, style and sophistication, a Patrician beauty who oozed sensuality and beautiful beyond belief with high cheekbones, swanlike neck and a sharp nose that gave her a classical Nefertiti look. Her oval hazel eyes were so mesmerising one could drown in them, as every male who had the privilege of meeting her could swear to. Her lips, like the rest of her, were too inviting to ignore. Her skin, unblemished, like the most delicate of fine porcelain, set off by her luscious eye-

7

lashes and shimmering auburn hair. She was blessed with a sharp intellect too, a pulsating sense of humour and tranquil nature. Overall, she was the perfect specimen of womanhood, and we three creatures were the lucky kind to have lived with and been loved by her. However, there was a more stunning beauty about her, far greater than her visual persona, an inner one that was the essence of her being – a beauty to live on beyond memory, even beyond the realms of time.

Her real name was Germaine Lefebvre, born and bred in Toulon, France, to middle-class parents who wanted for nothing. You could say she enjoyed a life of privilege. The style, grace, and poise she was to be so well- known for was there as a child – an inbred strain, gifted to her by the gods. Those who knew her realised she was no ordinary child, but one made from a different mould altogether, one to stand out from the crowd, always to be noticed, always on the lips of those she met. Nature blessed her with such exquisite beauty that the Divine Sculptor must have chiselled it out of the marble of Paradise, polished and tweaked it to perfection.

At the tender age of seventeen, she set out on a path that would introduce her to the world, which would mark her out as one of the iconic beauties of her generation. In the late fifties, she caught the eye of a Parisian photographer and soon signed up as a model with the famous fashion houses of Paris: Givenchy, and Christian Dior. Within a short time, became their premier model – a photographer's dream and fashion designer's delight. Being very much a non-conformist, she would always do things her way. Therefore, when she joined the fashion houses, she adopted the name Capucine, after her favourite flower, nasturtium. Wanting to be different, she

8

thought a single name would give her an air of mystery, not realising just how mysterious she would turn out to be.

She was well educated too and a linguist and would use these attributes to her credit as a young model as she reached the dizzy heights of fame, savouring every moment of her success. She enjoyed the glamour of it all, the glitz, buzz, and razzmatazz that surrounded the fashion world and the benefits it brought. In Paris, she was the one that men wanted to be seen with. Any man worth his salt would want her on his arm, to parade himself about the City of Light, showing off his prize and what a prize it was. As well as possessing talent as a model, she achieved fame and success in her profession as an actress. This brought her financial security and many friends, amongst them, unfortunately, the fair-weather kind. However, she was blessed with many good friends and three who were to be the anchors in her life. It was in Paris she met one of these, another natural beauty, probably the most iconic of them all – Audrey Hepburn, who was to be her best friend and confidante and, on several occasions, lifesaver. They became, not just good friends but soul mates, not only sharing apartments but on occasions, lovers, a kind of pass the parcel game you could say. Yes, they were kindred spirits, always destined, whatever fate had in store, to remain friends forever.

Capucine's penthouse apartment was something to see; to experience and savour and we three felines did just that. She decorated it to the highest standard of elegance. It was a delicate mix of the old and new, magnificent antiques along with modern sculptures, paintings, and porcelain. When it came to the arts, she certainly had a sharp and discerning

9

eye. She owned a piece of delicate Meissen porcelain and in-herited two priceless pieces of furniture from her parents, a Louis XVI writing desk along with a 16th-century Jacobean oak table. The desk was eye-catching in its look and artisan-ship and on its highly polished top was her beloved tortoise-shell pen, considered a rare piece that she often used for pri-vate correspondence or signing photographs for her adoring fans in her distinctive handwriting. On special occasions, this well-crafted oak table was used to wine and dine her friends and for her Christmas celebrations. On it, she always dis-played fresh flowers in a Waterford crystal vase, a gift from Peter O'Toole, the Irish actor she starred with, in the 1960's movie *What's New Pussycat*. Her rugs were something to see and we had the privilege and pleasure of stretching out on them. The one in front of the fire, which was our favourite resting place, she purchased from an auction house in Berne. This was a Persian one of autumn colours, rich in texture and magnificent in its artisan finish. The circular one at the en-trance door she acquired in the United States when filming on location. This was of a thick pile and designed in different shades of blue with a bright red dot on one of its corners. Her eye for fine art was second-to-none. Many of the paintings that hung on her pale peach walls were ones she picked up at galleries around the world of up-and-coming artists. Every-thing about the apartment was the best of all possible taste and style. When it came to the finer things of life Capucine was out on her own. Yes, a class act in every possible way.

However, her beauty came at a high price. Mother Nature didn't only bless her with exquisite beauty and talent but also cursed her with a lifelong burden – bipolar, that insidious manipulator of the mind and destroyer of the soul. She suffered a life of torment, pain, and psychological trauma because of it and in the end paid dearly for this injustice in her life. Audrey was able to help her through many of her bad times, those desperate, painful episodes when she would stand on her balcony rail screaming out to her mother – to God, for deliverance from the excruciating mental pain that was tearing her apart and then threaten to jump, to end it all, to end forever her mental torture. Audrey understood all of Capucine's moods and erratic behaviour and though she was an extremely busy actress and duties as a UNICEF ambassador, always found time to sit and talk her friend through her anxieties and depression and help ease her unbearable inner pain. Our lovely Capucine was a sufferer – a sufferer of the worse kind and I, Cheyenne and Tutalou were her carers, the soothers of her nerves, the guardians of her heart and the protectors of her soul.

This is our tale of love, laughter, and devotion to a very precious soul.

Strangers in the Apartment

Three wailing cats confronted inspector Lewee as he entered the apartment. His colleagues followed him to assess the incident scene. This was a difficult and emotional moment for the Inspector. He had known Capucine for eight years, had discussed her condition on several occasions, and was a source of good advice and reassurance to her. Their first meeting was after she was seen sitting on her balcony by a neighbour who became concerned by her behaviour and called the police. Lewee was the senior inspector sent around and managed to calm her down and coax her from the edge after a good heart-to-heart. Over the years, they would meet, and a gentle friendship emerged.

The Inspector was looking for one thing only, a letter or note, convinced Capucine would have written one, trying to give a reason why she ended her life. In these circumstances, there is usually a note or letter of some kind. However, if it were suicide, he didn't need proof of a letter to know the reason as he already knew, just as many of her friends and family did – that she'd had enough of life, that her mental torment had become insufferable, and life no longer had meaning, and she wanted out. It was a simple as that. He found no note. He checked the message box of her phone but there was nothing apart from a message from her housekeeper saying she would be late arriving. A note would be of value to the coroner to help understand her state of mind, to understand what led up to the tragedy. He was also aware there is always more than one factor that makes people take their own life. Nothing, in his experience, is simple when it comes to suicide. Could it have been an accident, after all, the inspector thought. Perhaps she had fallen whilst doing some chore or other. Knowing her as he did, he was as near as certain that was not so. He knew Capucine well enough and the nature of her condition and the reality of the situation. She ended her own life, as she had often threatened to do, and did so in a violent and horrifying way.

On another occasion, he visited her apartment for what looked like attempted suicide, this time by an overdose of barbiturates and alcohol. She swore it was unintentional but by the state of her, he was not convinced. On this occasion too, there was no note, so he gave her the benefit of the doubt, that it was indeed an accidental overdose.

He was visibly upset as he stood on the balcony. He examined the scene and felt himself retch as he imagined her last moments, imagined what was going through her mind as she leapt from the balcony. Did she have second thoughts as she plummeted to the ground? Did she cry for help? Did she cry out to him? He bit his lip, trying to keep back the tears, trying to keep his composure.

He had attended many incident scenes; however difficult they were he dealt with them professionally and in a dispassionate way. It was part of the job. This one, however, was different, as he personally knew the victim. Bending down he tenderly stroked Océane's neck, then softly patted the heads of Cheyenne and Tutalou as they sat between Capucine's wicker chair and the large terracotta pots of lavender that stood on either side of the French doors.

'Kenneth,' he called to one of his colleagues. 'Get some water or milk for these creatures. They are parched.'

The officer returned and the cats thirstily sipped at the milk as Inspector Lewee looked out over the balcony towards the lake and the mountains beyond, his mind full of memories of Capucine and the last time they met. It was at cafe Hemes in Lausanne where they chatted about a forthcoming flower show, and about his exhibit, he had submitted. He wiped away a tear then looked down at her devoted cats.

'They are distressed. They will need to be looked after, Inspector. Will I call the animal compound?'

'No, no! Ask around the neighbours gathered out there on the landing and see what can be done. They will be better off here in their familiar surroundings. The shelter will be the last resort. I'm sure a home will be found for them.'

Inspector Lewee again stroked Cheyenne, who was hyperventilating, then, in turn, Tutalou and Océane. He knew Capucine adored the cats as he had often talked to her about them. He always had a soft spot for Cheyenne, probably because her eyes shone every time he walked into the apartment. She had that effect on certain kind of men and the inspector was one of them, but this time her eyes were blank and despondent.

'This is her neighbour, Mademoiselle, Lucie Plessis. She already has a set of keys. She will feed them until things are sorted out.'

The Inspector gave her a reassuring hug as she sobbed into her handkerchief. 'That is kind of you to help.'

'This is terrible. Why, oh why did she do it? Why? Why? The last time we met, she looked so cheerful and relaxed. We talked about the Milan Fashion Week and the Spring Collection that I had recently returned from, and she was thrilled I was one of the leading models at the show. I suspected nothing, nothing at all. I was aware she had a problem but never thought it would come to this. I feel so guilty; I never noticed she needed help.'

He gave a look of resignation and hugged her again.

'I've looked after them before. I will take care of them now. They know me, so they will be OK. What will happen to them?'

'I don't know. It will be up to the family or the executives of her estate to decide. I will keep you informed.'

'Thank you.' She bent down and stroked each of them as they sipped at the milk then looked at the balcony and once more was in a flood of tears.

His assistant who was examining Capucine's bedroom called the Inspector.

'Excuse me, mademoiselle,' he said as he handed her his card. 'Don't hesitate to call me if you need any help.'

'Thank you,' she said in a low voice as she stroked Cheyenne.'

'There is medication here', the officer informed the inspector as he entered the bedroom. 'Only a few pills left. Do you think she was overdosed when she jumped?'

'I wouldn't say so. If she were, she would have swallowed the lot. Get them down to the lab and check out the doctor who prescribed them. The post-mortem will make matters clearer. My opinion, sergeant, it is sadly a clear case of suicide.'

Bad News from Gossip Camille

It was the fourth day since Capucine's departure and a horrific time it had been. We had cried oceans of tears. For the first three days, we were in a stupor not knowing what to do, think or say. We always knew this day would come but prayed it never would. This was always going to be Capucine's way to die, in this horrible manner without any semblance of dignity, even so, the shock of her departure was devastating and overwhelming. We had lived under the threat she would finally carry it out, but the manner of her end was so different to who and what she really was. She was in essence, a very private and in many ways reserved person, so to end her life in this public way was so different from her true nature.

Her illness had eaten away and worn her out to such an extent she was no longer able to carry the burden of her condition, and finally wanted out of life, wanted peace, a permanent solution to the agony of her mental pain.

We were trying to come to terms with her loss and the new reality of our lives – life without the one we love. Slowly there was an acceptance she would never return – a realization that our lives would never be the same again – that the wheels of fortune had turned against us, and our fate left in the hands of others, perhaps the hands of uncaring strangers. Since that horrible day, we had spent our time not just crying but also fretting and agonizing over whether we had done enough to save her. We were always vigilant in our care but felt we had let her down and were finding it difficult to imagine our lives without her, without her humour, laughter, and her caring and loving nature.

We curled up in front of the hearth and talked about Capucine and her life and how she would have wanted everyone she knew to remember her, not by the manner of her going, but how she lived and embraced life. We agreed we should celebrate her life as she had wished and not be morbid about her passing, so, as we rested in front of the hearth, we regained our humour by recalling those happy times and laughed aloud at many of her antics and her quirky philosophy of life. We were uncertain as to our fate but wasted no time in laughing about it and better still, at those unfortunate sufferers of the human condition.

So, there we were in deep contemplation about Capucine and the mysteries of life. We were good at this philosophising lark – I would say very adept at it – our most popular pastime, next to snoozing, eating, and lazing about the place. We would forever discuss and philosophise about life and the peculiarities and perplexities of the human condition, which was a never-ending source of amazement and amusement to us. You would never believe the mileage we got out of it and the hours of pleasure enjoyed, laughing at the antics and behaviour of humans.

'What will become of us, now that the lovely Capucine is gone,' Tutalou lamented, rubbing her eyes with her paw.

'What indeed?' Cheyenne replied as she stretched her sinews and gave a satisfying yawn.

'How much longer will we be left here, not knowing what will become of us,' asked Tutalou? 'The tension is killing me. It's four days now since we lost her. I miss her so much. I

17

miss her presence, her kiss, her touch, her loving embrace but most of all her smile.'

I was to be the bearer of bad news for my two friends. I received the missive the previous day and was reluctant to divulge it, but I had to, and this seemed the most opportune moment to do so. What I had to say would without doubt cause anxiety and traumatise them more than they already were. Whether what I had to reveal had any substance or truth to it, I did not know but I could no longer keep it from them. They had the right to know. I took in a good intake of breath and blurted it out, 'Camille, our Persian neighbour says we will be destroyed because now Capucine is gone there is no one to care for us – nobody wants us.'

They sprang to their feet, their fur raised, astounded by my unexpected revelation. 'DESTROYED!' they cried in harmony.

'Whatever do you mean, DESTROYED! – You mean – to DIE! That we will be KILLED! Is that what you're saying?' Cheyenne cried, her eyes wide in terror, her whiskers beginning to tremble with fear.

'This can't be so! To kill us – it would be *murder.*'

'Yes, Tutalou, if it's true, it will be murder, there is no other word for it. Camille says we will be taken from our cosy home to someplace, and there injected with a fluid that will put us to sleep forever. It would be a quick and painless death, she says, then our bodies incinerated, and our ashes cast to the wind.'

'*Cast to the wind!*' They both squealed.

'*Cast to the wind!*' Cheyenne repeated, gasping for air as she said it.

'Yes!' I replied. 'That will be the end of us. It will be as though we never existed. Camille was very definite about it. She also said Capucine's ashes are to be cast to the wind and we will follow her in due course. That is the way it will be. That is life – life is cruel, she says.'

Tutalou and Cheyenne looked forlornly at each other. They didn't know whether to laugh or cry. They either thought I was deadly serious or lost my mind completely and indulging in some kind of black humour. Tutalou sank to the floor as though her breath had departed her body, and Cheyenne closed her eyes and sighed deeply. They digested the bleak news in deadly silence, stunned and unable to utter a word.

'But... why?' Cheyenne quietly asked, breaking the silence, her eyes misting over. 'What have we done to deserve such a fate? All we have ever shown is love and affection to our Capucine, our lovely, tortured friend, to help her through her illness – her pain, through the traumas and episodes of her horrible affliction. We soothed her suffering, didn't we, with our love and tender care? We were her carers, her friends – like the children she so much wanted but unable to have. Are we really going to die for showing love and tenderness to a wounded soul? Is that how humans reward love, the love they say is the essence of humanity – by an act of violence?'

'Well, it seems so. Camille was quite adamant about it. As you know, she is not one for exaggeration. When she says something, something serious she is usually right. She says nobody will want us, as we are too old, to set in our ways to adapt to new surroundings – too old for anything. Who would want three old ones like us, she says.'

Cheyenne and Tutalou swallowed hard. This got Cheyenne back on her feet and out of her stupor.'

'*Old ones!*' she cried. 'She's not serious! Could we really be killed – murdered, dispatched like rubbish, *cast to the wind*, just because someone thinks we are *old*? Capucine would not have liked that. She would be horrified if they destroyed us for any reason, never mind for being *old*. She adored and loved us. I can't believe this is happening. Camille must be wrong, she must be, and she's just stirring things up as she always does. That's what she's like, nothing but a malicious stirrer. I'd guarantee she'll be getting immense pleasure and mileage out of our predicament. Must we listen to her? Most of what she utters has no truth to it at all, as this probably doesn't. She's the worst kind of feline – the gossiping kind.'

'Well, I'm not *old*,' Tutalou announced, taking umbrage at Camille's effrontery. 'I am in the prime of my life, I would let you know. My blood pulsates through my veins like a young one. I have a few years behind me, I will grant you that, but I am far from *old*. I can match any young one. Old is when one can't get around, can't function, when you don't know the time of day – when you no longer see the beauty of life about you. We are far from that. We are alive, active, mentally alert, and far from *old*. Who does this *Camille* think she is? She's a right little madame.'

'I'm far from old, too,' cried Cheyenne as she ceased walking around in circles. 'I'm also in the prime of *my* life. I'm fit too and can give any cat half my age a run for their money. I wouldn't believe a word Camille utters… anyway, she's just an agitator; we know that so why are we worrying – why are we letting her get under our skins? She's been at it for years, so her latest declaration is just another of her ramblings – she's like her owner, full of hot air and nothing more... a gossip of the worst kind. I never trusted her and always thought her *odd*, so not surprised by her nasty utterances and insinuations. I'm sure it's just more of her malicious gossip designed to put us on edge, of which she is succeeding.'

The three of us never had a good relationship with Camille. We did try to be friendly but never warmed to her in any way and she certainly didn't take to us. She had an inferiority complex, carried about unresolved issues, and took out her frustrations on others with her nasty and acidic tongue. I always thought she was jealous of us, jealous of our relationship with Capucine. Camille, unlike us, was unkempt and neglected by her owner and perhaps that was the source of her dislike of us as we were always well-groomed, fed and loved, something I'd say she had never experienced – must be nothing worse than going through life without love. There was always resentment in her nature, so we had to be cautious about her utterances and her implied threats but on this occasion, she seemed so well informed about our fate and took sadistic pleasure in dishing out the bad news. Gossip Camille was no friend of ours.

'If Camille is right, then we must do something about it; we can't just sit around and do nothing. We must save ourselves. This calls for action! I for one do not intend being exterminated – exterminated – We will see! We are made of sterner stuff. No one will get rid of us without us putting up a good fight! Come now, let's stick together and get out of the jam we're in – Are you with me?'

We both nodded our agreement.

Tutalou was back to her normal plucky self. If there was ever any chance of us getting out of this, then she was the one who would fight harder than Cheyenne or me. We were no slouches when it came to standing our ground, but Tutalou was in a league of her own. If she suffered from the human condition, she would have been one of those students demonstrating with placards for any and every cause and up for anything and everything and causing havoc in the process – a natural rebel – a feline one with a lot of spunk.

'How long have you known about this?' Cheyenne asked.

'Only since yesterday morning – I was reluctant to tell you as I was uncertain as to its truthfulness. As it came from Camille, I had to be sure, so after digesting it I thought there might be some truth to it so decided to tell you about it – best to take it as true and see what we can do about it. We've sure as hell been left to our own devices. Apart from Lucie next door feeding and watering us, it seems we've been all but forgotten.'

'But what can be done?' asked Cheyenne, still shaking from the revelation.

'Perhaps we could escape,' I suggested, trying to be practical. 'I'd rather take my chances on the streets than wait for an exterminator with a syringe to come and do me in.'

'But how... how can we escape? It is not as easy as you might think,' Cheyenne frowned. 'There's no way down from the balcony. It is far too high to jump. Anyway, I'm nervous of heights at the best of times. The only other place we can get to, is the roof, which is another dead end.'

'We could wait until someone opens the apartment door – then make a dash for it,' suggested Tutalou. 'We are still young enough to move fast if we have to, fast enough to escape if the opportunity arises.'

'That's unlikely. Even Capucine wouldn't let us out any further than the landing on our own apart from when she'd take us for walkies. It looks like there is no easy way out. We are doomed,' cried Cheyenne in a shrill voice. She was highly strung, was our Cheyenne. Everything to her was a disaster waiting to happen. She was the worst kind to have in an emergency – the panicking kind.

'Calm down, will you. We will not get anywhere if we get hysterical about it. We need cool heads if we are to get anywhere. There is always a lot of coming and going on the landing, so I suggest we wait until someone opens the door – then make our escape – make a bolt for it. It's worth a try.'

'Fat chance of it, Océane – the doors are never left open... they're electronic. The only time they are open is for maintenance, when there is an emergency or an electrical fault. Even if we could find a way out, where would we go? What would we do?' Cheyenne cried. 'We may not be old but we're not young ones either. How would we survive out there in that big bad world? Who would care for us? Who would feed us? Where would we sleep? I am too refined a cat to sleep rough. I'm a delicate creature. I need the comfort of Capucine's boudoir, not some drafty alleyway, and what about my nails, my beautiful nails – who would manicure them? Who would groom me like Capucine did?'

Tutalou's fur was on end at the remark. 'This is no time for vanity, to worry about manicures and cosy boudoirs. You and

23

your vanity and self-indulgence – will you ever give it a rest. We must put our minds to survival otherwise we are finished – do you not understand – finished! We are feline after all, so putting our minds to survival shouldn't be *too* much a burden as it's an integral part of our nature. We will have to make a run for it; after all, we don't have too many options, do we? A drafty alleyway is preferable to the alternative. I'll give anything a try at the moment, anything, including sleeping rough and forgoing manicures.'

'I won't survive on the streets. I know I won't, I'm just not that kind of cat.'

'God, Cheyenne – don't be so dramatic! We have no option but to get out of here as soon as we can, so focus your mind on survival and nothing else. Stop whining and sit down and stop walking around in circles – you're driving us nuts.'

'We won't survive,' Cheyenne insisted, her whiskers trembling. 'I know we won't! I'm scared! I'm scared!'

'Calm down, will you. Yes, we will if we stick together and keep focused. You need a good dose of optimism, Cheyenne,' Tutalou suggested.

'Optimism,' I sighed. 'I'm afraid it's in short supply. It died with Capucine, but I do agree, we must try something – anything. How about the balcony – We could get out our normal way through the cat flap and make our way up onto the roof, then down between the flashing and along to the rest of the apartments. We can climb down a few floors that way but not to the first three because of the barrier. We could watch and see if any of the apartment doors are open and find our escape there. It might be worth a try.'

'Good idea,' Tutalou agreed. 'We should do a wander about the place – do a reconnaissance as they say. The apartment at the far end of floor three might be an ideal escape route as it has stairs on the balcony leading down to the second floor. If we can get in through the small window by the door that is often open, we could climb in and hide and once the French doors are open, we can skedaddle. The oak tree leans over towards the balcony, so we can jump onto it then climb down to safety. It's a bit of a long shot, I know. I'll check it out and report back.'

Therefore, as matters stood, escape was our only option. This at least was agreed. Tutalou wasted no time and dashed out the cat flap onto the balcony, along the flashing and down the chute on route to floor three to carry out her reconnaissance. Problem was, if we did escape, where would we stay and how would we survive – like finding food and a safe place to live. We may be cats but had never caught a mouse in our lives and as for getting around to doing it, we were clueless – would not know where to start. It's supposed to be instinctive, this survival lark, so we'd find out sooner or later whether we're real cats, able to catch our own prey or just nothing more than domesticated cats, a sad facsimile of our ancient lineage. Cheyenne would probably run a mile from the sight of a mouse, never mind catching one and Tutalou, although a tough one when she wanted to be would also have no notion on how to stalk a prey, never mind getting around to actually killing it. Behind her strong exterior lurked her squeamish side. As for me, I would probably want to make friends with a mouse rather than chasing, killing and having it for dinner. I'm a feline pacifist who has no desire to kill anything, especially a wee mouse.

These were the questions going around in our minds as we again settled down on the Turkish rug to try to work out an escape strategy. This survival lark was new to us. Survival or any worry about our welfare was never of any concern to us as Capucine always took care of it.

Tutalou returned from her reconnaissance. She was down in the mouth and very sullen with her tail between her legs.

'What's wrong?' I asked.

'It's no good, it's no good! Escape is impossible as the apartment on floor three is empty with not a stick of furniture in it and the window firmly shut. Suzanne, the stray was sitting outside the door and said the tenants vacated it three weeks ago. That escape route is out. We will have to find another way.'

My heart sank at the news and Cheyenne became tearful. We lay down again feeling deflated and out of sorts.

'Surely Suzanne must know how to get out. She is a stray after all and knows every nook and cranny of the place,' I reminded Tutalou.

'I've already talked to her about it. She says she hasn't been out of the complex for a few weeks and residents on the top floors are feeding her. A few invite her in to eat and if their front door is open, she wanders off again on her adventures. That's how she gets out and about and every now and then she manages to make her way down the floors and out onto the street.'

'Maybe we should give it a try.'

'Don't be silly, Cheyenne. It's hard enough for Suzanne to do it. Can you imagine the mess we would make of it – the three of us, not being noticed trying to get into an apartment? As she says, she never knows where she will end up so can you imagine where we would.'

There was silence once more, as we tried to collect our thoughts.

'If escape is not possible, perhaps one of the neighbours will take us in,' suggested Cheyenne, breaking the uncomfortable silence. 'There's Lucie next door – she's as cute as they come and has been feeding us since Capucine left and we sort of know her – She's a kind soul with an intoxicating smile and would look after us well. She has kindness radiating from her.'

'Don't be ridiculous!' I snapped. 'She doesn't even like cats. We give her the creeps! She is only feeding us as a kindness and respect for Capucine. You can tell by her demeanour that she is nervous being around us. She's usually in here in a flash, gives us our meals, cleans out our litter boxes, says a few hellos, nervously smiles, waters the potted plants, then she's off as quickly as she came and never stops scratching whenever she's near us. She's so bad she even makes me itch. Only yesterday, as she fed us, I'm sure I saw her twitch as well. Even when she is holding the watering can, her hand is trembling. Give her another few weeks coming in here and she'll be a wreck. She was always like that on the odd occasions she looked after us in the past.'

'You're exaggerating. I find her OK. She was the first to volunteer to look after us, had no hesitation in doing so, and always gives us a pat before she leaves. If she didn't like us,

27

she would never have offered to feed us never mind touch us and don't forget she sat with us most of the night Capucine died. That makes her special. I know she is a little nervous of us but given time, I'm sure she'll warm to us as everyone does. We are felines after all and irresistible to most women so give her a little breathing space and she'll soon succumb to our charms. Just wait and we will have her hooked. She looks good too and is the most elegant woman around the place. Well, the best now Capucine is gone.'

'You're dreaming again, Cheyenne,' I replied. 'Once humans are nervous of cats there's no hope for them and want nothing to do with us – It's only a certain kind of human... the good and wise ones who take to us. Yes, they are mostly women. We unnerve men. They know we felines have them sussed out; that we have their number and subsequently keep their distance. Men are stupid in general as we know but wise when it comes to us felines. It's always a *wise* man who knows his limitations, not only with women but also with the feline.'

'How about Madame Lumiére, then – we could be good company in her old age. She has a kind face, and we could add a little spice to her dotage,' Cheyenne suggested. 'She has no family to talk of. Maybe she'll take a shine to us, spoil us and tend to our fancy whims and give us a manicure, a good grooming and even rub our tummies – may even whisper sweet nothings in your ear, Tutalou. Yes, I fancy her.'

Tutalou gasped. 'You're not serious – Madame Lumiére whispering sweet nothings in my ear! How could you even suggest such a thing? How could you think her suitable to care for us, that we could ever let her near us? She is a woman of little patience at the best of times, one of little compassion and as cold as they come – we'd freeze at her touch. I wouldn't let her near me. Can you imagine her giving our nails a manicure? Uh! The thought of it makes me queasy. She is so heavy-handed she'd kill us in the process. What we need is someone with a softer centre; you know the kind, someone with the tender touch, someone who understands our delicate nature and the rhythm and beat of our souls, just as Capucine did. Don't forget, Madame Lumiére also had no understanding of Capucine's illness or suffering and never could, as she was incapable of showing any kind of compassion. Surely, you haven't forgotten the time when we tried to get her to help Capucine when she was going through one of her blackest episodes after she collapsed in the foyer, and we cried out for help. She reluctantly came but when she saw Capucine in a convulsive state on the floor, she rang the ambulance then turned her back on her. She didn't show any compassion towards her – none whatsoever – didn't even hold her hand or ease her through her torment or give words of comfort until help arrived. I don't think she knows what compassion is. No, no, she just left her there until the medics arrived and never asked afterwards how she was – that's the measure of *that* woman. She hasn't a caring bone in her body, and you think we should go and live with her and be exposed to her cold nature – let her loose on us, on *our* nails – are you mad altogether?'

'Oh, I wasn't thinking,' replied Cheyenne, rather ashamed she had forgotten Madame Lumiére's indifference to Capucine.

Madame Lumiére always passed some harsh words about Capucine's choice of lovers, her lifestyle, even her dress sense, which was hilarious seeing Madame Lumiére was always unkempt and had no dress sense whatsoever. She was never out of that bottle green rag of a dress of hers and had the dirty habit of a permanent cigarette dangling from her thin purple lips. Her hair resembled a nest, and as for her perfume, it was the cheapest in town and what a whiff. She was very judgmental too – another unsavoury element inherent in the human condition we observed and worse still, she had it in abundance – had a real bad dose of it. Whenever Capucine arrived with her latest beau, especially if he were much younger than she was, she'd always pass a smutty remark to a neighbour about her and her gigolos, as she called them. She had a vicious tongue, didn't she just, this Madame Lumiére – always thought the worst of Capucine – never dawned on her, perhaps the men were just friends or acquaintances and not lovers at all, even if they were it was no business of hers. She was a nosey old crow – made an art form of nosiness. No, not her, we could never have had her near us – she had a one-track mind – It was sex and nothing more she thought of when it came to Capucine. In essence, she was a nasty piece of work, as nasty as Camille was. Worse still, she even envied Capucine her beauty. Any woman who envies another her beauty as Madame Lumiére did is a very sad case indeed. She was, without doubt, an unsuitable carer for delicate souls like us.

'We need someone sensitive, someone, who understands our needs, someone with a nature just like Capucine's, which

I'm sure will be hard to find,' Tutalou suggested. 'We must be fussy in our selection.'

'Then how about Mademoiselle Fanette,' I suggested. 'She also lives on her own. We would be great company for her. She has a lovely manner and a wicked sense of humour that will suit us just fine. On many visits here, she often had Capucine doubled over with laughter. She always gives us a cuddle whenever she sees us. She has a divine taste in perfume too. The last time she cuddled me I caught a whiff of that exquisite scent *Chloe Fleur de Narcissi*. Another time she wore Capucine's favourite, *L'Interdit.* Fanette knows her perfume too and has style just as our lovely Capucine had. She will do nicely. It will be a delight to be around such a chic woman. Let's be honest, a woman who knows her perfume can't be that bad, can she? She's not in the same league as Capucine, but she's gorgeous all the same and has a beautiful and tranquil nature about her. I think she'll adore having us. We couldn't do better than her.'

'Pfff! Problem is,' Cheyenne reminded us, 'she travels a lot. She's always away on an assignment or other to some far-flung part of the world. She's in great demand, as we know, one of Europe's top fashion magazine editors. Yes, it would be delightful to be with her, I'm sure, but it would be an inconvenience. Career women don't have cats or children, only jewellery, perfumes, disposable income and men without commitment.'

'But are we not her three jewels – Capucine always called us her sparkling jewels. Aren't we the most sparkling of them all?'

'Without doubt, Tutalou, but I don't think we're the kind of jewels Fanette wants to hang around her neck,' I laughed. 'I'd say she'd have no shortage of admirers to give her jewels far more sparkling than us dazzlers.'

'Talking about dazzlers,' Cheyenne remarked. 'You remember the young girl who moved into the vacant apartment on the sixth floor the other month. I like her. She is from Burkina Faso, so I'm told. She would do nicely.'

'Where on earth is that?'

'In Africa, you clot. Do you not know that?'

'Never heard of it...'

'You mean the French translator,' I asked. 'She seems awfully shy, though. Do you think she could cope with three far from shy cats?'

'Perhaps she's only shy on the surface,' Tutalou suggested. 'A lot of women are like that, you know. Anyway, she already has a cat – can't see her wanting to take on another three.'

'Who else is there, then?' asked Cheyenne.

There was silence as we pondered this quandary. We were not short of people within the apartment complex as possible carers, but we had to consider seriously an escape plan in case no neighbour takes us in. Why would they anyway? Taking in three cats is just too much to ask.

As we lay deep in contemplation, I had a sudden moment of feline inspiration. I have moments like these on rare occasions and this I thought was sublime, the solution to our dilemma.

'How about Concierge Courcelles and his wife,' I proudly announced. 'They will be perfect.'

'Pfff, that's impossible – They are not allowed to keep animals, well, apart from goldfish and hamsters. It would be a good choice if only they could.'

'What a pity. I know they like us. Every time concierge Courcelles sees us he always gives us a rub and tickle under the chin. You never can tell, Cheyenne, perhaps an exception could be made.'

'Maybe... Who else is there?'

'Well, there is Monsieur Sablon, the retired cabinet maker.'

Tutalou and Cheyenne looked hard at me as though I had lost all of my sensibilities.

'I don't think *so!*' gasped Tutalou.

'Why ever not – he'd be the perfect candidate – an excellent choice.'

'Océane, you can be a fool at times. Monsieur Sablon has little patience with animals. He hates them, especially cats. I thought you knew that. He's a philistine when it comes to animals. He has little patience with his fellow beings, and you think he'd have the patience to look after us sensitive creatures – No chance! I can't believe you even suggested him.'

'But every time Capucine called him to do some work or repairs or whatever he was there in an instant. We didn't seem to bother him then, did we?'

Tutalou gave a riotous laugh. 'That's because he thought Capucine was a divine goddess, Aphrodite or the likes and was willing to put up with us creatures just to get near her. Men are like that. They are so weak, so shallow, so blinded by sex and the female form they can never see the real person before them. What a sorry shower they are. Thank God, we felines don't suffer like that. Aren't we blessed to be as we

33

are, wise, sensible and near perfect in every way? Anyway, his dislike of animals is not the real problem... its Madame Sablon. She has an allergy to cats – to us and any other furry creatures that comes her way. When Capucine used to take us out and we'd pass her door she'd always wheeze, her eyes would bulge, and she'd get the shakes – just one look at us and she comes out in a cold sweat with beads of perspiration suddenly appearing on her furrowed forehead. She's a nice woman, I'm certain, but unfortunately allergic to us. It's bad enough the poor dear living with Monsieur Sablon without her having to suffer discomfort from an allergic reaction from us. She'd need to be tranquillised if we lived with her.'

'Pfff. We'd need tranquilised if we lived with her husband,' Cheyenne quipped.

'Good job we have a sense of humour otherwise we'd go mad waiting to see what fate has in store for us,' Tutalou laughed. 'Best to leave this life with a laugh, if that is how it's to be instead of bawling our eyes out.'

'I'd rather not leave at all,' I dolefully added.

The Model Neighbour

There's not much more we can do,' Inspector Lewee said to his team. 'There's nothing here that can cast any further light on the investigation apart from the medication.'

'Will they be OK, inspector,' his assistant asked, looking over to Lucie, who was sitting in the wicker chair with Océane and Tutalou cuddled up to each other at her feet and Cheyenne resting on her lap. They were in absolute shock.

'Yes. She will look after them OK,' he replied as he walked over towards the balcony.

'We must go now, mademoiselle. You know where to find me if you need help,' Inspector Lewee said as he prepared to leave the apartment.

'Yes,' she murmured 'I think I'll stay with them for a while as they are traumatised and need company. I don't want to leave them alone.'

'Very well – I'll be in contact with you in a few days to keep you updated. We have a lot to attend to and clarify so this will take time. Another visit may be necessary. I will let you know. Are you sure you will be, OK?'

'Yes.'

'Then I'll say good evening – my condolences mademoiselle for the loss of your friend – our friend.'

'Thank you, Inspector.'

After he left, she sat in the dark looking out over the lake as the cats pined away. She was desolate and numb with grief. Her fear of cats seemed to have eased as she sat with them until the early hours. She recalled the kindness

Capucine had shown her in the eight years she had known her. Not long after her career as a model began, she moved into her apartment only to discover her neighbour was no other than the famous Capucine. She was in awe and nervous about meeting her, as she knew she eventually would. She always admired her but never dreamt she would one-day meet her, never mind being her friend and neighbour. With Capucine, being a top model in her younger days, Lucie wondered what she would think of her – a new wave model, in a fashion world that had changed so much since her heyday.

She was only eighteen when she moved in. A few days later there was a knock on her door and standing before her was Capucine, holding a bunch of lilies and wearing a welcoming smile. Lucie was speechless. Capucine soon put her at ease, and it was not long until she was relaxed and at ease in the company of this icon of divine beauty. She was surprised how approachable and friendly she was, and far from the cold, aloof and distant image, some had of her. To Lucie, Capucine was a goddess and adored everything about her.

It was hard for her to believe Capucine was gone as she sat with the three sorrowful cats. She stroked each of them and wondered what fate awaited them.

Lucie later returned to her apartment after making sure the cats were asleep then flung herself on her bed and wept for the lovely Capucine. It was a long night with many more to endure.

A Choice of Neighbours

Again, there was silence. We were lost in our own thoughts. Within less than a week, our cosy home turned from a secure and loving place to a potential death cell. We felt like prisoners awaiting execution and innocent ones too. We had done nothing wrong, nothing to deserve being so shabbily treated. Tutalou, for one, was determined to escape, to be free from the threat of extermination. While unsettled in my mind, I thought the other two were being overdramatic, even becoming paranoid about what Camille had said, although matters would take a turn later that I would join them in their paranoia.

Once more, as we lay on the rug, we contemplated rescue by a neighbour.

'Well... there's the beatnik a few floors below. You know, the lanky woman, the one with the bohemian look about her, always with a flower in her long curly red hair – the one with the sallow face and always dressed in colourful outfits. She seems a cool character – seems with it. I think we should give her a try.'

'Cool character – with it! Really, Cheyenne, where are you coming from?' I asked, flabbergasted by her suggestion. 'She's always as high as a kite and her boyfriend is on a different planet altogether – He's wired to everything going. Have you seen the cut of him? She might look good, but he's grotesque. He's a washout and hasn't bathed in ages – smells to high heaven and those jeans, God, did you ever see the likes of them. He's so attached to them he's probably swarming with lice and other unmentionable creatures. He's tetchy as hell, sarcastic and obnoxious and they are his good points. Have you heard the music they play? Cool indeed. It's so off the wall it would fry our brains if we lived with them. He's into that Heavy Metal stuff most of the times, banging his head on the wall to the beat of it. When he's not, it's the satanic noise of Black Sabbath and the likes he's swaying to. She's as bad. She's hung up on protest music and that folksy stuff too, you know the kind, singing through the nose and making no sense at all. They compete with each other to see who can make the loudest din. They can hardly see themselves in the haze of hash that surrounds them like a satanic halo, so, if we lived with them, they'd never see us. They can hardly look after themselves, never mind us. We are used to listening to the classical and soothing tones of Debussy, Ravel and Rossini and Capucine's collection of Count Basie, Ray Charles and Ella Fitzgerald, not the head-banging delirium they blast out at all hours of the day. I'm far from a prude when it comes to music, but really, there is a limit.'

'You are right,' Tutalou sighed, agreeing with me, which was a rarity. 'Can you really see us living there, listening to that racket, worse still; we'd end up as junkies breathing in their polluted air. We would be better off dead and *cast to the wind* than having to suffer their antics – to lower ourselves to their level. She's worse than he is. That stuff she sniffs up her nose keeps her on a perpetual high. I doubt she knows what day it is. I can't remember her ever having her feet on the ground. Not happy with that, she has to drag on those reefers that completely make her gaga and the smell of it always drifts up to the balcony, polluting our environment. Capucine had words with her several times about it. Her reaction was to offer her a drag. 'Breathe it in, love – let yourself go – set your spirit free,' she'd say, dangling a reefer in front of Capucine's face, who would push it away with a disapproving look. Her drugs and addictions go well with her bohemian and 'love in' image of the sixties. She's stuck in a time warp. She's a perfect match for him and his Heavy Metal trash – best to keep them at arm's length if we want to keep our sanity.'

'I must say,' exclaimed Cheyenne, 'I'm quite partial to a bit of Heavy Metal myself – Not so much Black Sabbath, more like Dep Leppard. Now they are as cool as you could get – in a league of their own.'

'What!' I cried.

'Yeah... I like AC/DC too. I dig them. It took me a while to get to grips with Metallica, but once in the blood there is no shaking them off, but the truth is there's no beating Dep Leppard! Something about Heavy Metal really gets me going, gets my pulse racing.'

Tutalou and I looked in astonishment at her.

'What do *you* know about Heavy Metal?' Tutalou sniggered. 'You're a classical freak, aren't you? Since when, have you been into that rubbish and what's this *cool* and *dig* talk?'

Cheyenne, with her nose in the air replied, 'Pfff... It's far from rubbish, all a matter of an acquired taste. Something you have or you don't. You two obviously don't and are lacking in the taste department. I would often sit outside their apartment window to listen and appreciate their choice of music, which is a good antidote to the music you two indulge in. Every time I hear Heavy Metal I'm off into a different world – takes me out of myself.'

'You can say that again, you're well out of it now,' I laughed. 'Perhaps you should join those two crackpots on their psychotic planet and fry whatever little brains you have left – you and your Heavy Metal.'

'Pfff – you two need to broaden your horizons. You'll be surprised how healthy it can be. It rather liberates the soul. Anyway, it's not becoming of felines to be so narrow-minded, so *Luddite* – it's not part of our genetic makeup. You two don't know what you're missing by being so blinkered in your musical tastes.'

'Blinkered – Luddite! What are you on about? We're far from blinkered. You know we are intellectual in our outlook and very cultured in our ways. It's part of the character of our breeds; yours too, so don't give us that trash of intellectual superiority,' I replied, a little miffed by her attitude.

'Yes, you are. At least I open my mind and allow in the fresh air of change, allow in new ideas and give things a chance. Every time I whisper words of wisdom, your minds close and you drift off not wanting to embrace anything different, anything new, just wanting to leave things as they are. At least I take in everything about me and don't stagnate in my own indifference and I'm willing to embrace any challenge put before me.'

'Oh, yes, we'd forgotten... you're the enlightened one, aren't you?' I laughed 'The ultimate intellectual feline. We are so humbled to be in your presence. You're all talk, Cheyenne, as for you embracing any challenge put before you, then how come you are so scared of the challenge of surviving on the streets, having to seek out your own food and live without the life support of humans?'

'Ah, that's different,' she replied with a chuckle. 'I'm not stupid altogether. Wanting to survive on the streets is not an option by my way of thinking – too high risk! Why take risks if you don't have to?'

'Go back to sleep, Cheyenne,' I advised, 'and give your 'intellect' a rest.'

Every now and then, we were like this, getting on each other's nerves but it rarely lasted long. The truth was we enjoyed a good healthy argument. It was a kind of stimulant, kept us on our toes and felt better for it. Silence once more descended as we contemplated our options that were getting narrower by every passing second. I thought the other two were getting carried away with themselves, thinking Camille was right, that we were to be disposed of. It seemed so unlikely, yet, like Cheyenne and Tutalou, I was scared stiff – still laughing about it but behind the smiles was fear, an icy, stalking fear that intensified with each passing day.

'We're not having much luck, are we?' Tutalou asked, breaking the silence, 'We are not good at this survival lark at all – useless is more like it. The problem is, we've been spoilt rotten. Let's be honest with ourselves, we have been so indulged and pampered by humans we've lost our natural survival instinct. What kind of felines are we? We're a disgrace to our ancient lineage if we can't find a way of surviving against all the odds, to hunt, to seek out our prey, to rely on our own instincts instead of those of humans. What failures we are.'

'Pfff! It's too late for all that,' Cheyenne lamented. 'Survival... it's bred out of us, that's why trying to escape to the streets is such a bad idea, or I should say a stupid one. Humans have manipulated us for centuries, as far back as the ancient Egyptians and probably way before that and will continue to do so as long as we allow them. We are nothing remotely like our ancient ancestors and have nothing in common with them. We are deluding ourselves about our exotic pedigrees. Humans – they've bloody well ruined the lot of us.'

'I wouldn't say ruined. No! No! All they've done is spoil and over-indulged us because we are so desirable, so irresistible but you are being too dramatic to think they can take away our natural instincts.'

'How right you are, Tutalou,' I agreed. 'Our problem is we can't resist the human touch. We're addicted to their caresses and titbits. If we have been manipulated by them, then it's been by our willing consent and encouragement. We love being indulged – That's our fault, not theirs.'

Cheyenne was having none of it. 'No,' she said with some authority. 'Not all of it was willing. Humans, don't forget, interfere with our breeding, by messing about with us in an outrageous way, the result being we have the oddest of breeds. Don't forget too, they also manipulate us and use neutering to control, not just our breeding but robbing us of any sexual pleasure or desire. Humans, a sadistic lot they are. Pfff, by all accounts we're not missing much. Capucine went further than that on occasions, saying she'd be far better off without sex. Didn't she once say there is more pleasure in a glass of fine vintage than sex? That her most pleasurable times have been sitting with a friend sharing a bottle of wine rather than rummaging about in bed with a demented male trying to find himself and when he does, he's so confused he leaves the unfortunate woman utterly frustrated and unsatisfied. Humans are cruel by nature. They have ruined us in so many ways. I still would have liked to know what sex was like, what all the fuss was about and allowed to form my own opinion of it. Instead, they have robbed us of it, so now we'll never know.'

'Sex... It's the human's Achilles' heel,' I laughed. 'They would be far more civilized if they weren't so hung up about it, they are so obsessed. Anyway, let's forget about sex and get back to finding someone to look after us.'

'There's always, Deputy Bourbon, the politician on the sixth floor and his wife Esther.'

There was laughter from Cheyenne and me at the very mention of his name.

'Tutalou, do you not remember what Capucine used to call politicians? Have you forgotten?' I asked after the laughter subsided. 'Let me remind you of a few choice ones: liars, two-faced lackeys, shysters and toe rags and these were her polite ones. Could you imagine what she would have said if we were adopted by a politician, especially Deputy Bourbon, that pretentious drip from Caen.'

'Just because she didn't like politicians is no reason for us not to. He seems alright to me as does his wife and their son Daniel is a smart young man with a roving eye for beauty, so he'd be sure to like us.'

'Pfff. You'd soon change your mind if you lived with him and forced to listen to the political diarrhoea he comes out with. His wife, if you haven't noticed is always away on some holiday or other to get out of his sight and you think we should be exposed to him – If she can't stand him what makes you think we will. No thank you, Tutalou – go on your own if you wish.'

43

'Wait a moment,' Cheyenne cried, as she raised herself up on her front legs. 'What about – what's his name? You know – the young one with the cello, the one with the gaunt looks and facial twitch who lives at the far end of floor four. What's his name now?'

'Didier!' replied Tutalou with a chuckle.

'That's him. He would do, wouldn't he? He's rather a pleasant young man – handsome too. I'd say he'd spoil and pamper us.'

Tutalou rolled over, her legs in the air as she roared with laughter. Tutalou's a gas at times – laughs at the most unusual of things and always at the oddest and inappropriate of times.

'What's up with you? Did I say something funny?'

Tutalou looked at her. 'Funny, you're hilarious! – Didier, the cello player – You've missed your calling, Cheyenne. You should be on the stage – you're a born comedian! – You may enjoy his playing but that's about all you'll enjoy. That Heavy Metal nonsense has gone to your head and rusted the little brains you had.'

Cheyenne hissed at her.

'How come you know all this?' I asked.

'Suzanne keeps me informed and up to date with that part of the complex. She often wanders into his apartment and sniffs about the place, says it smells of incense, just like a church. She likes him in a strange kind of way. By what she tells me, I just can't see what it is she likes about him. Didier always feeds her and whispers in her ear, which she likes. She can be cheap at times, can Suzanne. She's probably his best and only friend. Shows how strange he is if his only friend is a stray cat who he whispers sweet nothings to. He's not quite the fellow you think he is, far from it.'

'What are you on about? He is far from strange. There's nothing wrong with him.'

'Oh yes, there is! He's not only strange – he's weird! He has fixations too!'

'Fixations!' Cheyenne cried.

I was astounded at Tutalou's assertion. I always knew Didier was a little bit *different*, maybe eccentric and a loner but as for being weird, well I found nothing weird about him in the least and as for having fixations… never noticed them.

'Yes! Fixations, fixations of every kind – you name it, he has it. I can assure you, there is none quite like him. These fixations are a regular occurrence in the human condition – another one of its many peculiarities. I think the whole condition is peculiar if Didier is anything to go by.'

'You know more than I do. What fixations?'

'I thought you both knew about them, especially you, Cheyenne, seeing you're a know-all.'

'Well, I don't. Please, enlighten us.'

Tutalou was a dedicated observer of the activities and the peculiar habits of humans. It was her pastime and took a lot of pleasure from it. She was quite an expert, like a doctor of humanities. I thought she was just a nosey old parker, but Tutalou thought herself as merely an observer of the human condition. She watched and took mental notes of every utterance and action, clinically dissecting them to see what made them tick. Tutalou, apart from being a nosey parker, was also strong-minded, said what was on her mind, and didn't care what anyone thought. Many a time she would send us mad

45

with her detailed observations of the coming and goings of our neighbours. We would turn our minds off, sleep, and let her ramble on. However, the cello player and his fixations, well, that was something new. We weren't sure if she was only teasing us, as she was apt to do, or what she said was true.

'But didn't I discuss this with you lot not long ago. You remember when the police arrived last Good Friday and took him away in the most undignified manner. The whole neighbourhood was out to see him manhandled into the police car, him screaming and shouting for his beloved cello, saying he never lets it out of his sight and can't live without it.'

'I don't remember that Tutalou. I mustn't have been listening.'

'Pfff! I don't remember it either. You must have been talking to yourself, again,' added Cheyenne as she pruned herself. 'You are getting very adept at it lately – talking to yourself. It can't be healthy.'

'Well, if you'd bothered to listen, instead of dozing you would know what I was on about.'

'You had better tell us, then. I always took Didier for a decent skin, a quiet and gentle kind of chap who kept to himself – a harmless and reserved kind.'

'He's quite alright but far from harmless,' Tutalou stated with certainty. 'He has different kinds of cameras dangling from his neck and quietly sneaks about the place taking photos.'

'What of,' muttered Cheyenne, already bored rigid by Tutalou's ramblings.

'Women...'

'Women... What on earth is wrong with that?' Cheyenne naively asked.

Tutalou was flabbergasted, her whiskers twitching with irritation. She was getting herself into a bit of a tizzy. 'What's wrong? Are you serious?'

'Women are always being photographed, just as Capucine was in her acting days and more so in her modelling career. She seemed to relish all the attention – most women would.'

'She consented to being photographed – it was part of being a model and actress. That's different. Can't you see what the cello player is doing is wrong? For heaven's sake, Suzanne says the walls in his apartment; especially his music room are covered with photos he's taken of women, including Capucine, Audrey, that hippy and many other unsuspecting women, even Madame Lumiére, for pities sake.'

'Again, what's wrong with that?'

'WHAT?' Tutalou exclaimed, annoyed at my indifference. 'You don't think there's anything wrong with a fellow hiding away in his apartment, playing his cello at all hours of the night, and surrounded by photographs of women, all of which were taken without *their* knowledge or *consent*. You see nothing *odd* or disturbing about it?'

'Maybe he just likes women.'

Tutalou was apoplectic at my remark. I thought she was about to expire. 'That's not *liking* women; it's abusing and demeaning them in the most invasive way. Can't you see that?' she cried, getting on her high horse. 'The man's a menace to women. I can't believe you don't see how weird his behaviour is. Any reasonable and rational man would not behave in such a way – and you think we delicate creatures be left in *his* care – the man's as deranged as they come as well as dangerous – Best kept at a distance – a good distance. You notice he has no girlfriends. You never see him with a woman on his arm, only on his walls. Suzanne also says his apartment is very sparse. She says he's a minimalist too.'

'A what!' Cheyenne cried.

'A minimalist – you know the kind that lives with the least amount of clutter, one with few possessions, and one with little sense. Their homes are bare, stripped down to the bone. They are so obsessed about it they are freakish – and Didier, I'm afraid is one of them.'

'Well, some people don't like clutter, so there's nothing wrong with living like that,' replied Cheyenne. 'Most humans are obsessed with material worth, so he seems to be one of the enlightened ones, living a sparse lifestyle rather than an extravagant one. He's not odd or weird in my eyes, just a wise young man, I'd say.'

'That's not enlightenment – that is being unhinged,' Tutalou laughed.

'Maybe the photos give him inspiration in his composing and playing the cello,' I suggested. 'These artistic lot are like that, aren't they, needing to be stimulated – inspired by someone or something, like nature, fine words or more likely, by women. Some even have a muse to get their artistic juices flowing.'

'What!' cried Tutalou? 'Are you saying he can be inspired by someone like Madame Lumiére? That she could be his *muse*! She couldn't inspire a fly never mind an artist – and that beatnik – a muse! What could she inspire? Anyway, he is not a composer. He only plays the cello and not very well.'

'He must be good as he's in an orchestra.'

'Not so,' replied Tutalou. 'He might play in an orchestra for mediocre and unhinged musicians for all we know.'

'Pfff! Anyway, what on earth is a muse?' asked Cheyenne, much taken by the word.

'I thought you knew everything, you with your intellectual superiority and all, you *must* know, surely. They are usually women who hang out with artists, such as Manet, Picasso, Monet and Dali, or writers like P.G. Wodehouse, James Joyce, Rimbaud, and Hemingway and even poets like Robert Graves, Dylan Thomas and Byron or composers such as Ravel and Bizet. They inspire them to produce great pieces of artistic excellence by their very presence.'

'What Océane is saying is they are not only there to inspire or soothe their artistic brows and get their creative juices flowing but also to attend to their sexual needs.'

'No, I didn't mean that at all. You are being totally unfair to the muse,' I interjected. 'Many of the greatest artists in the world have had a muse without any sexual connotation or contact whatsoever.'

Tutalou laughed. 'Dream on Océane.'

Tutalou was always a cynic, a common trait in us felines, but had an offbeat sense of humour to go along with it that made her cynicism less toxic.

'What about his other fixations, then?'

'How many times, Océane, have we watched him from the balcony, avoiding cracks in the pavement? He skips

49

around them like a fairy. He's been doing it for years. It can't be right.'

'What's wrong with that? It's quite common. People often do it and worse – it doesn't make them weird – simply different.'

Tutalou again raised her eyes to the ceiling. 'Tell me, Océane; can't you see by not wanting to walk over cracks is the sign of a dysfunctional individual, one on the side-lines of society, someone with a psychological disorder? He's always counting to himself as well. It makes me freak. Do I have to give chapter and verse on the weird and bizarre working of the human mind? If I did, we would be here forever. You can go and stay with him if you like but count me out. I value my sanity too much to allow myself to be exposed to him or his likes. Just the mention of his name gives me the creeps.'

'It could be an illness,' I suggested. 'If it is, then surely you shouldn't criticise him over it. That would be unfair, unjust. It's compassion he needs, and understanding, not criticism.'

'Illness – no,' laughed Tutalou. 'I think he's just an oddball. He's certainly out of the running as our carer. I couldn't live in a minimalist house with a mediocre cello player with a twitch who fixates on anything that moves, has a fetish about women, talks to himself and skips over cracks, who's only friend is a stray cat. I'd rather be in the gutter.'

'You may well be unless we can find someone who'll take compassion on us, or we manage to escape. Still think you're being unfair on him and overcritical to the point of being cruel. He needs kindness and understanding instead of being put-down and ridiculed because of his condition. You are far too hard on him!'

'We have to be cautious; after all, we don't want to go to a dangerous environment. We need a safe haven so we must be careful in our choice. We must be cautious, Océane, we must be.'

'But not too cautious otherwise we'll never escape or be rescued. We're quickly running out of neighbours and options,' I warned. 'We need to take a few risks.'

Once again, we curled up on the rug, no wiser than when we first started, no nearer as to whom our saviour maybe, that's if there was one.

'Hang on! There's that fellow who lives in the other penthouse on the far side of the complex, the one with the crewcut,' Cheyenne cried as she sprang up. 'What's his name, now?'

'Oh! Guy, you mean,' said Tutalou.

'That's him. Capucine was always fond of him and his wife whose name I can't recall.'

'Well, to start with, Guy wasn't too fond of Capucine. He said nasty things behind her back, cruel things – then, when he met her, he was as smooth as they come, a real gent and full of her praises. He may have been a fine film producer in his day but he's far from sincere and as two-faced as you can get. It was his wife, Yvette who liked Capucine.'

'Nonsense, Tutalou,' I replied. 'Guy was a fine man, one of the best. He adored Capucine. He couldn't keep his eyes off her. He had a lot of time for her, often down here to visit and seemed a nice kind of chap. Yes, a real cultured gentleman.'

'They say he's pernickety and fastidious, a stickler for punctuality, rules and timetables. We couldn't live in that kind of environment. Can you imagine us living to a timetable and

51

having to tiptoe on eggshells as not to disturb his regulated and regimented life? No thank you – I'd rather suffer the antics of Didier or even cuddle up to Madame Lumiére.'

'Excuse me, Tutalou, I think you need to remember, we're not in a position to be selective, and we are not exactly showered with choices, are we? The alternative, if Camille is correct, is not worth thinking about, so I'll settle for his pernickety and fastidious ways any day,' replied Cheyenne. 'If we can't find a neighbour to care for us then there's not much hope, so let's take whatever is offered, even Guy and be thankful for it and stop bellyaching and being so fussy.'

'Anyway, let's face it;' I butted in, 'it's clear that being cared for by any of our neighbours is not on. It's highly unlikely any of them will offer to take us in. We are deluding ourselves to think they will. We could go through all the tenants and still not find a solution to our dilemma. Best to wish for the ones we fancy coming to our rescue and praying we don't get the ones we can't stand, like Guy, Didier or the beatnik, but seeing rescue is highly unlikely, let's try to escape as I first suggested. Let's be brave and make our escape. It's our only realistic option. There must be another way out. Who's with me?'

They looked sadly at me and nodded their heads in agreement.

We again contemplated our exit strategy in peace. As I lay there, I did begin to think about what our fate might be. One thing was certain, Cheyenne was right; we would not be able to survive on the streets for long and stay together as we were clueless and had no survival instinct left in us, yet escape was our only realistic option. I thought, perhaps we had got it wrong, and rescue was at hand after all, that something was being arranged or an out-of-the-blue saviour might descend and liberate us. Capucine was so well organized, so for her not to provide for us seemed highly unlikely but by the look of things, it was difficult for us to be optimistic. And where was Marcia, Capucine's devoted cleaner and confidante, one of our most reliable of friends. She vanished without trace. We couldn't understand why she hadn't called to see how we were. Even Audrey was nowhere to be seen, which was more disturbing. It was so distressing. We felt abandoned by the ones we love. We were three very unhappy felines. The only human contact we had was with Lucie and Inspector Lewee.

The Florist and Her Lost Love

The weather changed suddenly from clear spring skies to menacing brooding ones, drenching Lausanne with pulses of heavy rain, adding to the gloom and despondency of a city in mourning.

Cécile Charon looked tense and distracted as she sat in the café Lemon on Avenue de la Harpe, her head lowered, cradling a double espresso in her trembling hands, her swollen eyes still moist and reddened from the many tears she had shed for her lost love. She nervously lit a cigarette but after a few puffs stubbed it out in the glass ashtray. With one gulp, she downed the espresso then looked out of the window, casting her eyes toward a newspaper kiosk at the headlines and the accompanying photos of Capucine. It had been four days since she died but Capucine was still very much front-page news for the national papers, many after writing about the initial event now began delving into her background and scrutinizing and speculating about her personal life. She lowered her head again, dabbing her eyes. Her pale, frowning face said it all, all what Lausanne was thinking, why, why did she do it. Why did she not call for help? Could nobody save her? Did nobody see the warning signs? The tears began to flow once more as she stood up to leave, wiping her eyes with the back of her hand.

'Adieu, mademoiselle,' the waiter softly said as he handed her a fresh napkin.

She didn't answer but nodded an acknowledgment and took the napkin. Outside she stood in quiet thought as the rain streamed down. She held a bunch of red roses and her saffron umbrella, given as a gift from Capucine on their last visit to the Christmas Fair in Lausanne. She didn't open it to protect her from the heavy rain as she slowly walked towards the elegant apartment block at the far end of Chemin de Primerose. Her short-clipped silver-grey hair was soaked. She never thought a person could hurt so much, could suffer such excruciating pain they could no longer see or feel the world about them. Her world was dying with every fallen tear, with every drop of rain her reason for living flowed further and further away down life's river of regret.

She reached the spot where her dream had ended on that fine March day, where the love of her life had lain broken and battered, where her reason for living had disappeared. Looking up at the balcony, she whispered a prayer then knelt and placed the roses alongside the mass of flowers already there from the people of Lausanne. In amongst the flowers, she noticed many cats sitting as though guarding the spot, their eyes following her every move. As the rain mingled with the flowers and her heartbroken tears, they looked at her with compassionate eyes as though they knew who she was.

The final act of her lost love made the world a greyer place and made her tomorrow not worth living. However, life goes on as it always does and always will. She turned and slowly walked away leaving her umbrella amongst the flowers and the guardian eyes of the cats of Lausanne.

The Three Feline Philosophers

So, this was the scene of the aftermath of Capucine's sudden departure from our lives, three philosophising cats in want of a home: in need of rescue, three broken-hearted and despairing cats facing an uncertain future and in need of care. We had no idea what was to become of us. If Camille was right, then we were done for – if she was wrong, where did our destiny lay.

***

Before we go any further, let me introduce myself and my pals, Cheyenne and Tutalou and a few others that were part of Capucine's life.

Océane

I am Océane – the narrator of this tale. I am a sleek eighteen-year-old Abyssinian with striking almond-shaped green eyes, with a grand bearing and because of my breed, I have a superior air about me. Cheyenne and Tutalou do not agree but I know I'm the best of breeds and not shy about telling the world about it. I have an aristocratic gait and fully aware of my ancient lineage. I can trace it back before the pharaohs. My ancestors would have prowled the great palaces of ancient Egypt; Abyssinians would have surrounded Cleopatra as she soaked in her bath of asses' milk and purred when Mark Antony came a-courting. I'm not a large cat. I have a slim body and long shapely legs. My coat is a silky rusty brown with dark specks with pads and paws a darker shade as are areas of my hind legs. My tail is very sleek and oval-shaped and tapers to a point. I'm a natural extrovert, an excellent mixer and like to play and have fun and better still, blessed with a nonchalant demeanour – the truth is, I'm as cute as they come.

Capucine had rescued me from a pet shop window when on a visit to England to make one of her movies. You may wonder what a highly bred cat was doing in a local pet shop. Well, let me tell you.

One morning, as Capucine made her way to the railway station at Purley, in Surrey, to catch a train to the city, she passed a small pet shop situated on the narrow alleyway that led towards the station. It was a wreck of a place. It was like many that then lined the alleyway to the station. To her horror, lying exhausted in the shop window were three kittens in a terribly dehydrated state – my two siblings and me. There were originally six of us in the litter but three had been sold. We were wilting in the heat as the sun beat down on us through the shop window. Our owner, who wanted us disposed of, dumped us in the shop as though we were rubbish. He had inherited a fortune and indulged in many a scheme but was soon bored with them and breeding was one of them. A friend told him it was a good investment to get into cat breeding, as it could be very lucrative if he acquired the right bloodline and the rarer, the better, so he said he would try it. He registered with the Cat Breeders Association, paid his dues, took a few courses in feline know-how then set about

57

his breeding career. He secured our mother, Lavinia, one of impeccable pedigree to begin his cat-breeding career. At first, he was keen on the idea, but his enthusiasm didn't last long. When we were born, our poor mum died, and he found he couldn't handle us. Instead of selling us to other breeders for a price and especially to the breeder of our father, Durer, one of an even more prestigious line than our mother, he decided in a fit of temper to get rid of us by dumping us in the pet shop, all against the strict rules of the Cat Breeders Association. He must have been madding after spending so much time and money on our breeding programme to dispose of us like that. This episode was my introduction to the weird and odd phenomenon that masquerades itself as the human condition.

I noticed Capucine looking in the window at us scrawny cats as we gasped for air as the shop front became hotter and hotter. She looked aghast, shaking her head in disapproval and pursing her lips in annoyance. She opened the shop door, trying hard to keep her temper in order as it was beginning to simmer. There was an angry look on her beautiful face. She walked smartly into the shop, letting the man behind the counter know exactly what she thought of him, leaving animals in a state of dehydration. It was not only cruel but also criminally irresponsible. He was one man not immediately struck by her stunning looks and told her to sling her hook. She was fuming. Furthermore, he added, if she was so concerned about their welfare, she should buy them and stop pestering him and added, he didn't take kindly to a bossy Frenchwoman like her parading herself in *his* shop, dictating to *him* – 'buy them and get lost,' he snarled. This she did. Not the three of us but the weakest, which was me. The shop-keeper, a lanky, long-haired man with a scrawny beard and long fingers, grabbed me by the scruff of the neck and roughly put me in a cardboard box and thrust me at Capucine. 'Here, take it', he snarled. 'Hope it brings you nothing but misery.' She glared at him, throwing the fifty pence coin at him, the miserly sum he thought I was worth. When turning to leave she remonstrated with him once more, telling him he was a cruel individual and not fit to own a pet shop. He didn't take kindly to that. He once more told her to sling her hook, this time with a few well-placed expletives thrown in. He had better things to do, he said than to listen to a cranky woman on a day trip to London, looking to browbeat a man, quietly going about his business. She told him, as well as being cruel he was also a rude and an obnoxious blackguard and she intended to report him to the RSPCA. He ignored her; then, grabbing her arm, guided her roughly to the door, 'Now madame, on your way,' he snapped, slamming the door behind her.

Once outside and calming herself, she looked at poor me in my little brown box. I was a sight to behold, all skin and bones, shivering and dying of thirst. She looked in the window and sighed at the sight of the other two cuddled up to each other. 'Can you imagine how he must treat women if he treats innocent little creatures like this,' she said to herself as she made her way to the station. Once inside she headed straight to the café and bought me milk. I looked as though I had had my lot, but the sight of the milk soon revived me. I thirstily sipped at it and when I licked the last drops, I looked up at my saviour with my large watery eyes and Capucine's heart melted as our eyes met. It was love without a doubt. Giving a sigh, she pondered the practicalities of the situation she had gotten herself in – buying a cat on impulse was probably not a good idea. She had an important meeting in the city, and she didn't think the producer and director would be too pleased if she turned up with a skeleton of a cat for company. As she looked at me it dawned on her, I was no ordinary cat but a thoroughbred. She knew a thing or two about cats, did our Capucine and cared for many in her life and it was clear to her I was a breed with exotic origins. How I ended up in such a hole as that so-called 'pet shop' she would never know. By the look of her, she wasn't going to let the pet shop owner get away with such cruel treatment of animals. It was later I discovered she did just that and filed a complaint with the RSPCA and the shop, after being examined was shut and the shopkeeper prosecuted. I would say he rue the day he ever set eyes on the lovely Capucine.

When she arrived at the director's meeting, she left me with his secretary who wasn't too happy as she couldn't stand the sight of cats, not just cats, but any household animal. She had a thing about furry creatures. This irrational fear of things is another peculiarity of the human condition that we found hard to fathom. This young lady had it bad and far from amused by my appearance. After a little coaxing by Capucine, she reluctantly agreed to look after me as long as she didn't have to touch me.

On return to her hotel, Capucine called a vet, who, after taking one look at me suggested he should put me out of my misery and took out a syringe and a dose of death ready to do his dirty business. He made matters worse by saying she did not deserve having an animal if this is how she treated it. She was seething with rage and flabbergasted by his remark and quickly put him to right, furthermore, she would not have me destroyed but would take care of me and restore me to good health. He was far from impressed as he put away the syringe but wished her good luck, saying it would take a miracle to save me.

I was destined to live in her cosy penthouse apartment in Lausanne but first, there was quarantine. Not having documents, the required inoculations and being unhealthy the authorities in Switzerland made an order of quarantine against me. It was not a good experience, I can tell you, three months without seeing Capucine. The quarantine vet informed her, in his humble opinion; I was of the Abyssinian breed and a very rare one too. He was right of course and told her when I gained weight my dark coat would change, and the true Abyssinian colours would emerge. After a lot of love and tender care given to me by Belinda, one of the quarantine nurses, I began to revive but was worried that Capucine might have forgotten me.

The day finally arrived and there she was waiting for me, all dressed up in the latest fashion, looking stunning. She smothered me with kisses, whispering words of love and hugging me tightly and told me my name was to be Océane. I liked the sound of it. Yes, I thought, I like this, Capucine. How lucky I was she caught the train that day from Purley station.

In Lausanne, she introduced me to her penthouse apartment, which was heaven, compared to the shop front at the railway station and the quarantine centre in Switzerland. To my surprise, there was another cat there. Her name was Ve-

61

ronique and did not appreciate my trespassing on her patch. She was old and did not take well to a young one like me suddenly appearing, upsetting her routine and tranquil life.

By the time I arrived at the apartment Capucine was making The Curse of the Pink Panther with Peter Sellers, her second Pink Panther movie and the laughs she had rehearsing her lines with him was something to behold. He would often visit. She liked him but found a lot of his behaviour odd and at times, tasteless. Peter was another one of those men who thought himself a Casanova, believing he was irresistible to women but not to this one and would brag incessantly about his virility. He was forever sniffing about Capucine and was not the kind to understand the meaning of the word no. It didn't take her long to realise his sole mission in life was to bed as many women as he could. She made it clear she was not to be one of his conquests at any price and was fussy whom she allowed into her boudoir. He was miffed with his nose put out of joint – being turned down by a woman was alien to Peter and couldn't handle it. Finding he was out of luck, their association cooled rapidly but they still met on the rare occasion over the years. Peter never liked me, always hissing, kicking out at me, and swearing as though it was going out of fashion. He may well have been a genius of a comedian, but I was glad to see the back of him, as I was not one of his admirers. When he died, Capucine was surprised to find he left her a bequest in his will. He must have liked her far better than she thought.

That is how I came to be a pet of the lovely Capucine, by a chance meeting on the way to a railway station. Unknown to me, I was destined to become the guardian of Capucine's heart.

Tutalou

Tutalou was a 16-year-old *Egyptian Mau*. Her breed was the real blueblood of the species. There is nothing to match the *Egyptian Mau*. They have everything the rest of the feline world wish they had, poise, elegance, style, and sophistication. You name it they have it. I never let her know she was of a far higher and rarer breed than I was, as I didn't want to give her notions of superiority.

Capucine acquired Tutalou on one of her many trips to the market in Lausanne. As she was buying her groceries, she noticed a cat at her heels. By her bearing and look, she was no ordinary cat. Before her was the most exquisite of creatures. She was well groomed – her coat, a subtle shade of grey with dark spots and uneven horizontal stripes on her legs leading to graceful oval-shaped feet. On her forehead was the 'M' scarab that distinguished the breed, continued in dorsal stripes from her nose to the tip of her tail. Her eyes were a sparkling seductive goose green. An elegant feline beauty if there ever was one.

As Capucine made her way along the stalls, she noticed the cat still at her feet. 'Hello,' she said as she knelt to stroke her. Tutalou hunched her back to receive Capucine's hand. Her touch was soft – the hand of a caring and sensitive soul. 'Are you lost my pretty one? I haven't seen you around here before. Come, let's see who you belong to,' she said as she examined her collar. There was no nametag or address. But to her surprise attached to the collar was a diamond-studded silver cross. There was nothing cheap about Tutalou. Engraved on the back of the cross was *'mon beau Tutalou'*. 'What a curious name that is – that's if Tutalou is a name at all and why would anyone attach a cross around your neck – very peculiar! Well, you can't come home with me because you belong to someone else. Look at your nails, so beautifully manicured and the silken look of your coat. You are well looked after. Off you go now. Go home,' she said as she shooed Tutalou away. She continued walking but Tutalou was still close at her heels. Again, she shooed her away then continued her journey home. After a while, she looked back and there was no sign of her. She called into her local florist and as she stepped back onto the pavement, there was Tutalou sitting waiting for her, the silver cross sparkling in the morning sun.

'Well, here you are again, cheeky. Whatever will I do with you? Off you go. You can't come with me.'

Tutalou meowed. Capucine put down her messages and picked her up, giving her a cuddle and kiss on the head. 'You are pretty, aren't you?' Tutalou nuzzled into Capucine's shoulder, purring as the caring hand stroked her head and caressed her ears. 'You must stop following me and go home. I'm sure your owner is looking for you.' She put her down and once more shooing her away. 'Off you go now.' Tutalou meowed again as Capucine went her way. She looked back. Tutalou was gone and thought she had returned to the market. On arriving at the entrance to the apartment complex and

64

searching for her keys, she noticed Tutalou sitting on the step looking up at her. 'Well, you cheeky little thing, following me home like that – whatever would your owner think, following a strange woman home. What will I do with you?' Tutalou looked sheepishly at her. 'Oh, you'd better come in then.' She opened the entrance door to the foyer and Tutalou sprang up the steps and followed her, rubbing herself against Capucine's legs as they walked towards the lift. 'You can't stay here for long. I have a cat already,' she warned as the lift door closed. 'I don't think she'll take too kindly to another joining her. She is the jealous kind. You can stay here until I find your owner, who I'm sure is frantic with worry trying to find you. You are very naughty running away like this.' Tutalou looked up; squinting at her newfound friend, then gave her a hungering meow. She was famished and in need of sustenance.

I wasn't too happy with the new arrival as she skipped into the apartment and wondered why Capucine had brought this stranger to my patch. She gave Tutalou milk, and I prowled about keeping a sharp eye on the interloper who took no notice of me as she sipped from *my* porcelain bowl.

As a new edition to Capucine's household Tutalou was in for a surprise and about to enter a feline Paradise, a Paradise I thought I had had to myself. Everything around and about Capucine had class, style and sophistication and this new arrival was in for a treat. Although I had Capucine to myself, she could have up to three cats living with her at any one time, which was her normal quota. Cats were always around her – an integral part of her life. When I arrived, there was only Véronique, an American Bobtail. She didn't like me at first, but I managed to win her over. Although old, she was a cool cat and filled me in about her time with Capucine, about her bipolar condition and all the gossip about the apartment complex. She passed away six months later. Being the only cat, I was getting used to being the centre of attention and spoiled in every possible way, this however changed with the arrival of this stranger with her elegance, expensive tastes and her seductive goose green eyes.

As for the sleeping arrangements, well they were something out of this world. I had a specially designed basket made by CeCe, a well-renowned craftswoman from the outskirts of Besancon and linen blankets made by Porthault's of Paris. These were real fancy things, too. Capucine spared no expense when it came to her feline friends. I even had an *Art Nuevo* designed grooming brush she picked up in Paris on one of her many trips.

Capucine was fussy too about the bowls and plates her cats ate and sipped from – No ordinary ones for her, only the best, a set of three 19th century Samson China ones. In fact, they were soup bowls, but Capucine thought they made perfect watering bowls for her exotic cats. As well as these, she had silver-plated eating dishes for us. These were no ordinary ones either but stylishly designed with our names engraved in fancy French script. It wasn't just our eating utensils that were of the best but also our dietary needs. A feline dietary specialist, Madame Galignani was always at hand to make sure we ate only the best and our calorie intake didn't exceed what she considered healthy. No trash for us, only the best feline cuisine possible, made from the best lean cuts from the local butcher. Madame Galignani was well-known around Lausanne and its hinterland as the best in the business when it came to the health and welfare of the feline fraternity. She was a cranky, ill-tempered and rude mannered individual but tolerated because of her knowledge of all things feline. She had no veterinary qualifications whatsoever but was outstanding in animal welfare and had that special touch when it came to felines. Her own place on the outskirts of Lausanne was a haven for homeless cats – she never turned any away.

When it came to our medical needs, well, that was something special too. A well-known veterinary surgeon, Jean-Pierre Brioude, a friend of Capucine was always on hand to make sure we were in the best of physical health. He didn't get along with Madame Galignani but still held her feline expertise in high regard.

Capucine thought she must find out whom Tutalou belonged to, so she took a photograph of her as she made herself comfortable on the sofa under my jealous gaze, hissing at her to let her know I was far from pleased by her unwelcome presence. Posing seemed second nature to her as she settled down for her photo-shoot. She wasn't just pretty, this Tutalou, but also an inveterate show off. Capucine posted photos in and around the market area and notices in the local papers *le Martin* and *24 Heures.*

She called into her local police station to register that she had found Tutalou and the silver cross. The oddness of the find surprised them. They duly took note, and Capucine signed a document saying she would care for the cat and keep the cross safely stored and insured until the rightful owner turned up. The two officers on duty were goggle-eyed by her presence. They had a hard job keeping focused as she filled in the forms, giving them a quick glance and smile from under her long eyelashes – even the law became distracted by the lovely Capucine.

Time passed without any results. Strange, she thought. She couldn't understand why there hadn't been enquiries as Tutalou was a highly bred and prized creature with an expensive accessory. This petite but solid silver cross was a valuable piece, encrusted with diamonds and rubies with a well-crafted engraving. Whom in their right mind she thought would want to place it around a cat's neck – who indeed. She was also surprised nobody had noticed the cat before she had. Even an opportunist thief never took advantage of the situation to steal it – a perfect chance for any self-respecting thief. She thought that perhaps the cat lived nearby or within the market area so spent some time knocking on doors and asking around but with no luck. This cat was a mystery. Capucine would have been shocked to discover the truth about the origins of Tutalou and her cross.

She was also acquainted with a local radio station's director so asked him to put out an appeal. Like most men, he could not resist her allure and would do anything she asked. The radio appeal described to the listeners the rarity and special breeding of the *Egyptian Mau*, found at the market in Lausanne, asking the owner to contact the station describing the cat and its unique paraphernalia. There was a massive response and all of a sudden, Tutalou, at the time a cat with no name, was very popular indeed. Everybody wanted her and willing to lie through their teeth to possess her. Humans seem to have a habit of wanting to possess things that don't belong to them. Capucine received hundreds of letters from people claiming to be the rightful owners. She spent many a long hour sifting through them with the help of Marcia, putting aside those she thought genuine and disposing the rest to the garbage bin. Some of the claims were a bit fanciful and certain to be opportunists seeking ownership of her expensive find. She interviewed many but all failed to describe the cross. Even those she at first considered genuine turned out to be the worst kind of deceivers – absolute fakes and liars.

She was getting nowhere so decided to value the cross and insure it as she had informed the police she would put away for safekeeping in her safe, attaching a note stating its value and how it came into her possession, hoping, in time the owner would turn up. She was perplexed that whoever owned her had not contacted the police or posted a notice either in a newspaper or on the radio offering a reward for it and Tutalou's return.

She entered Dorsa, a well-known jewellery shop in Lausanne on Chemin des Chantres. She knew the owner, Daniel Dorsa. He had previously valued jewellery for her and was another man transfixed by her charm and beauty and like most had a soft spot for her. He looked at the cross and taking out his eyepiece examined it in detail.

'It's an exquisite piece of art without a doubt. Where, Capucine, did you get such a gem from?' he asked, not taking his eyepiece away.

'Around a cat's neck!'

He looked at her, astounded, his eyepiece falling away, '– a cat!'

'Yes, a cat. It followed me home from the market with it dangling from its neck.'

He scratched his head. 'Umm, around a cat's neck, you say. Umm, this has to be the most bizarre thing I've heard of concerning jewellery for a long time and believe me, I've heard many.'

'Well, if it's an exquisite piece of art as you say, what is it worth?' she curiously asked.

'A small fortune.'

'What!' She gasped, cupping her face in her hands. 'Are you sure?'

'Yes! You see, this is no ordinary silver cross, not by any standard. By the hallmark, here,' he pointed out to her, 'it's at least a hundred years old.'

'Are you serious?'

'Well, within a few years or so. You see these four tiny rubies, one on each arm and in the centre and the nine diamonds between them, each in their own right are valuable. They may be small, but they are extremely well-cut.'

'How much is it for heaven's sake?' she asked after regaining her composure.

Once more, he examined it, giving a sigh every now and then. He put down his eyepiece, shook his shiny baldhead, and sighed again. 'In my humble opinion, Capucine, this piece of superb craftsmanship is worth a minimum of 150,000 dollars!'

'Oh my God!' she cried.

'It's a crazy world we live in,' he replied handing back the cross to a visibly shaken Capucine. 'But who in their right mind would put a gem like this around a cat's neck? It doesn't make sense. They must be mad or recklessly rich.'

'You have me there, Daniel. They are probably both. Whoever it is must possess little sense about them to leave it around a cat's neck and let it wander around a busy market-place.'

'Have you tried to find the owner, who I'm sure will be worried sick?'

'Yes, but so far to no avail. I can't believe nobody has missed a rare cat never mind the silver cross. Even the police have had no enquiries about it – not a word. It's weird.'

'I can ask around my colleagues to try and trace its origins if you like. It's somewhat distinctive and members of the trade may be able to trace its origin. The hallmark will be helpful. It might be worth a try. I'm as curious as you to know its origin.'

'If it's not too much trouble – it would be of great help. Thanks.'

'What will you do with it?'

'Well, it won't hang around the cat's neck again, that I can guarantee. I will have it insured and hope the owner finally turns up to claim it. I can do no more than that. Would you be kind enough to certify it for the insurance?'

'Very well, but I strongly advise you to get a second opinion. The value I've put on it is the minimum, so seek that second opinion,' he advised as he wrote out the certificate. 'As for insuring it, I'm afraid you'll have difficulties as you are not the rightful owner. The law is very specific about it.'

'Oh God, I never thought of that. Well, if I can't insure it, it looks like the safe or the bank is the answer.'

She was rather dazed as she walked home after Daniel's valuation and began to wonder where the cat came from and why nobody had claimed her or the cross. They must have missed it. She was confused, to say the least, and concluded that unfortunately, no one was going to claim her soon so decided instead of taking her to the animal compound she would keep her at the apartment. However, she did leave details with the animal compound in Lausanne who assured her, they would circulate the details to other compounds and outlets in case the owner contacts them.

Once home she looked curiously at her new housemate. 'What will I call you?' she mused as I prowled the place in an agitated state, my fur, and nerves on edge as she tenderly stroked her. It was so annoying. I had no time for this new member of the household, and I let Capucine know about it in my many demonstrative ways. I continuously circled her feet, meowing as loud as I could and hissing at her until she lost patience and ran me into another room. I was soon back to annoy her and the newcomer as she settled down to snooze after she fed once more from of *my* dish. She took no notice of me, just closed her eyes, and drifted off. She wasn't shy about making herself at home, was this goose green-eyed beauty.

'I can't just call you cat, can I? I'm sure you have a lovely name already but seeing I don't know what it is, I must call you something,' Capucine said as she looked at the cross again and its inscription *mon beau Tutalou.* 'I know, how about, Tutalou, how about that, then? I have no idea what Tutalou means, but it sounds good. Maybe that is your real name after all.' Tutalou looked up at her and squinted, wagging her tail as if approving her choice of name. 'Yes, Tutalou it is. Tutalou will suit you fine.' She looked over at me. 'Well,

Océane, come, make friends with Tutalou, your new house-mate.'

I scowled.

'No need to be like that. Take no notice of her, *Tutalou*,' she laughed as she hugged her new ward. 'Océane, poor dar-lin' has had her pretty little nose knocked out of joint.'

She was right, and it was too painful to endure.

A few days later, as Capucine rested on the sofa, she again pondered where Tutalou came from and who her owner might be. What she did not realise, Tutalou was not from Lau-sanne or anywhere near it and the cross was more valuable than Daniel Dorsa could have ever imagined. Her story was not a happy one. This is how Tutalou described it to me. She belonged to a young woman from Toulouse called, Carolien Junas. Juliette was Tutalou's real name and given to Carolien as a kitten by her boyfriend, Pablo, a well-to-do Italian of Rus-sian extraction, which accounted for his irrational nature that was to be the cause of Carolien's misfortune. This Italian, to dazzle his lover for her twenty-first birthday, managed to find a kitten of a rare breed. He did his research well and at the party, with full fanfare, produced Juliette, who he had paid quite a lot for. She was an inspired choice as Carolien adored, pampered, and spoiled her and they were insepara-ble. After a few years, however, the relationship with her Ital-ian lover began to cool and wane and there was a lot of an-tagonism between them. Terrible fights followed, mostly over his roving eye. They fell out then made up and so it continued until finally she had had enough of his philandering ways and told him their engagement was off and their relationship over and wanted him to leave her villa. She threw her engagement ring at him along with some choice words. He was raging and raised his hand to hit her then thought better of it and in a fit of temper left with the ring grasped tightly in his hand, knowing this was the end of the relationship, that his eye for women had lost him his finest catch. Out of spite, when Carolien was away visiting her parents in Italy, where she had fled for sanctuary, he took Juliette. With him, he also had the silver cross, a Junas family heirloom. It was a present given to Carolien by her parents for her 21st birthday. It originally belonged to her great-grandmother, Matilda, also given for her 21st by her parents who had it specially designed. Tutalou was a family pet name for Matilda, hence the inscription. It was then given in return to Carolien's grandmother, then to her mother and finally to Carolien.

Pablo had taken the two things she most treasured knowing it would cause acute distress to his former lover – the cat he gave as a love token and her most precious possession of all, the silver cross. When he arrived at Gare Lausanne, on route to his home in Tuscany he removed Juliette from her basket and replaced the nametag with the cross. He then placed her on the platform and continued his journey, laughing as he looked out of the train window, waving goodbye to the poor creature, standing bemused and meowing on platform two of Gare Lausanne.

If that was the kind of man he was, Carolien was well shot of him.

Juliette missed Carolien terribly and her home in Toulouse but had a good replacement in Capucine. Would the cross or Juliette ever be returned to Carolien? Well, you never can tell how fortune turns, but it seemed highly unlikely.

Juliette warmed to her new name and settled in well. After being moody for a while I soon got used to her, then had to go through it all again with the arrival of another intruder – Cheyenne.

Every year on the anniversary of finding Tutalou, Capucine would take out the cross, attach it to Tutalou's collar for the day, and let her wander about the apartment showing it off. This was the highlight of her year. She acted as though she was royalty with her nose in the air and flashing her jewel about like some highbrow tart. We were always glad when the day was over.

Tutalou did not know it at the time, but she was destined to become the guardian of Capucine's mind.

Cheyenne

Cheyenne was an almost pure white fifteen-year-old *Khao Manee* and a right little madame when she wanted to be and was the youngest of the household. She was striking to look at and fully aware of her feline beauty and vain about it too. She had a black spot, the size of a button on her front left paw, very attractive and cute but this only added to her vanity. There would be very few humans as vain as this feline beauty. She just loved to watch herself walk past the mirrors or catch her reflection in the windows, never failing to stop and have a good admiring look as though she was a model or heartthrob. She was in love with herself, and the vainest cat I ever came across and unfortunately, there is no cure for this kind of vanity.

Audrey gave her to Capucine as a gift to help recover from one of her most serious episodes, one in which she fell and bruised her ribs and had to be confined to bed, to be cared for by Marcia and Audrey. Cheyenne was one of six kittens born to a prize-winning *Khao Manee*, with the odd name of Dorette Doe. Cheyenne was a class act without doubt, and she knew it too. The only one who had more style and sophistication about her was Capucine, who Cheyenne absolutely doted on. If she had been human, she would have been a prima donna of the worse kind and a handful for any man to handle, but even with her personality flaws, we loved her all the same.

Cheyenne was gorgeous, I must admit. Her coat was so silky-smooth it made Tutalou and me jealous. I had never touched such a soft and luxurious coat before and her eyes were so mesmerising, one blue, the other a dark yellow – the classic sign of her breed. This gave her a seductive and dreamy look. No wonder everyone fell in love with her.

Capucine was left physically exhausted and mentally drained by her fall and Audrey was at a loss to know what to do to help. She first thought of taking her to *La Paisible*, her home, in the village of Tolochenaz, that overlooked Lake Geneva and the Alps but knew Capucine would not agree, as she would consider herself a burden. Audrey knew she was far from that and relaxing in her garden would revive her spirits but when Capucine said she did not want to do something, it was a waste of time arguing with her as she could be so stubborn at times. There was Audrey's villa outside of Marbella. That would have been perfect for her recuperation, but Capucine wasn't up to the journey. Tutalou and I were of great comfort to her, but Audrey thought she needed some-

76

thing extra special to cheer her up and another cat would do just that and bring her quota back to three again. Audrey would never disappoint when it came to what was required for any occasion and this was one of them. She had already sent a bouquet of roses and boxes of her favourite Belgium chocolates but something else was needed, something that would spring her back to life. I was resting on Capucine's chest with Tutalou next to her head with one paw on her perspiring forehead when Audrey arrived the next day carrying a spectacular round white box decorated with pink lines, tied up with a blue ribbon. She placed the box on the bed. Capucine was still exhausted and slow to recover and didn't want to see any visitors but when she realised it was Audrey standing at the bottom of her bed, she revived enough to give her a broad welcoming smile.

'Take a look at this, my friend... a little pick-me-up.'

Capucine raised her weary body, scattering us in the process and untied the ribbon, carefully lifting the lid. Her bloodshot eyes widened with surprise and delight to see a pure white kitten curled up in the box on a pink satin cushion. Lifting it up and looking into its odd, coloured eyes, her spirits rose. Yes, this present was 'something special'... *too* special. However, Tutalou's and my spirits took a nosedive as we looked at this unwelcome arrival being smothered with kisses. We were far from impressed. The truth was we were madly jealous of this wee kitten being cooed over and lovingly embraced by the woman in our lives. We knew the moment we set eyes on her that she was a little too cute for our liking and far, far too adorable. We had competition and didn't like it.

'This one is special, Cap,' Audrey enthused as she stroked the white bundle. She always called her Cap on happy occasions like this but when being serious or wanted to make a point; it was Capucine with a strong emphasis on the first c.

'She is extremely rare – the only survivor of six. It was a weak litter, beset by all kinds of problems.'

'Oh, I'm sorry to hear that. What a terrible thing to happen,' sighed Capucine as she stoked the new arrival.

'It's amazing she's survived at all. We are lucky to have her – a miracle kitten indeed.'

'Has she a name?'

'No – I'll leave that to you.'

'Haven't you any suggestions?'

'No, not really... you select one.'

'Oh, that's difficult. You've caught me on the hop.'

'I'm sure you'll think of something.'

'Where did you get her from?' Capucine asked as she tickled the kitten under the chin, who purred with delight.

'From Cheyenne Guérina, you remember, the breeder from Berne. She had never lost as many in one go and was heartbroken by her loss. I called her last week saying I wanted something special for you... told me to come over as she had a little surprise that would tickle your fancy. She offered me this bundle of joy saying you would adore her. How right she was. She's gorgeous.'

'It was good of her to remember me. I know what I'll do, I will call her Cheyenne in her honour. What do you think?'

'Yes, a perfect choice. I'm sure she'll be delighted. Because of the bad luck involved, she decided not to sell the survivor but give it away. The moment I mentioned you, she had no hesitation in offering it as a get-well gift. I have her papers here,' Audrey exclaimed, handing her an envelope. 'All that is needed is to fill in the name and have it registered.'

Capucine read the certificate. Cheyenne's bloodline was certainly impressive. Yes, she was certainly no common house cat. Well- bred was she with a pedigree that made her one of the bluebloods of the feline world, nearly as impressive as mine. However, it made poor Tutalou feel inadequate as at that time her lineage was uncertain, as there was no documentation to prove her pedigree credentials.

Capucine would have expected nothing less from Audrey when it came to buying the most appropriate gift for any occasion. Again, she had succeeded. Now she had three cats again and was delighted with her gift; however, Tutalou and I were not! When Cheyenne introduced her to the household, we were curious at first but rather put out by the commotion of her arrival. I took to her better than Tutalou did. Of course, she had been there before. It took her long enough to get used to my whims and ways when she arrived on the scene, now she had to see what this newcomer had in store. Cheyenne was too adorable of a creature for Tutalou's liking and I was not too impressed either.

Until Capucine was well enough to rise from her bed, she allowed Cheyenne to sleep on her pillow and indulged her in every possible way, very much to our annoyance. I'm sure she was trying to tease us as we squirmed every time she kissed and cuddled her. However, Cheyenne's arrival hastened Capucine's recovery, so our displeasure with her soon dissipated.

Cheyenne settled in well. It didn't take her long at all. She thought she owned the place. Tutalou and I, however, after many difficulties warmed to the new addition to the household and in no time became firm friends.

However, not all was well. Cheyenne was only a year old when she developed abscesses on her hind legs. Capucine was frantic with worry and called on the services of Jean-Pierre Brioude who after assessing Cheyenne's condition concluded it was linked to the loss of the litter and the breed was susceptible to this kind of condition, decided an operation was needed. Cheyenne was poorly for a long time after the operation that was at first thought to be a success, but shortly afterwards she developed a fever and infection. It was touch and go whether she would survive. We were all in a terrible state thinking we would lose her but Capucine, with love and dedication nursed her back to health. However, there was worse to come and poor Cheyenne had to once more battle for her life. A second operation was needed but this time she was in danger of losing one of her legs. Once more Capucine with Marcia's help nursed her back to health. She made a full recovery and never looked back. Her only legacy was a slight limp.

Tutalou and I took her under our wings and the three of us settled into a cosy regime of co-existence, only interrupted by the intrusion of Capucine's illness and worse still by some of her dubious male friends, and not forgetting another four-legged creature that trespassed on our lives every now and then – More of that creature later!

Cheyenne did not know it when she arrived that she was destined to become the guardian of Capucine's nerves.

The Insidious Invader
(In memory of Philip)

What was it? What was it that made Capucine want to say goodbye forever to family and friends? What was it that caused her to no longer to see the beauty of life – that caused her so much pain; so much suffering that she opted to end her life in such a horrific and dramatic way? What was it? – It was bipolar, that insidious invader of the mind and soul that rips asunder the lives of its victims that have the misfortune to come its way. It not only passes through one's life but controls and subjugates it. It is a demon deep within the sufferer, dictating and manipulating every thought, deed, and action. It is unforgiving and a curse of the human condition.

The term bipolar was unheard of until the nineteen nineties. Before that, there was an accumulation of terms such as manic depression, anxiety, paranoia, and compulsive behaviour or to those who fail to understand mental health: mad, loopy, or crazy and a never-ending line of adjectives to stigmatise the sufferers of this cruel and merciless condition. Many people get confused by the term and say it is a way of sanitising the condition. Others say it's the accumulation of many ailments banded together under the term of bipolar. It doesn't sound as hard and disturbing as manic or clinical depression, but the truth is, whatever words one wishes to use, if not controlled, it is a life-threatening condition, which should be handled with care and compassion.

Our feline friends are fortunate to be able to understand mental illness far better than humans do, to understand its character and its manipulative power. Do not ask why they have this capacity because nobody knows, and it has been a source of many a contentious argument over the years. Some say it is all a load of hogwash, whereas others say it is true and all sufferers from depression would be fully aware of the therapeutic value of the presence of the feline. They have a natural empathy with sufferers and can detect changes in their moods and therefore soothe and relax them.

The illness had been with Capucine since she was a child, although in her younger days it was in a mild form but still disturbing enough to cause her acute anxiety. She could never remember a time in her life she did not suffer the symptoms of this invisible intruder. It was so much part of her life she would often fight with the unwelcome interloper. Throughout her teens, when an episode came on, she would do battle with it, often screaming at it to let her be. 'Can't you leave me alone – can't you give me peace? Please, go, go away and leave me alone and never return.' Of course, it never let her be, would never give her peace, and would always return. It would return and return until it finally consumed her. Her battle with it would exhaust her, leaving her distraught and mentally drained. Her parents were very understanding of her condition and procured for her the best of treatment that allowed her to enjoy life in between her mood swings. This condition was the curse of Capucine's life and the curse of all her fellow sufferers.

The Six-Minute Lovers

As Cheyenne and Océane snoozed away on this, our fifth day of confinement, I got to thinking about the male of the species. When it came to them, we were always amused and saddened by their ineptitude. To us, it looked like they couldn't help themselves, whatever they did or said always left a question mark about their sanity – a huge one. Nothing quite like the male, is there... nothing genuine about them whatsoever, well, that was our honest assessment of them. Of course, the only grounds we had to come to this conclusion was our exposure to men that passed or should I say trespassed through Capucine's life. We didn't agree on many things but when it came to the male of the species, we were in complete harmony and agreed they were an absolute waste of time and space – well, most of them anyway and not worth the effort women make to appease them. There were, thankfully, a few exceptions. Poor Capucine, however, was not of the same opinion as us, she just liked men and men adored and drooled over her and did so in the most nauseating fashion. She was not the kind of woman to go long without the company of a man – a few weeks without and she would suffer severe withdrawal symptoms. Men flocked to her side like bees to honey, honey she did not give away lightly, but when she did, it was, in general, to the most undeserving of males. Men buzzed around her ready to steal her nectar and give nothing in return. We discovered the male was like that... taking and giving very little in return, especially when it came to women. We would sigh every time she brought another undesirable home, either a friend or a so-called lover. Sometimes it was hard to know the difference. It was disturbing to watch. She didn't have to do much to attract men – just one look was enough. If a man didn't see her face, he wouldn't miss her divine figure, her pose and sensual walk – she had it all. Her very being was a turn-on. She sizzled with sexuality; even the coldest of men would melt at the sight of her. She sent out signals few could ignore or resist. Just a look, a smile, a flash of an ankle or a swish of her hair would be enough to send most men into orbit. All she had to do was walk down the street and men would have palpitations, come out in hot sweats, or become disorientated as she glided past. Men are so weak when it comes to women, so easily led, and aroused, so easily taken in. Women always seem to have one up on them, but men never seem to realise it. They need to be pitied, do they not, these males of the species. Of course, she was very much aware of her effect on the male, of her sexuality, her beauty and style. Apart from her looks and her sensuality, her intellectual prowess also attracted admirers, especially other women. Men – well, they are different. They always feel intimidated and threatened by intelligent and emancipated women as though it was a threat to their masculinity. However, there were men who intellectually stimulated her – more of them anon.

In essence, Capucine had everything, everything except the freedom from her depressive condition. Even with the many attributes she possessed, all the admirers she had, and the love received, she was desperately unhappy, having to suffer the indignity of the soul-destroying bipolar. She would have willingly exchanged her exquisite beauty for a life without mental pain.

When at the market in Lausanne, eyes would follow her every move. The local butcher, Denis de Buc was in rapture every time she stepped into his shop. Denis was a man in his prime but terribly seriously minded, and in general, a very dull person. Worse still, had little interests in women – only politics, his abiding passion. It is reasonable to deduce that only fools and knaves prefer politics to women and poor Denis was one of them. All that political manoeuvring, skulduggery and two-faced nonsense was the one thing that turned him on, well that was until the lovely Capucine stepped into his world. The moment he met her he was hooked and in absolute rapture and politics were soon forgotten. Denis was possessed – mesmerised by her. Every time she entered his shop, he couldn't keep his sparkling blue eyes off her. As he often said to his friend, Theo Blanc, his neighbour, and owner of the local boulangerie, that the lovely Capucine was the best tonic any man could take. He would never fail to tell anyone he met how wonderful she was and would wax lyrical about her at the drop of a hat. She was a lucky woman, always guaranteed his best lean cuts. If you can't afford to turn a woman's head with diamonds, give her your prime cutlets instead – it can't fail to impress. Nothing was of trouble to him. Whatever Capucine asked for he would always go out of his way to get it. Locals would say the highlight of his existence was to serve Capucine – to be in her presence – to share the air she breathed. They would often whisper that he was a sad case in need of treatment. He didn't care what others thought – he was very content with his lot and happy to be acquainted with

85

her. Just knowing her was paradise itself. There is no cure for the likes of him and he wasn't looking for one either. He had it bad and was a very happy man indeed to be near the lovely Capucine, even if it was on an irregular basis at the far end of his butcher's table. When it came to obsession, we rated all the men in her life and Denis, God bless him, scored ten out of ten – a real top of the class obsessive.

He was far from the only one who lost his head over her. Although Theo Blanc would tease Denis about his devotion to Capucine, he himself was as bad and mesmerised by her. His only trouble was, he had to keep his feelings to himself otherwise his wife, a jealous kind, would make his life hell if she thought he had eyes for any other woman than herself, albeit only friendly ones. Theo was a wise man. He admired other women from afar and saved himself from a good verbal hiding in the process – a wise man indeed.

A florist in Lausanne, Mademoiselle, Cécile Charon, who attended to all Capucine's floral needs, was madly in love with her. They first met when Capucine called into her shop on Lausanne's rue Tailo for a bouquet of roses. Cécile had only recently bought the florist shop and Capucine was her first famous client to call, wishing her good luck with her new enterprise. At first, she didn't recognise her famous client but instantly found her an interesting woman. Cécile was an attractive looking woman, very stylish, preferring a 1920's look to the more contemporary one. She was ten years younger than Capucine but looked much younger than her years. It was only after Capucine's third visit when ordering flowers for a soirée she was hosting; she asked whether Cécile would do the flower arrangement. She didn't realise who her client was. On arrival at the apartment, it finally dawned on her she was in the famous Capucine's home after looking at the photos on the wall. She was awestruck as Capucine showed her around the apartment and introduce her to us. All she could say was how cute our names were – never mentioned how beautiful we were – or any endearments to stimulate and massage our egos. We, in turn, watched in wonder as she set about arranging the flowers. They were getting along well and were soon on first name basis. To Cécile's surprise, Capucine invited her to the soirée. I remember the evening well, with Cécile wide-eyed as she was introduced to many famous people and when shaking hands with Audrey Hepburn, nearly passed out. Dirk Bogarde cornered her for a good deal of the evening, probing to find out some snippets about her life, especially how she met Capucine. She was so dumbstruck by his presence she could hardly speak. What she didn't realise, it was she, amongst all the Beautiful People, who was the centre of attention with everyone asking, 'who is she'.

Capucine suffered a breakdown at another soirée Cécile attended, hosted by a film director friend. It took Cécile by surprise and the disturbing nature of the episode she witnessed upset her. After managing to calm Capucine down, she escorted her home and with our assistance, sat with her most of the night as she struggled to come through her trauma. This episode was to last twelve days and Cécile's introduction to an illness she had previously known little or nothing about. She could have taken flight and avoided the trauma of bipolar but stayed and took all the abuse Capucine would throw at her when in her manic state. She didn't understand the illness but with the help of Marcia and a few tips from

Audrey, was soon well versed on it. She quickly understood the importance of patience while dealing with mental illness. Cécile was far from a cat person but soon realised how essential we were to Capucine's well-being and so warmed to us and surprised by our capacity to help, that our very presence was soothing to her mind and soul. Capucine never forgot Cécile's kindness and a beautiful friendship, already steadily growing, blossomed. From then on, whenever she held a soirée or was invited to a reception, she would always remember to invite her, although she rarely accepted as she was not comfortable in the company of strangers, especially the theatrical and film set kind. Cécile was in love with our lovely Capucine. It was so obvious to us, but did she know of Cécile's love for her – I doubt it. If she did, she never let it interfere with their friendship. She preferred Capucine's friendship, one that could last a lifetime rather than declaring her love, a love that may be rejected. We could see the love she had for her. It was in everything she did – the way she talked and looked, and her body language said it all. Yes, Cécile loved Capucine with a passion, a passion only deep emotional love could arouse.

Another devotee was the Spanish coiffeur, Philippe Selis from Jerez. He was the lucky man, who on a regular basis would run his long fingers through her hair. His trainees dreamt of one day having the honour, but Philippe was the only one Capucine wanted, and he made sure it stayed that way. No amateur would be touching her silky-smooth hair. When visiting his salon, the whole place was alighted by her presence. He was her confidante in many ways. As he clipped away, she would tell him of her troubles and often asked for advice, which he would freely give. He would visit the apartment on occasions to ply his trade and we would lay back and enjoy his theatrics as he toyed with her hair and delighted her with his short and tall tales. He was a good teller of yarns with a never-ending stream of them. He made her laugh – always a good way to a woman's heart. She made him tingle – always a good way to keep a man's attention. He knew he was lucky to have the ear of this stunning icon. Men! Well, he was like most of them… easily led by stylish hair, pouting lips and sparkling eyes. I am telling you; men are suckers when it comes to the female form and the prettier the better! He was, however, fully aware of her depressive illness and understood her vulnerability and anxieties and was very attentive in his care of her and at any sign of a downward slide in her health he knew how to deal with it. This came about one day in her apartment when she confided in him about her condition and the complications it brought to her life and how at times, she was unable to cope with it. She was very candid about it, and at first thought he preferred she had never told him, but after mulling it over realised it was a cry for help and he was privileged she had so much confidence in him to lay her soul bare before him. He had access to her apartment and the contact numbers of Marcia and Audrey in case of an emergency. He was a stalwart friend, keeping a protective eye on her. There was no hint of romance between them, just two very good friends who enjoyed each other's company and a good laugh.

As for her choice of men, well, we could do a thesis on them; we, of course, had these men summed up the moment we cast eyes on them. Reading body language is second nature to us felines. It's in our genes, so it didn't take us long to mark their cards. We soon selected pet names for each one of them: Foolish David from the University of Delusion, Inadequate Samuel, a minor actor in life, the cretin Jaques, still attached to his mother's apron strings and poser James, he was a minor English aristocrat who thought he was a major player in the art of snobbery. There were many more, like tetchy Nicolas from Passy in Paris and an inheritor of a fortune but carried around a chronic inferiority complex. He may have had wealth but received no pleasure from it. He would become very defensive and aggressive every time someone mentioned money as though it was an affliction. Capucine became afraid of his volatile temper and thought he would hit her on a few occasions. One day he made a lunge at her, and Cheyenne was at him in an instant, scowling menacingly with extended claws at the ready. He tried to grab her on another occasion and Cheyenne leaped at him and dug her claws in his arm, to let him know you pay for showing aggression towards a woman. He threw her off and grasping his bloodied arm dashed from the apartment in a huff. She finally realised she was on to a loser and sent him packing back to Paris and another romance fizzled out. We had no hesitation of giving him ten out of ten on our table of Nasty Slobs. Tutalou was a devoted observer of the men who traipsed through Capucine's life; using her and irritating us with their platitudes of devotion that were often shallow and hollow. You would never believe the crassness of some of them. Tutalou was of the opinion that men in general, believe good one-liners were enough to impress a woman and a few well-placed stanzas enough to get her into bed. What a deluded lot they are.

They are a sad bunch and need pitied. The maxim that men are from Mars and women from Venus has a lot of credence to it.

One thing we observed was these 'lovers' if that's what they were, didn't care or want to or understand her condition or the trauma she suffered. They only wanted to use her and brag to others that they were an item and the latest beau of the lovely Capucine and the envy of every man in town, yet she would continue to select this kind as her friend and some-time suitor as though she had no say in it. What she saw in most of them was a mystery and completely lost on Tutalou. She called them cads. I favoured drips and Cheyenne pre-ferred shits. With a few exceptions, they were the most unre-liable and unstable of men. The exceptions, well, I'll get round to them later. Yes, these undesirables, on the surface would be well-groomed and successful men. However, we observed most were fatally flawed and self-obsessed slobs. For an ex-tremely intelligent woman, one would have thought she need-ed intellectual stimulation but not with this crop of losers. As I said before, she received it from women more than she did from men – but there again; seeing men are intellectually infe-rior to women we shouldn't be that surprised. Men take a lot of understanding we discovered. The only way men will ever be understood is if every woman was a psychiatrist. Worse still, men can't understand themselves. They think they do, but they are all deluded. No wonder they and the world are always in chaos.

We were of the opinion that the worst kind of male lover has the brain the size of a pea. Take Heinz, for example. He was a first-class act of an ass if there ever was. What she saw in him baffled Tutalou, perplexed Cheyenne and bamboozled me. I thought maybe there was something about him we'd missed... but nothing ever materialised. We called him 'The swine from the Rhine.' He treated her like dirt, showed her little respect but thankfully stopped short at hitting her – what a man he was! I had to restrain Tutalou from clawing the eyes out of him on a few occasions. There was an incident when Capucine was in the throes of a violent rage and instead of comforting and reassuring her, he went into a rant saying she was a self-obsessed control freak and an attention seeker. This only made her more unstable, but he didn't leave it there. No, this ass then called her mad and neurotic and left her shattered as he told her they were finished. He was no loss to her, and we were relieved to see the back of him, but she wasn't. For days on end, she cried and fretted at his loss – her fragile world once more began to crack and fall asunder.

Then there was Peter, the stud from Montenegro. He was some lad. I remember him so well. He was handsome and mad as hell – thought he was a Casanova, bragged that in his native Montenegro and in particular in the capital, Podgorica he bedded more women than he cared to remember. I thought it was all macho talk and nothing more as most men of a particular persuasion talk like that. His rugged looks and impeccable manners captivated Capucine. That was her problem; all of her men were like that, handsome and suave but behind the masquerade were weak and unstable men. Peter was one of them. She knew of his reputation and the rumour he was sleeping around, yet for a time ignored this. In doing so was taking a terrible risk with her health. It finally dawned on her he was a liability, and he received his marching orders. He didn't take kindly to this and when she threatened to call the police, he wisely left. She had a lucky escape from the grip of the Casanova of Montenegro.

Although we observed her lovers took different times during their amorous adventures, one thing was certain, they were all in a mighty hurry, so we labelled them her six-minute lovers. We got this from a term used about former President of France, Françoise Mitterrand. He was a womaniser. It was said he didn't hang around much in the bedroom. He would slip the key in the door, say hello; make love, have a shower and leave. He was nicknamed the six-minute lover by one of his critics and the label stuck. He always professed to love women but any man in such a hurry to get away from them can't in any way love women – Sounds more like he had an aversion to them.

One place we weren't allowed to stray was into her bedroom when she had a lover on-board – It was non-negotiable. There were no exceptions. When we did try, she would chase us away and told not to be so nosey.

Men and Capucine – It was never easy. She once declared '*I used to think I needed a man to define myself. Not anymore.*' How right she was. Don't get me wrong, she wasn't an absolute failure with men – far from it! She may have had her fair share of weak and unsuitable men trespass through her life, but she did have some who were the complete opposite. When making the film, *The Lion*, she fell in love with the actor William Holden, fifteen years her senior. He was gorgeous and we loved having him to stay. Cheyenne would be in ecstasy every time he appeared and left in a trance for a few days after every visit.

Unfortunately, William was married but Capucine still fell for him, unaware at the time he was carrying about his own illness, his own burden in life, that of a chronic alcoholic. He was a strong and caring man, and she had found someone she could finally relate to, not only socially but also emotionally, sexually, and more important to her, intellectually. He was an excellent conversationalist and intellectually stimulating which appealed to her. It was on the film set he first noticed she was carrying a burden around with her but had no inkling as to what it was. Although she was beautiful, he noticed dark rings around her eyes marred her beauty. He thought she must be fatigued or run down or recovering from an illness. They began seeing each other socially and when enjoying a meal at a restaurant in Los Angeles she confided in him she was a manic-depressive. His response was not what she was expecting. There was no uncomfortable shuffling on his seat, fidgeting with his hands or eyes diverting – how most react to the realisation the one they are talking to is suffering from some form of mental illness. Instead, she discovered a caring and understanding man. She thought he would run a mile at the revelation, but no, he sat with her for hours listening to her explain her condition – how it was affecting her life, and how she was coping with it. She was surprised that he could be so attentive and sensitive to her condition. He asked many questions and showed a genuine interest. That night when she returned to her hotel, she thought, even though he had been sympathetic and understanding, the next day after a night of reflection, he would be cool towards her. There was no filming the next day, and she heard nothing from him. Again, she thought, maybe it is not a good idea to tell others

94

of your condition. Perhaps, for your own sanity, it is best to keep your mental state to yourself.

When filming resumed, she was surprised, when arriving at her dressing room to receive a boutique of flowers. '*We all have to suffer mentally in life in some form or other and understanding each other's pain is the key to mental rehabilitation,*' the blue-tinted and lavender perfumed card read. She was impressed and felt relief he hadn't abandoned her. They met again and romance blossomed. She was always conscious he was married but she couldn't resist him. Audrey had warned her about his amorous side and wandering eye, but it didn't make much difference. For the first time in her life, she had a lover who didn't leave or threaten to leave when an episode occurred or when she flew into a rage or suffered one of her morose periods – he was there and able to cope and comfort her. He stayed to take all the verbal abuse and still be there when she came out of it and soothed her troubled mind as no other could. Her time with him was some of the happiest and most fulfilling in her life. She knew it wouldn't last, as his track record with women did not inspire confidence. He was not the kind of man to stay with a woman long as the chase and conquest of a woman was his thrill in life, after that he was seeking pastures new, but she didn't care and was content to hang onto him and enjoy his company as long as it lasted.

He underwent a vasectomy. Having two children already, he didn't want more or to be more accurate he wanted to be free to have relationships without any risk of fatherhood. It didn't concern Capucine as all she wanted and desired was him. She always gave the impression it was with William she would have settled down if given half the chance. He understood the nature of her condition and she was madly in love with him and valued every second of their relationship and the friendship that grew from it. William – he was far from a six-minute lover. However, the romance didn't last long, two years to be precise, mostly because of his chronic addiction to alcohol that she found difficult to handle, but out of it came a solid friendship. He never stopped caring for her and would do so for the rest of his life.

Before he met Capucine, he had a short affair with Audrey, but it fizzled out. She had talked to him about Capucine on a few occasions but never about her condition. Capucine was worried this new relationship might sour her friendship with Audrey, but far from it. She discovered their friendship was solid, an unshakable bond and nothing would ever come between it, especially men and certainly not William.

Ah, then there was Dirk, the handsome and suave, Dirk Bogarde. We loved this man and when he visited, he brought us out in goose pimples, and she bloomed at the very sight of him. He would spoil us in every possible way as he did Capucine. He adored her and worshipped the ground she walked upon. He loved her, of that I'm sure but she always held back with her emotions. They were lovers – if they weren't, I'd love to know what they were up to in the bedroom – they certainly weren't talking politics or praying together. They first met in 1960 on the set of *Song Without End* and since then he became a constant presence in her life. He wanted to marry her, but she dithered, never saying yes or no. They were the perfect couple and looked so good together. What a pity they never married. We couldn't help but laugh at the gossip and the innuendo by the press that he was the other way inclined. If he was, he sure knew how to handle women. We watched him in operation, especially with Capucine, and I can tell you he was all male, make no doubt about it. This all came about because of his friendship with Tote; his close friend and manager, who he lived with. Gossip being gossip the innuendo soon becomes fact to some people. The modern trend is to label people. If a man lives with another man and is not married, or has no girlfriend, he is gay, or if a woman in a similar situation, she is lesbian.

On a few occasions, we visited his home at *Le Pigeonnier* at Grasse on the Cote d'Azur where he would indulge us in every possible way. Capucine often complained about his excesses, and he must stop spoiling us. His response was always the same, 'yes dear', and then he would continue feeding us titbits when she wasn't looking.

So, this is a little insight into her love life, a love life that she could never fully embrace. However pathetic, good, or understanding her lovers were, it was her condition that ruled her emotions, her thinking and her very existence.

Speculation

For the dead, there is little rest if in life they happened to have been beautiful, famous, and mysterious. So, it was with the beauty of Lausanne. Before she was even laid to rest speculation began about her sexuality, the men in her life, her reclusive lifestyle, but the illness that drove her to her demise was all but an afterthought to most media mogul and their editors. The only time they take an interest in mental health issues is when they wish to demean the sufferers as they did on occasions with Capucine. It is only sex and scandal that sells papers and that is exactly what they were looking for when it came to Capucine, this tormented, fragile and faded star.

Capucine was a very private person, at times shy and retiring and resented the constant harassment and intrusion in her life by the paparazzi. Her sanctuary away from their preying lens was her penthouse apartment that was out of their reach, her haven from the madness of the world where she could relax and be herself in the company of her three feline friends. She accepted the paparazzi interest concerning her profession but found it intolerable they would not allow her a private life away from their lens and the gutter press. The constant pursuit of her caused a lot of stress and anxiety that worsened her condition. Because of this, in the latter part of her life, she became reclusive, which only added to her mystique and compounded her already fragile state.

Now that she had departed this world, it was open season for the filth peddlers and speculators to put their boot in and tear her apart, to portray her in any way they wished. Forget about the goodness of the woman and her humanity, all they wanted was scandal, sexual innuendo, and sensationalism. They said she was lesbian and concocted scenarios to fit in with their allegations citing so-called relationships. When investigated there was not a modicum of evidence to justify the claims, yet the allegation persisted. Not content with that, they intimated she was a man-eater, bordering on nymphomania. The list of men she allegedly sank her teeth into was endless. The most outrageous claim of all, she was a man masquerading as a woman. There was no stopping them. How could anyone suggest she could possibly be a man? There was never anything masculine about her, not in her manner, stance or looks. That is how tabloids and dirt rags get their kicks by demeaning, belittling, and bullying others until they run them into the ground and get their money's worth of dirt, unconcerned by the damage they have caused.

Ah! the danger of being beautiful, famous, and mysterious.

The Reality of Capucine

As the other two slept soundly, I was wide-awake. We were now facing our sixth day in the apartment. I had a fretful night, sleeping on and off with Capucine very much on my mind. I was thinking about one day in particular when the reality of her illness showed us how devastating and soul-destroying it was and what a curse and injustice to its unfortunate sufferers. I remember the day well. It's seared into my mind.

It was a Monday, a bright and sunny May morning with Lausanne in full bloom, as spring burst forth in all her opulence and colour. The balcony doors were open. The fragrance from the flowers and herbs that festooned the balcony drifted into the apartment. The bees were busy with a couple of willow-tits twittered away on the balcony rail. Capucine adored her penthouse apartment with its panoramic view of Lake Geneva, with Mont Blanc and the soaring Alps in the distance and the peace and tranquillity of the neighbourhood. It was home to her restless soul and her sanctuary away from the glitzy and shallow world of showbiz and a world that didn't understand or want to understand her condition and the mental suffering it brought.

Capucine loved Lausanne with a passion. The city gave zest to her life and a buzz no other city could, not even Paris with all its beauty and temptations. Although a lover of Paris, it was here she was at ease and at home. It was here she put down her roots and was very much part of the fabric of this fashionable lakeside city.

She had guests arriving later in the day, a visit from Phillipe Selis and lunch with a publisher who was keen to sign her up to write her memoirs, something she was not too keen in doing but the publisher, Léon Roulet, a pugnacious kind was not interested in her saying no. He was not a man to give up easily. The truth was she preferred to leave her past behind as there were too many painful memories of what might have been, too many ghosts of past demons, broken romances, and family traumata. The thought of having to recall all for an autobiography filled her with dread, even more disturbing, would be someone writing a biography about her.

It had the makings of a good day, but her depressive illness had other plans. It would dictate how her day would be in every possible way, and she would have no say in it, absolutely none. She awoke to the bright sun streaming through the open French windows and the chirping of the birds but didn't see or hear them or feel the refreshing breeze from the lake on her skin or hear the soft snoring of Cheyenne, snuggled up at the foot of the bed. What consumed her was the blackness and bleakness of her condition and hadn't the energy to rise from her bed or to focus on the world about her. This was nothing new. It was the reality of her life – the burden of her life; the cross she was destined to carry. It became heavier and heavier after every soul-destroying episode. She would fall many a time under its weight until she could bear it no longer. This was bipolar in full swing, in its most vindictive mood, unsympathetic to anyone, to suffering or pain. It was not just a yoke for her to carry but the curse of her life, the curse of so many lives. This sinister condition we had witnessed so many times was indifferent to race, creed, sex, or class, and has ruined millions of lives and ended many and will continue to do so until there is a cure or a universal understanding of it. Since her early teens, she had awoken to many mornings like this when the demon within tore into her, ripping her apart and eating away at her soul, chipping away at her self-confidence and her ability to cope with life. There was little release for her once in its grip. Years of torment had taken its toll. Some days were worse than others – some manageable, others, a living hell. She had routines that gave her life a framework, a kind of structure so she could function. In general, these worked, but there were episodes she had no control over, so destructive, so devastating they threatened the very foundations that were so essential in allowing her to function as a normal human being. Once these episodes occurred, she had no rational control over her physical or emotional being. When the black dog got a grip, she couldn't shake it off. Once it had its serrated teeth into her there was no relenting, it gripped harder and harder, deeper, and deeper, tossing her emotionally back and forth and physically draining her. Try as she could, it would not loosen its grip until it left her physically and mentally shattered and crying for deliverance from this injustice in her life.

Not the most religious of women, although a spiritual soul, she did on occasions cry out to God to set her free, to have pity on her, to end this burden of a life that was becoming tiresome and heavier to bear by each passing day, but He didn't hear her agonizing cries. She often cursed her life, cursed the God that had inflicted this disorder on her, then relented and let God off the hook, then cursed Him again. She had fallen in and out of love with God so often and would continue to do so until her tragic end. Oh, the times she had screamed at Him, swore at Him, then begged to Him to have compassion on her, to show her the love and tender care He says is there to be ours. It can be hard to believe in a compassionate God when one is in agonizing pain and torment when your inner demon is tearing you to threads.

She needed relief and would seek it wherever it could be found. On many occasions, she visited Lausanne cathedral where she would sit in quiet contemplation in the chapel of St-Ruiane. She rarely attended a service, instead settling for private prayer.

The three of us would often sit and discuss the phenomenon that is religion. We felines don't have a need for it, as we already know the secrets of the universe, unlike humans who are still searching and can never see the truth before them and the secrets within. Capucine, however, would find solace in prayer that was all-important to give her some release from her mental pain.

She tried so hard to understand the nature of the illness, read everything there was available. Devoured every kind of medical journal you could think of, reviews, clinical reports, trauma testimonies and papers by the most knowledgeable and prominent experts in the field of mental illness. We would often snuggle up to her on the sofa as she read them, such as *The Lancet* or *The Jama*, sometimes reading them out aloud. She studied in detail the conditions that make up the bipolar disorder, reading testaments of sufferers and videos of which she would spend hours viewing. We would watch them with her, but I found them too disturbing. However, Cheyenne couldn't take her eyes off them, taking in everything like she was a medical student. As for Tutalou, her attention span was short and would soon nod off. Capucine also attended many lectures or symposiums to try to get to grips with it but all to no avail. The truth be told, she was so well versed on mental health and bipolar as any consultant or expert, yet her mind was set on a cure, even though throughout all her studies it could not be made any clearer, there was none – no cure, only containment. We put this obsession for a cure down to her inner demon dictating her thought processes.

She would reflect a lot on life; was an inveterate philosopher, not as good as we felines but good all the same. Yes, she was an excellent deep thinker – would ask the unanswerable questions, you know the kind insecure humans always ask, something we felines never do – what is life about? What purpose does it serve and does it have any rhyme or reason to it. Apart from these questions, she would often ask why her, why did she have to carry this burden and suffer the indignity of it all. What had she done to deserve this fate? She never found the answers as there are none. Questions, questions – she would forever question everything, not just the evil that is bipolar but the mystery of life itself, which in her condition was not the best path to take. Many of her family and friends believed she taxed her mind too much about life's mysteries that the only outcome was anxiety, confusion, annoyance, and more depression, making her illness more profound and potentially life-threatening.

She and Audrey would often sit cross-legged on the rug in front of a roaring fire discussing life and, on many occasions, her depressive illness. Audrey had a good grasp of its makeup and was always good counsel to Capucine. They had many an argument about it but always ended with an embrace and kiss. They would never, on any occasion say goodbye or sleep on an argument or any kind of disagreement. Audrey was the main anchor in her life, who she treasured dearly. The great thing about these two beauties, they were not only devoted friends but also soul mates – soul mates to the end and nothing, not even bipolar, men or we three feline philosophers could ever come between them.

On this fine morning, Capucine was drenched in sweat after a restless night, her eyes swollen, and face contorted with the pain she was suffering. She tried to focus on the world about her, but it had all but disappeared. All she could see were dark, brooding, and menacing shadows that danced and hovered over her like demons gathering for the kill. All she could hear was the erratic beating of her heart, a heart grown tired of life, in need of rest, or repair – a heart dying from within. The beautiful day was irrelevant to this broken soul, prostrate on her bed, crying for deliverance from her mental pain, wishing she were dead – wishing she had never been born, wishing she could sleep and never wake up.

Cheyenne had been observing Capucine her since the early hours, knowing she was heading for a breakdown. She knew her moods and swings so well she could always detect when they would arise. Capucine had been on a high the previous evening, the last of thirteen days of accelerated euphoria, dashing about the house, singing, and calling friends, stirring them from their sleep to tell of the new TV film that was up and coming or just idle chat and how much she loved them. Her mind was racing, her speech rapid, then, within a short time sank into a deep remorseful low, weeping uncontrollably. She prowled the apartment with her arms wrapped about her then suddenly dashed out onto the balcony, her eyes wide and wild, her nostril flared. The night was clear with a large blue moon shining down on her. Sitting between the large pots of lavender, she cradled her aching head and cried hysterically. We could do nothing but sit at her feet, watch, and share her pain as she cried and screamed out into the darkness of the night. Her shrill cries made our fur creep. She called out to her mother as she often did; begging to be held, to be rescued, and to be assured all will be well.

It was late when she staggered to her bed, unable to keep her eyes open then drifted off into a well overdue sleep. We sighed with relief, but it wouldn't last long until the demon had its way. When she awoke, we knew she would quickly sink into the lowest depth of her depression; we were always ready for whatever it might bring. There were times when she just lay in bed for days on end, dishevelled, with her hair matted from lack of care and rarely washing, so different from her normal self. She only managed to stagger from her bed to feed us then back again, hardly eating or drinking herself. It was only when Marcia or Audrey called around would she eat anything substantial and with their encouragement, shower, dress and return to some kind of normality.

Cheyenne nudged me as I curled up, trying to sleep.

'Wake up!'

I opened my eyes and knew instantly something was amiss as there was tension in the air.

'You too, Tutalou,' Cheyenne whispered as she gently pushed her with her paw.

Capucine was restless and tossed back and forth until she was exhausted, then fell heavily onto the floor, screaming and clutching her hair, her knuckles white from tension. We looked on in despair. She struggled to get to her feet, then ran from room to room, screaming, her eyes ablaze, her heart thumping as the growing anger within made her shudder violently. Her perspiring face was ashen, her chiselled features contorted as the pain of her mental torment tore through her.

I jumped down from the bed and ran, meowing towards her. She kicked out, screaming, 'Out of the way, you horrible shit – away with you.' I avoided the kicks and the vase that followed, splintering across the lobby's black and white marble floor. This was her prized porcelain vase, a family heirloom. We knew she would regret its loss once she recovered, that was if she was able to remember. This was the first time she had ever sworn or kicked out at us in a violent manner or thrown anything. She was dashing from room to room, kicking out and screaming obscenities as she ran then stood in front of the open French doors of the balcony and cried out, her screams filling the clear morning air.

Tutalou and Cheyenne followed behind me, crying, knowing what Capucine was experiencing was something different. Her condition had reached a more serious level. It was scary – it was alarming to see her completely out of control and in the throes of her debilitating condition, in the grip of her inner demon and unable to do anything to free herself. We could only help when she began to ease out of the trauma after her demon had done its worst. Bipolar was like a slave master, whatever she did, she couldn't escape the sting of its painful whip. On this occasion, the whip was relentless as it cut into her, driving her further and further towards the edge. She screamed again and clenching her cheeks, dug her nails into her flesh. Dashing from the balcony, she headed for the bedroom still clutching her face. We ran after her, frantic with worry at what she might do next. She tore off her negligée, throwing it across the room; then slumped onto the bed, thumping her chest, and screeching something inaudible. Her ghostly face was smudged with blood as pearls of perspiration formed on her forehead. Her eyes were wide open and darting to and fro in an erratic fashion as she clutched the eiderdown tightly, her nails digging deep into the fabric. Screaming, she buried her face in the eiderdown as she tossed and turned, her guttural groans eerily echoing around the apartment. We sighed with despair as we patiently waited for her pain to subside. However, many times we witnessed an episode, we could never get used to it, but this one was more disturbing and deeper in its intensity than any other. It was painful and soul-destroying to observe, to listen to her plaintive cries and helpless to do anything to comfort her. All we could do was to be with her and wait until her pain eased.

Cheyenne tried to get near her, but she kicked out. Her cries became shrill, her naked body now soaked in sweat with strands of hair clinging to her distorted face. She was now in the violent throes of bipolar, out of control with no one to hear her painful cries except us, her faithful cats, who died inside with every agonizing cry. They had no end; they raged on and on until they finally began to subside as exhaustion set in.

After she calmed down it was time for us to do our tasks. Cheyenne crept towards her, gently stretching out and touching her trembling feet with her paw. She violently kicked the paw away, screaming at Cheyenne, who, not one to give up, again crept slowly towards her and gently stretched out her paw, this time managing to softly touch the big toe of Capucine's left foot. She gave out a sigh but did not reject the softness of the caring paw. Cheyenne tenderly touched each toe in preparation for her stimulating and healing treatment.

Meanwhile, Tutalou crawled on her belly towards Capucine's head. She managed to get close to her face and gently touched the sweat-soaked cheek with the tips of her whiskers that sent an immediate relaxing sensation through-out Capucine's body. She quivered and gave out a submis-sive cry as her contorted face began to relax with her darting eyes returning to some kind of normality. Tutalou continued to let her whiskers do their healing work as I began my task. Once I was certain she was reacting positively to Tutalou and Cheyenne's touch, I made my way onto her chest and rested upon her heart. She made no resistance but laid her hand on my head, gently stroking my ears. My purring soon relaxed her and gradually regulated her racing heart to its normal rhythm. She momentary opened her eyes and looked at me. There was relief on her face and began to relax and even managed a slight smile, the dullness in her eyes beginning to show a glimmer of life. Cheyenne, in the meantime, continued manipulating her toes. She worked on each one until she felt the tension easing out of Capucine's body, then touched the big toe of her left foot, manipulating it to allow the sensory nerves to send relief to her tense and knotted muscles and nervous system, then touched the big toe on the right foot en-abling the muscles in her shoulders to loosen. Cheyenne had a natural flair for reflexology, became an expert, and never failed to stimulate the nerves of our tortured friend. She was as dexterous with the ear technique as she was with the toes but could only perform this when Capucine was in a more congenial mood. Capucine enjoyed the feline touch and would often relax on the sofa as Cheyenne performed her skills. It was there she would allow her to manipulate her ears.

Once we had exercised our expertise, it didn't take long for her to finally unwind and fall asleep and allowed us to close our weary eyes and recharge our emotional batteries.

Later that morning, Phillipe Selis arrived but could get no reply on the buzzer. Capucine would rarely miss an appointment, so, feeling a little concerned he let himself in. He was one of the select few of her trusted friends who had a key to the apartment. The moment he opened the door and caught sight of the shattered vase he realised something was amiss as her normally tidy apartment was in disarray. Jumping down from the bed, we ran out to meet him, meowing for his attention. He called out for Capucine but there was no reply. Noticing the balcony doors open he dashed outside with his heart in his mouth. She wasn't there and nervously looked over the balcony and sighed with relief, realising his fears were unfounded but felt guilty that such a thought passed through his mind. We ran crying towards the bedroom, and he swiftly followed. He entered to find the room in a mess with Capucine naked and sound asleep on the dishevelled bed, grasping a sprig of lavender in her limp hand. He tried to waken her, but she just moaned and turned over. He checked her for any signs of injury and once satisfied she was in no danger cleaned the blood off her cheeks and dried her sweat soaked body then covered her with the eiderdown. He phoned the doctor and Marcia, explaining the situation. He tidied up the room and the rest of the apartment whilst waiting for them. Marcia was the first to arrive and took charge of the situation with the doctor following shortly afterwards. It was a day we could never forget. It left our Capucine devastated and us traumatised and emotionally drained.

Many a time as we lay on the rug, we would discuss mental illness and its devastating effects and why humans suffer from it and not us felines, or, as far as we knew, other animals. Many experts contend that all animals suffer some form of depressive illness, but if they do, we certainly don't and not the symptoms of bipolar and all the horrors it brings. We have our bad days OK but not on the scale as bipolar sufferers do. Many of our philosophical discussions would be about why humans are so indifferent to the sufferings of others and those who suffer with what they class as 'mental disorders'. Humans are odd, one moment they are doing everything possible for those suffering from illnesses of the body and injuries caused by accidents but mention anything to do with the mind or mental health, and they take flight. They are a disgrace apart from a few enlightened souls, like Audrey, Marcia, Cécile, Philippe and Capucine's psychiatrist, a most humane man and those dedicated to the relief and care of those in mental bondage.

So, this was the reality of this charming but damaged woman, to the outside world an iconic beauty, successful, engaging, and mysterious but behind this veneer was a fragile and tortured woman, a sufferer of a terrible condition, locked in a prison of pain and on a downward spiral to disaster.

Instead of trying to accommodate her condition through a strict medical regime, she wanted to do battle with it and beat it into submission. This was never to be. She was always going to lose. There was no cure or deliverance, only containment within the structures of medication, through therapy and the help of friends, including us. That was the truth of the matter, but she refused to see it. She always fought the medication, the medication that would have been her saviour, if only she could have accepted it.

The Warmth of Petit-Chéne

Memories – that was all Cécile Charon had left as she opened the door to her florist shop. She sat in her wet clothes unable to stop crying and thinking of Capucine.

She had no idea what was to befall her friend the last time they met as they walked arm-in-arm to the top of Petit-Chéne to visit the annual Christmas fair in Lausanne. The city was alight with festive warmth. Wrapped up against the fierce cutting wind that swirled around Rue Grand St-Jean and the sprinkling of the first winter snow they enjoyed the excitement of the night as the crowd mingled around the stalls buying last-minute presents, chattering, and laughing as they went with the carol singers on the corner of Petit-Chéne in full voice. They stopped to listen to all of the popular carols: The Holly and the Ivy, Away in a Manger, Little Donkey and many more. There was a warm and cosy feel about them as they linked arms, swaying to the festive music, and joining in a few choruses.

After shopping they retired to Chez Lou, a once favourite haunt of Capucine before she became reclusive, to enjoy a Christmas meal together. This was a rare visit as Capucine seldom left her apartment as her illness was taking its toll, not just on her mental health but also her physical health. She was feeling more isolated and alone than at any time in her life. Her zest for life she experienced between her bouts of illness had all but disappeared. Cécile, aware of this, persuaded her into going out and it was a welcome break from her insular routine. Her only excursions were to partake in the odd

TV drama or a photo shoot. Even this took a lot of effort. Her looks were starting to fade, and her increasing social phobia was beginning to control her life, making her paranoid and a prisoner, not just in her apartment but also in her mind. It took Cécile a lot of coaxing to get her to go and was delighted she came, although she did not know at the time it would be their last meal together, their last embrace and final kiss. They were relaxed and chatted, laughed, and enjoyed the seasonal meal and life for those few hours could not have been better.

Cécile accompanied her home, but she was in a very reflective mood talking a lot about her mother and things past and what might have been. She never mentioned anything about the future or anything positive. Every time Cécile tried to lighten up the conversation, it did not take long until it returned to the negative.

Capucine gave her a Christmas present of a saffron umbrella. Cécile in return, a headscarf she bought when visiting her brother in Vienna. They embraced and Cécile left not knowing she would never see her friend again.

On arriving home, she checked with Audrey and Marcia to ask if they had noticed any change in Capucine's demeanour of late. They had not, apart from their concerns over her increasing reclusiveness, so she put her concerns aside thinking she was just having an off day.

Cécile was always grateful for the quality time spent with this delightful and fascinating woman. She relished these periods of calm and relaxation because dark clouds would always follow Capucine and the darkest cloud of all was hovering not far away.

The Problem with Humans

The days were getting longer, and we were becoming rather mournful, lacklustre, and worrying about what might be. To snap out of this, I started reminiscing about some of our happy and wacky times and no other cat can be as wacky as Cheyenne.

I well remember the day when she surprised us with her latest revelation. This was a few years before we lost Capucine. It was typical of how we drifted into physiological discussions. It usually came out of nowhere, just as this one did. Cheyenne, always one guaranteed to come up with something different, or should I say weird, surpassed herself with this gem.

'Tell me, Océane, did you ever wish you were a human being?'

I looked at her through narrowed eyes and gasped, my whiskers bristling at her audacity. 'A human being – Are you mad? Have you lost the little sense you had?'

'Mad! What's mad about it? It's been going through my mind a lot of late. I wouldn't have minded being one, that's all I'm saying – not forever – I'm not that mad – just for a little while to see what it's like, to see if it is all it is made out to be.'

'Whatever for,' I asked, bemused by her logic.

'I just do!'

'You forget who and what you are, Cheyenne. Do you not understand your lineage – your bloodline – your majestic background? Nothing is more superior to being feline. Why would you want to change that to be one of *them*, with all their hang-ups and peculiar goings-on? Why?'

'Well, I must remind you it's one of *them* that feeds us and tends to all our needs – It's one of *them* that spoils, pampers and indulges us in every possible way. Our Capucine, I'm talking about.'

'Yes, she does, and others too but why would you like to be one of *them*? It's such a crazy notion and even crazier for a fellow feline to suggest it. What have they got we don't? Tell me because I don't know.'

'Do I have to answer that?'

'Yes, seeing you have a fancy to be one.'

'It's far from a crazy notion – they have a lot we don't – a lot. To start with, they know how to live, to have a good time, don't they and always live their lives close to the edge. Their lives seem to be exciting and fulfilled – not like ours that can be dull and boring at times, just lazing about the place. They have a structured life and know where they are going even if it is over the edge. They also know how to laugh at themselves and have a good time.'

'Are you saying we don't,' Tutalou asked as she stretched out on the windowsill.

'Well, we are not exactly a barrel full of laughs, are we?'

'Talk for yourself,' replied Tutalou, 'I have a fantastic offbeat and dry sense of humour. If I were human, I'd make a great stand-up comic or better still, a politician.'

'Lazing about here all day doing nothing but eating, snoozing, and philosophising about life is far from fun. We don't exactly set the world alight with our talk and laughter, do we?' Cheyenne replied. 'Humans, as well as having a good time, know the meaning of humour, laughter and fun. They fit so much into their lives whereas we stagnate in our uneventful lives, boring each other rigid with our worn- out philosophy. They always find time for the basic pleasures of life too, like travelling the world, soaking up culture, eating, relaxing in the sun, and being pampered by their loved ones, and I can't forget the best of all – sex!'

'You may not be full of laughter, but I am,' I informed her. 'I can see the funny side of everything and don't have to imagine myself as one of *them* to enjoy it. I'm happy in my feline skin as you ought to be.'

'I am, but still think I would make a good human, though, that's all I'm saying.'

'Would you now and what kind would you be?'

'The best of course – what else – I'm not daft altogether and aware how peculiar they can be. Although mindful of the many serious and unstable fault lines in their structure and behaviour as we have often observed and debated, there is a good side to them too. Yes, their good side appeals to me. I know I would enjoy the experience, only for a short period. I wouldn't want to over-indulge in their condition – that would be bordering on insanity – just a little exposure would suit me fine. Just a taste would do, to see what it's like.'

'You don't say,' I cynically replied.

'Yes, I do. I can also see the joke that is the human condition?'

We both looked at her in amazement.

'Whatever do you mean, Cheyenne? What joke?'

'Tut! Tut! Océane, must I explain to you the peculiarities and complexities of the human condition? For a cat, you know very little if you don't know what these are. You're not even curious for heaven's sake. What kind of cat are you if you're not curious?'

'A wise one…'

'A wise cat – nothing wise about you I'm afraid if you don't understand the basic instinct of a cat, like being curious. You are far from *wise.*'

'Of course, I'm curious. I'm always curious to know every-thing, especially these peculiarities, these complexities you are on about. What are they?'

'Do I have to list them?'

'You mean to say there are lots of them?' Tutalou laughed.

'Yes, a never-ending stream. They have so many it would take a lifetime, or eight of ours to describe them.'

'Well, off you go. Let's hear them?'

'For heaven's sake, aren't we always laughing at them? They're a complicated lot, that's for sure. I always thought we felines had a few peculiarities and complexities to contend with but these humans, well, they're in a league of their own – leave us standing with their hang-ups, rituals, habits, and ad-dictions. They get hung up on the most peculiar of things.'

'Hang-ups – peculiar – such as,' Tutalou asked, as she stretched out after her slumber that was disturbed by Chey-enne's ramblings. 'They had better be good. I hope you didn't wake me from my slumber for some nonsense or other. I need to be intellectually stimulated, not verbally assaulted with your usual insane and neurotic ramblings, so make it good and snappy. Let's get this right. You say our human friends are peculiar, with loads of hang-ups.'

'Yes.'

'Not just peculiar but also serial addicts in every possible way, with bad habits and worse still, you'd like be one of *them*?'

'Yes!'

'And you want to experience the human condition?'

'Yes!'

'And you say you're not nuts?'

'Far from it – I'm as sane as you can get.'

'I've never heard such rubbish before, wanting to be human. Even humans don't like being human most of the time. Just be content to be feline and realise how lucky you are.'

'She's right about one thing, Tutalou,' I replied. 'They are peculiar, as we know darn well. There's another word or several I can use to sum them up than peculiar, like weird, mad, and how about psychotic and a few rude words too but being of good breeding I won't utter them. As for wanting to experience the human condition, you must be deranged to even think about it. Now that we've heard about their bad side let's hear what's so fascinating about them that you want to be one?'

After having my say, Cheyenne flexed her muscles and gave a good stretch, as she was apt to do when inspiration got to her, then lay down, resting her head on her paws.

'Well, naturally, it's only the good parts I want to experience not their peculiar and irritating habits – that would never do.'

'Are there any good ones?'

'Yes! They wear clothes, don't they? That's a good trait to start with. They have what they call style, class, and sophistication as our Capucine and Audrey have. Of all the things I would like to experience, it is their fashion – it is sublime. To indulge in little *haute couture* therapy would be heaven – oh, it makes me tingle just thinking about it.'

'What, to wear *clothes*?' cried Tutalou, alarmed at such a thought.

'Yes. Just look at the clothes Capucine and Audrey wear. They are superb. It must be thrilling wearing all those fashionable things – fantastic clothes designed by those fashion houses of Paris and Milan – made from all those delicate fibres that are great to the touch – not like us with our one coat that we can't change. What about their lipstick, false eyelashes and fancy hairdos – oh, yes, I fancy all that, and the shoes they wear and those fancy stocking and leggings with their superb designs. Ah! It makes my head twirl at the very thought of it.'

'Yes, I can imagine you in your fancy stockings and high heels, done up to the nines with your lipstick, false eyelashes and hairdo, smelling to high heaven and strutting about the place like a high-class tart,' laughed Tutalou.

'Pfff! You may snigger but I'm the one with style and imagination, not you,' Cheyenne indignantly replied. 'Do you see what they eat? Not like our limited cuisine. They have an appreciation for good food. Their cuisine is spectacular and the names they give them are beauty itself and they have fine restaurants to indulge this pleasure, whereas we nibble away on our limited cuisine in engraved silver plates on a cold marble floor and have no choice – no menus to choose from, nothing to whet the appetite.'

'You need to see a psychiatrist,' said Tutalou. 'A feline one to get you back on track.'

'Yes, I can understand what you say, but a little exposure to the human condition wouldn't do any harm at all and would be a great experience – it would suit me just fine. I like their restaurant way of life. Apart from food and fashion, they are into those exquisite perfumes like our Capucine uses, such as Chanel, Christian Dior, Yves Saint Laurent and Givenchy and they have fantastic names for each range like *J'adore* and *Mademoiselle*. Um, yes, I fancy it. Bring it on, bring on the human condition!'

'You're barking mad,' replied Tutalou. 'As for the perfumes you're so taken with, well, they kill animals in the manufacturing of them, too, I'll have you know. They test their perfumes on defenceless animals, causing untold suffering and many die agonising deaths in the process, all to satisfy their vanity and vulgar habits of humans. We don't need their perfumes, restaurants, clothes, or any of their other bad habits. They are not like us felines who have an exotic natural perfume that is superior to any of their brands.'

'They take drugs,' I reminded Cheyenne, 'not the kind our Capucine takes, but ones for pleasure and relaxation. Recreational drugs they call them – they always have great names for their follies, do our human friends. And you say you want to experience that, all that head banging stuff, that delirium of the mind, with their heads in the clouds or heads down the toilet carry on, just like the beatnik and her way out fellow on floor seven.'

'Of course, I don't,' replied Cheyenne. 'It's one trait I wouldn't like.'

'Oh, you want to be an *à al carte* human, do you?'

'As I said, only the good parts – nothing wrong with cherry-picking the niceties of life.'

'Then they mustn't be happy with their world if they want to get out of it in a purple haze,' I exclaimed. 'So many of them indulge in it – takes them out of themselves, so they say and into another psychedelic world. A few of Capucine's men attached themselves to their reefers too. I'm telling you, we felines are so superior to them in every possible way. Can you *really* imagine us dragging on a reefer or sniffing powders up our noses and going all-gaga? I suppose they've some good points, these peculiar humans, but taking drugs is not one of them.'

'I agree, however, they're not *all* peculiar! We know quite a few who are not. There is Capucine to start with, nothing peculiar about her. She is one of the good ones. She's kind and loves us dearly and what about Audrey, she's as cool as they come, and Marcia, we can't forget her, can we?'

'Yes, Cheyenne, they are first-class human beings,' Tutalou agreed.

'Don't forget, Cécile. She's always so kind to us and look at how she loves and cares so much for Capucine – such a dependable woman. And don't forget humans have music in their souls too,' Cheyenne reminded us. 'What a quality that is to possess. Capucine always plays us divine music. Humans compose the most wonderful of works. Some have heavenly voices too, like Nina Simone, Eartha Kitt and all those other blues singers, then there are the classical tones of Pavarotti and Joan Sutherland and don't forget my favourite, Def Leppard, so why wouldn't I want to experience the human condition and the beauty that is music.'

I looked at our poor deluded friend. 'Yes, they have music and the other indulgences you are so hung up on, but we can listen and enjoy their music without being one of them. Yes, they may have music in their souls but don't have what we have.'

'And what is that?' Cheyenne nonchalantly asked.

'You mean to say you don't know?'

'Yes! You seem to know everything, Océane. Well, what is it we have that they don't?'

'Karma! Good karma.'

'What!'

'Karma – tranquillity,' I reminded her, 'you know – peace of mind and all that. Humans are always uptight whilst we are calm, serene and at peace, not just with ourselves but the world because we generate good karma. You are a sad case, a sad case indeed if you want to swop what we have to be one of *them!*'

Cheyenne allowed this bit of wisdom to sink in. She didn't say anything, but her demeanour said it all. I think she knew exactly what I was saying. She exercised her whiskers then lay down after the exertions of her mental walkabout.

Tutalou gave a boring yawn, and I turned over, closed my eyes, and ended another session of feline philosophy, allowing Cheyenne, the poor creature, to dream on.

If Only She Had Noticed

The passing of Capucine devastated Marcia d'Orsay, and she suffered greatly from it. She had only been chatting and having a laugh with her three days before and was in sparkling form. Since then, she had gone over in her mind the hour they spent together, trying to see if there were any give-away signs, she had missed that could have alerted her to the disaster that was to unfold. There was none. They had talked about Capucine's intentions of visiting friends in the US in May and was excited about it as over recent years she rarely left her apartment, and this trip would be a boost to her sagging self- confidence. Marcia was concerned, like many of her friends by Capucine's increasing reclusiveness. Her illness was taking its toll and the more intense it got the more reclusive she became. With work very much on the wane she became more and more concerned about her finances that were steadily depleting, even considered selling off many of her treasured artwork and jewellery and more alarming, her family heirlooms.

When Capucine was a busy actress and model and away from home quite a lot, she relied on Marcia to feed the cats, clean the apartment, and attend to any unexpected occurrences that arose within the household, then when Capucine's mental health deteriorated, her duties changed to that of a carer. This was no burden to her. She was like a mother to Capucine, with a deep understanding of her illness and was one of those fantastic gems that descend on this earth on the rare occasion, this one landed on Capucine's lap, and the accidental benefactors of this were her three cats. Marcia was blessed with a caring and nursing character that all would benefit from. For years she had been a tower of strength to Capucine and knew her weaknesses and masterfully was able to give balance to her life but in the last few years, she became concerned for her as she had lost interest in life and unable to focus on anything positive.

Marcia and Capucine had little in common, both from completely different backgrounds and beliefs, but there was something between them that clicked. From the moment they met at the job interview, it was clear they would be good for each other.

Marcia was born not far from Capucine's apartment and was of Swedish extraction. You would not think so looking at her, as she was only five feet tall, round figured, and dark-haired. She was married but had no children and no animals and was a devout catholic who attended mass on a daily basis. She would never fail to say a prayer or light a candle for Capucine at the chapel of Saint Jude, to whom she was devoted.

Marcia adored the cats and spoilt them in every possible way. She would never arrive without a packet of 'Kitty Kavier' titbits in her pocket. Capucine would remonstrate with her when she found her dishing them out, but Marcia couldn't help it as she was a softie, and the cats knew it. She also suffered a sweet tooth herself which was responsible for her round figure. She had been with Capucine for eighteen years. When told about a vacancy for a housekeeper by her local agency she had no idea who the client was until she arrived for the interview and told it was Capucine. She was extremely nervous and in awe of her who she knew as the famous actress and one of the beauty icons of her generation and felt a little intimidated and had second thoughts about the position. She also knew Capucine was known for being standoffish and reserved with strangers, but she received her warmly and after introducing her to the cats, which looked curiously at her, sat down and over coffee chatted away as though they had known each other for years.

'I hope you like cats as these are a handful, especially Cheyenne,' she said pointing mischievously at her with a spoon.

'I certainly do,' she replied, 'the cuter the better.'

'Oh, they will love you if you call them cute. They can be vain at times.'

'Don't worry, I won't spoil them.'

'I've seen you before, on several occasions,' Capucine informed her.

'Oh, have you... where?'

'The market, at the vegetable stall and a few times at Leo the butchers.'

'Oh! I never noticed you,' Marcia exclaimed, a little embarrassed that she hadn't noticed her, hadn't noticed such a striking looking woman.

They clicked and Capucine had no hesitation in offering her the job. She always went by instinct and in her bones; she knew she had made a good choice. Once they discussed terms, they celebrated with a large brandy and another long chat. Marcia left the meeting floating on air. She had a feeling she would enjoy working and getting to know Capucine better *and her cats too, who never took their eyes off her throughout the meeting. They were psychologically summing her up.*

It was not long into her job that she observed her employer was carrying some kind of problem around with her. As she cleaned the apartment, she noticed medication on Capucine's bedside locker. Looking at the labels it soon dawned on her that her new employer suffered from a psychological condition. She did have some understanding of bipolar as her second cousin suffered from it, although, as she was soon to find out, not on the same level of intensity as that of Capucine's.'

One day about a month later when they were having a coffee break, Capucine told her of her illness. It was a difficult admission for her to make, especially to someone she had only known for a short time. Marcia, being a practical woman took it in her stride. Capucine said she had to tell her in case she came across her in one of her moods or in the deep throes of an episode.

The day Marcia met Audrey Hepburn she thought she would die from excitement. Audrey put her at ease and being the thorough woman she was, left no stone unturned. She explained to her the ins and outs of the bipolar syndrome and the procedures to use when Capucine was in a depressive state. It was not long before she would witness one and so began her devotion to Capucine under the watchful eyes of the cats who after studying her gave her the green light of approval.

Marcia and Audrey worked with each other to make sure someone was always available to care for Capucine if she were in difficulties and would keep each other updated on her condition. Capucine was completely unaware of this ar-rangement.

Soirée with a Difference

It was a sparkling spring day, so after Lucie fed us, we decided to spend our eighth day up on the roof. It was easy to reach, a quick exit through the flaps, along the lead flashing and up onto the tiled roof. This was one of our popular resting places. We often made a race of it with Tutalou always getting the better of us. There we could laze in the sun and often joined by our other feline friends from the lower apartments and exchange all the gossip and tittle-tattle. It was always good fun and lots of laughter. Over the years, we had some good debates covering every possible subject – these could range from the obscure to the sublime – politics, philosophy, sport, drama and any subject one could think of – nothing off-limits to us. Camille would often arrive, but in general would sit on her own. It was only when she had some salacious gossip to impart would she join us and never failed to vent her spleen. She caused a few fights too. One morning she had a mighty go at Suzanne, saying she should not be up on the roof, as she was a stray and not one of the in-crowd, and then set about verbally abusing her. It was a big mistake, because Suzanne, not being the shrinking violet kind wasn't having any of it and attacked Camille with a vengeance and ran her ragged around the roof, with us cheering on and finally sent her scurrying down the chute with her tail between her legs. Camille kept well out of sight for a long time and when she did venture out, she looked to see where Suzanne was first. Camille – she would test the patience of the calmest of souls. It's

129

always hard to befriend an aggravating spirit like Camille. She was such a difficult cat.

'You remember that crazy soirée Capucine put on a few years back?' Tutalou asked as she basked in the spring sun. 'It was so much fun.'

'The one with the bodysuits you mean, or cat suits as they are called now.'

'Yes, that's the one. It was a real ding-dong of an evening, full of laughter, good food and chatter.'

'It certainly was,' Cheyenne agreed, 'a star-studded evening, a gathering of the Beautiful People, many with their halos slightly tarnished and dented and others glowing and basking in their fame.'

Capucine hosted many a soirée in the apartment over the years. They were all good and perfectly organised but this one stood head and shoulders over the others not only because of its theatrical nature but because sadly it was to be her last. She was never short of imagination when it came to suggesting a theme for a soirée. This one was different in every possible way. To start with, guests had to be dressed in a cat suit. Each suit had to be in a pastel colour only and all guests had to make sure their colour was different to all other guests so there was a lot of manoeuvring between the guests before the event, checking and double-checking to make sure their colours did not clash. The suit had to cover the entire body apart from the face and hands.

The theme of this one was to do with health; something Capucine felt a need to highlight, in this case, the health and care of the Body Beautiful. She had intended to have three in the series, the other two being, the mind and the soul. She

130

never lived to organize them, but this colourful event was a marvellous one to remember in every possible way.

On the morning of the soirée, Capucine and Marcia busied themselves cooking and baking and later joined by Cécile who arrived with baskets of flowers. We kept out of their way and just relaxed watching them having fun doing their chores. Marcia was good at baking all kinds of tasty cakes and pastries. These were well known and looked forward to by the regulars and never failed to grab the taste buds of other guests. Capucine's expertise was in Italian cuisine. Problem was she was very untidy whilst she worked and Marcia was the opposite, organized, orderly and cleaned as she went so there was always a little tension in the kitchen as they worked. After Cécile did the finishing touches to the flower display, she lent a hand in the kitchen.

The main guest for the evening was a prominent professor from the University of Berne who was to give a lecture on the mysteries of the Body Beautiful. He was reluctant at first to wear a cat suit but once Capucine sprinkled him with her magical charm, he agreed to wear a melon and pale blue diamond one, the only suit to have two colours on the upper body. Capucine's was powder pink; Audrey was in pure white with a black spot on her right ankle with Cécile in mauve. Marcia turned up in glittering silver.

It was the guests imitating us, so we had no need to dress up but Capucine, to make sure we didn't feel left out, tied blue pointed sparking hats to our heads. We enjoyed walking in between guests as they clicked their glasses and enjoyed the tasty food that Capucine and Marcia had spent the day preparing. The main guest, however, was not one to set a party alight. He looked nervous and out of place and would have preferred to be anywhere but where he was standing. He went through his presentation with a lack of enthusiasm. What he had to say was very illuminating, but most guests were hoping he'd finish so they could get back to more sociable activities. To our delight, William Holden arrived just as the professor was finishing the presentation. He presented Capucine with a bunch of lilies. She was thrilled to see him, as it was a while since they had enjoyed each other's company. William, just walking through the door was enough to set the soirée alight – all eyes turned on him. He was dressed in a grey cat suit, wore a rustic red Stetson hat, and looked as handsome as ever with a twinkle in his wandering eyes. The rest of the evening went with a swing as the Beautiful People swayed to the tones of Eartha Kitt and Ray Charles, clicking glasses, and massaging each other's egos. Capucine spent a great deal of time dancing with William. It was the last time she would see him because within the month he would meet a tragic end that would leave her bereft and triggering another serious episode.

'She was in such good form then. It was one of the golden periods in her life when she blossomed and lived life to the full – What a shame it couldn't last. How could we have foreseen the tragedy that was to befall her?'

'We couldn't, Tutalou, we just couldn't have,' Cheyenne replied as she soaked up the sun.

As I lay on the tiles on that sunny morning my heart was heavy after recalling the soirée and how happy and carefree Capucine was, relaxed and at ease amongst her friends and how it went so tragically wrong. Just thinking about it was painful – a pain I shared with Cheyenne and Tutalou. However successful the soirée was we didn't realise that a dark and heavy cloud was slowly heading our way, which would become darker and darker and threatening over the last decade of Capucine's life.

Cast to the Wind

It was to be a private farewell as she had wished.

Audrey had lost not only her soul mate but also her devoted friend of a lifetime. It was hard to take, that she was unable to save Capucine. She had done so on many occasions but failed miserably this time. Her heart was heavy with sorrow and deep regret – regret she was unable to comfort her in her hour of need, unable once more to talk her out of such an irreversible step. She knew deep inside this day might come but prayed it never would. This was of little comfort to her now as she arrived for the funeral at the small chapel with the rest of the mourners. The ceremony was simple in compliance with her wishes.

Capucine's continuous battle with her condition would always end in tears – always destined to end in tragedy. When bipolar spins out of control there are few happy endings, and Audrey was fully aware of it

Two days before Capucine's demise, Audrey was in Miami and had a premonition a dark cloud would descend on Lausanne. It preyed so much on her mind she could not sleep. She was up throughout the night, pacing the floor, but was unable to dissipate her anxiety. She phoned Capucine but there was no reply then called the concierge and he too didn't answer, so she left a message on his phone with the hope he might call with some positive news. Marcia was not contactable too. At last, she finally managed to contact Philippe Selis.

'Have you seen Cap? I've been trying to contact her – she's not answering her phone.'

'Is there something wrong?'

'I don't know. I just have this feeling, this terrible feeling. Will you check on her, check her apartment?'

'Of course – I'll call you back. Don't worry, Audrey, I'm sure she's alright.'

Audrey prepared for her performance, but her mind could not settle – it was elsewhere. It was in Lausanne. As she was about to leave for the performance, she was called to the phone. It was Philippe. The colour drained from of her face as she held tightly to the phone. Those near heard her cry, 'Capucine, Capucine – no – no!'

Her worst fear had materialised. She was in a stupor as the terrible news hit home. 'Capucine, Capucine, Capucine,' she whispered then let go of the phone and held her head in her trembling hands. It hit her hard; the realisation that Capucine did what she always threatened. It was terrible – a violent end for a pacifist soul. It was heart-breaking to imagine she would never see her again or enjoy each other's company or link arms and stroll through Lausanne, laughing and joking as they went. She would never have her to confide in again – that the special link in her life was gone forever. What was left were the beautiful memories of the special moments they shared in life, those endless hours spent together – forty years of friendship and companionship – forty years of a pure, pure, perfect love. Memories of the many times they sat and chatted over a glass of wine or relaxed over a meal at a local restaurant and many occasions at La Paisible or in the intimate setting of Capucine's penthouse. Life without Capucine seemed like no life at all. They had been friends most of their lives – more like sisters who shared their most inner thoughts and feelings.

Audrey felt as though her heart had been ripped apart as she took her seat for the service. She was so grief-stricken the service was just a blur. Later they cremated Capucine; then cast her ashes to the wind over Lake Geneva on a cloudless day, with a gentle breeze flapping the sails of The Daughter of Toulon that had taken a select few to witness the final act in the existence of Capucine, the lost and tortured beauty of Lausanne. Most who attended had suffered with her at some time or other through all the dark hours of her illness. Although it was goodbye forever, most felt relief that her suffering was at an end, and she was now at peace. All who gathered remembered the good times too as her ashes drifted on the crest of a breeze and up into a clear blue sky.

There was lots of talk about her after the funeral. Dirk Bogarde was heartbroken. He recalled how much of a privilege and honour it had been to have her in his life, to have loved her.

She was always on the lips of the folk of Lausanne, who adored her and always had a good word to say about her. Those who had known her reminisced about their association, her kindness and compassionate nature.

Cécile Charon was inconsolable. Although her love for Capucine was never returned, she never stopped loving her; always hoping that one day love would bloom. The realisation it would never happen only added to her grief and despondency. Apart from her love for Capucine, she also admired the way she coped with her suffering and yet still managed to conduct and manage her busy life with so much dignity and grace.

Denis de Buc would never be the same again. He knew Capucine was suffering from some kind of condition but had no inkling as to how serious it was, that it would end in such appalling tragedy. Unable to attend the private funeral, he stood outside the chapel as the service took place and remembered the beautiful woman that graced his shop. He could not imagine life or Lausanne without the presence of so gentle and generous a person. Since the dreadful news, his shop remained closed. He was not the only one crying. Surrounding him were many of the ordinary folk of Lausanne trying to come to terms with their loss. She had become part of the rich fabric of the city and it an indelible part of her life. People of all ages were there to show their respect, standing around the flowers outside the chapel, some in deep thought, others quietly exchanging words.

Philippe Selis was in complete shock. He was overwhelmed with guilt that he was unable to help and could not get out of his mind the way she died, the pain she must have suffered, the whole injustice of it all. He did not attend the funeral but stood on the shore of Lake Geneva as the service took place and looked out over the still water and prayed that she had found the peace she was desperately seeking. How he would miss her. He would be considered every inch a man's man, very macho and strong but as he stood on the shore with the water lapping at his feet, he cried out for his beautiful friend, repeatedly calling out her name as he let his tears flow.

Cécile Charon left Lausanne soon after the funeral and was never to be seen or heard of again.

The Visit of the Happy Chinaman

Another day passed and we were bored stiff. This lazing about wondering how long we were to stay locked in the apartment was starting to get to us. We were edgy and completely out of sorts. We had become creatures of habit living with Capucine and now were lost and adrift, prisoners in our home, in Capucine's once safe haven. Life was becoming very tedious indeed. The only highlight of the day was Lucie who brought us a quite different meal than usual.

'Here, I've something special for you. Made it myself,' she proudly announced removing the tin foil from the dish. 'Hope you like it. I spent a lot of time researching feline cuisine and this is the best dish I found. Tuck in!' It smelled so delicious it soon had our digestive juices moving. We tucked in as she suggested and was well worth it. She took a lot of delight in serving us this scrumptious dish, don't know what was in it but it was very tasty indeed and we soon devoured every morsel. Lucia's nervousness of us was easing with every visit. Gone were the cold sweats and shaking, now replaced with smiles and cheerful chatter. She had finally fallen for our charms and why not, after all we are adorable creatures. We were certain it was love. Then, after she bade us adieu and with our tummies well and truly full, we settled down and once more began reminiscing about life with Capucine and on this occasion, about many of the treatments she had sought for her condition which were many and varied.

'You remember the time she was persuaded into having a course of acupuncture with that Happy Chinaman fellow to try cure her condition?' I asked.

'I do,' replied Tutalou. 'I remember it clearly, as though it was only yesterday.'

'One of her six-minute lovers convinced her that this trickery was the answer to her affliction. Can't remember what his name was. He was as forgettable as his lovemaking,' uttered Cheyenne as she gave a satisfying stretch, ready for her morning snooze.

'Serge!' 'I replied. 'He was that pretentious drip from Dijon, the ski instructor she met at Statss up in the Alps on one of her vacations. Have no idea what she saw in him. He may have had the good looks but let's be honest, that's about all he had. He was tactless and insincere – a very shallow kind of man, certainly not worthy of Capucine's attention. He tried to give the impression he understood her condition, understood her suffering, but he was full of shit. If he had, he would never have treated her as he did and would have tried to understand her condition and never introduced her to that Chinaman and his alternative medicine.'

An acupuncturist had treated Serge for a severe ski injury, and he thought he was so good he recommended him to Capucine. Serge was one of her short time suitors, about ten years her junior. After he witnessed an episode, not long into their relationship, he made a bolt for it and left her in a distressed state. She, unfortunately, adored him and after recovering, begged him to return. He reluctantly did but it wasn't long before the relationship fizzled out after she exploded into a rage as another episode kicked in. She tried to explain to

140

him the nature of her condition – tried to explain that she rarely remembered what she had said or done when the black dog got a grip of her, but he was having none of it. He argued that when he tried to calm her down and reason with her, she continued spitting out filth and venom and fighting with him. He was a weak character and had no interest in trying to understand her condition. She failed to see it, but we did. We had him marked as a weakling within ten minutes of his arrival at the apartment. It can be disturbing and traumatic for someone to be confronted for the first time with the effects of bipolar but why can't people like Serge not try and understand and show at least a modicum of compassion. He didn't want to understand; it was as simple as that. As for compassion, well, it was truly lost on him.

Cheyenne was an out-and-out cynic of these practitioners of alternative medicine. You know, the ones who say all modern medicine and practices are dangerous, only designed to line the pockets of pharmaceutical profiteers and damaging to your health and welfare, then what do they do, peddle their own dicey alternative medicines, no doubt for a healthy profit too. Well, Capucine had the misfortune to come face to face with one of them in the guise of the Happy Chinaman, real name, Doctor, Lee Chang Dow. Cheyenne thought it was nothing more than trickery and those practising it were charlatans of the worse kind, and she should keep well away from them. Tutalou, however, was more open to it and thought any medicine, albeit an alternative one was worth trying if it would relieve Capucine's condition and ease her terrible inner pain. I could understand her thinking but I wasn't convinced. I would never give this kind of alternative medicine the benefit of the doubt, but Capucine would and did.

The Chinaman arrived early one morning to convince her that acupuncture was the answer to all her ailments. He stood in the doorway of the apartment as though he was a revelation, a fixed smile from one end of his face to the other, dressed in a smart well-tailored white suit and highly polished black shoes, laced in a fancy bow. What made him stand out was his fluorescence turquoise shirt and red tie. He was fully aware of his presence and paraded himself like a theatrical trooper. Capucine, at first, a little startled by his appearance was certainly impressed and poured him a cup of green leaf tea as he set about convincing her that his skill with needles and the practice of acupuncture was to be her salvation. He was a very confident and astute practitioner of this ancient Chinese art and had little difficulty convincing her – she took in all he said without question. Even though his appearance gave her some cause for concern, she thought him a sincere and honourable man and more so, trusted him. He assured her he knew his craft well and made it clear that he and his acupuncture technique, his relaxing programme and dietary regime was what she was looking for to relieve and cure her of her condition. My ears popped by his assertion. He used the term *cure,* which should have screamed caution at her, but it didn't, instead her eyes lit up at the mention of the word. His smooth talk had won her over, and even Tutalou fell for it in the end, after recently giving us a good lecture on its evils. Our Tutalou – how easily swayed she can be at times. Cheyenne, even she was leaning towards it, but in this case, I was convinced it was all a load of codswallop and would be detrimental to her mental health and physical well-being. It may be an ancient practice, and many swore by it, but I couldn't fathom how he could cure her when it is well documented there was none. If acupuncture were beneficial then surely the experts on mental health and of bipolar would endorse and prescribe it. They have not, therefore, I was right to be suspicious of the doctor's motives.

The Chinaman, however, wasn't too keen on us. Every time we went near him, he became extremely nervous, wiping his perspiring brow and panting. Wouldn't fancy the likes of him sticking needles in me, I thought.   He arranged the first course of treatment at the apartment for the next Friday morning and what a show it turned out to be.

'I like this fellow,' announced Cheyenne.

'I must say, so far, he looks to be OK, and Capucine is happy with him. He may dress in a bizarre way, but he seems to know his trade and knows what he's talking about,' declared Tutalou.

'You two are so easily led, so easily taken in. You were always criticizing alternative medicine, now you are all for it. Did you not hear him say he can *cure* her? You know damn well that is a load of baloney. He knows that too and is deliberately misleading her and managing to convince you too. He knows she is desperate for a cure and he's telling her exactly what she wants to hear. Nothing good will come out of this, mark my words. He has quack stamped all over him.'

'Océane, that's unfair – even if he can't cure her but helps to relieve her condition for a while then surely that will be beneficial and well worth the effort. She needs help, and he's offered to give it and explained how he can help her, so let's see what happens – let's be a little open-minded about it.'

'Hope you're right, Cheyenne,' I sighed. 'If not, then we will be the ones who'll have to pick up the emotional pieces of her decision. It's his assertion he can cure that is bugging me.'

When he appeared at the door for the first session on the following Friday, our Happy Chinaman was accompanied by his assistant. All that remained of the last visit was his fixed smile. He was dressed from head to toe in white. His attire was not the ordinary kind doctors wear, but a well-cut piece of work. The only colour was the red carnation in his lapel – He looked the part but was there any substance to him or his treatment. His assistant was in a light pink coat, matching high heels, pink trimmed glasses and pink rinsed hair. She was Danish, tall, and extremely attractive but had an air about her that didn't ring true. Capucine welcomed him with open arms as a long-lost friend, and embraced him, kissing him on both cheeks and his smile began to tingle. Was it the thought he was going to have this ravishing woman to himself for an hour every week that made him grin so much or that he honestly believed in this ancient Chinese remedy, that he could ease her condition or even cure her? Did he really believe in it or was it just another one of many moneymaking schemes aimed at sufferers of mental illness and the emotionally vulnerable?

'Well, Madame Capucine, I hope I find you well this morning and ready to receive the benefit of our acclaimed Chinese remedy.'

'I am indeed,' she replied, all wide-eyed at the prospect. 'But please, no madame – Capucine will do.'

'As you wish – this is my valued assistant, Sahoo.'

'She gave a traditional Chinese bow, which looked out of place being performed by a tall Dane dressed in delicate shades of pink. As Capucine and the doctor talked, Sahoo prepared the treatment area. Capucine had earlier changed into a white dressing gown and sat down on the cushions carefully arranged on the floor by Sahoo.

He began by explaining to her the essence of Yin and Yang and the importance of the unblocking of Chi to help relieve stress, anxiety, and any other symptoms that are disrupting the true flow of her body. Sounded great, but could acupuncture work for sufferers of mental illness, even in the absence of any real scientific evidence. Yes, we all agreed there was something in this Yin and Yang theory, but acupuncture, was it really the answer! I thought it highly unlikely, but Capucine wanted to find out and so succumbed to his oriental charm. I didn't.

After explaining the rudiments of the procedure, he wasted no time getting down to business. He first checked her tongue for signs of I don't know what and then took her pulse, which by the look on his face was perfect. Everything seemed fine on the surface but in his professional opinion, there were underlining problems that needed investigation, he said. He gave his prognosis, which was extensive, then outlined his treatment plan, which she listened to intently. After letting her think it over he asked if she was ready to proceed. She nodded her agreement and lay on the cushions. Then, in a theatrical manner, he opened a bamboo box held out to him by

145

Sahoo and took out a batch of needles, holding them up to the light and sighing at the sight of them. His eyes glistened as he examined each one of them. It was like a religious ritual with a hint of sensuality.

'I don't like the look of this. Is this fellow above board? Is he for real?'

'Of course, he is, Océane.'

'I'm not certain. I must say, I feel uneasy about this.'

'Relax, will you. Let's wait and see what he does and how Capucine reacts before we give our opinion.'

'It's alright for you to say, Tutalou, you're not about to get needles stuck in you by a very strange looking individual,' I said, dabbing my hot brow. 'I don't trust him one little bit and his assistant is very shifty indeed. I wish Audrey would come and put an end to this nonsense. She won't be too thrilled if she finds out about Capucine's latest folly.'

'Stop fretting! Relax – let's just watch what he does.'

He inserted needles carefully up and down her spine and other select locations. All of these, according to him, were the most advantageous spots to give maximum effect for the re-lief of her symptoms. Capucine was very relaxed as each needle penetrated her skin. He was very attentive and talked her through each movement he made. He certainly had a good bedside manner. However, each needle piercing her skin made me cringe. How can this possibly be good, I thought. It can't be!

So, he continued the treatment. Capucine was surprisingly calm and serene and didn't flinch as the needles were insert-ed. She was so relaxed after the first few insertions; I thought she had gone to sleep. Once the procedure was complete, he gently twisted a needle causing her to give a submissive sigh then he proceeded to flick every other needle in turn.

Once he finished this part of the treatment, he explained the importance of lifestyle change that she should seriously consider along with an exercise routine, good diet and reassessing her medication regime. He whispered into her ear that he was going to let her relax for thirty minutes before withdrawing the needles.

He retreated to the kitchen where Sahoo poured tea. As he sipped his organic brew, he caught my eye and soon began to perspire with his little finger quivering as he held the cup. I have that effect on certain people, especially the devious kind. I don't think he liked me, as he knew I could see right through him. He turned his back on me and chatted with Sahoo, every now and then looking over his shoulder at me, each time nervously dabbing his brow with his perfumed handkerchief. After calming himself down he returned to Capucine, eyeballing me as he went. He was now ready to resume the treatment – removing the needles. He whispered to her with his soothing voice that he was ready to proceed, and she nodded her consent. He withdrew each one carefully and she didn't even wince, but it made me squeal and feel sick at the sight of it. With each withdrawal, she sighed with satisfaction.

He turned and looked at us and his perspiration increased. Sahoo dabbed his sticky brow as she glared at us.

'Well, Capucine, how do you feel?' he said after regaining his composure and withdrawing the remaining needles.

She turned her head towards him, her face beaming. 'I feel invigorated. Thank you, thank you so much. What wonderful relief. I feel so light. Its years since I felt so relaxed – so at peace. Thank you, thank you.'

He broadened his already permanent grin as he cast a sly look in our direction. 'I'm here to please and to ease your condition. Before each session commences, I will assess your progress and decide on the next course of treatment. I will explain it step by step. As long as you complete the entire course, your life will change dramatically. You will see the world about you in a completely different light. Just relax for fifteen minutes or so. I'll see you at the same time next week.'

'Thank you,' Capucine said, again in a submissive tone as she rose from the cushions.

'No, no, stay where you are,' he insisted. 'We will show ourselves out –relax – just relax.'

'Perhaps, at last, I'll find release from my demons.'

'Indeed. I will wish you good day.'

He gave a traditional oriental bow, as did Sahoo. He smirked at me as he left, as though he'd had one up on me. Perhaps he had.

After they departed, we looked at each other. Tutalou had that certain kind of look on her face, letting me know she had backed a winner. He certainly hadn't convinced me, and Cheyenne was now in two minds about it, but give him his due; he seemed to know what he was doing and handled Capucine perfectly. I was surprised he was able to do this because sometimes she could be very distant, stand-offish or even stilted with people she didn't know well – more surprising for her to let a stranger so near her comfort zone.

Capucine relaxed for nearly an hour then got to her feet and gave a good stretch then walked out to the balcony breathing in the fresh lake air that mingled with the perfume of the potted lavender that was in full bloom. We followed and lay at her feet as she sat in her wicker chair. We hadn't seen her so relaxed for a long time. She was content and happy, smoking and blowing smoke rings, as she loved doing. This Chinaman, I had to admit, had the Midas touch when it came to stimulating Capucine. We certainly noticed a change in her demeanour over the next week. It was a transformation. She was so laid-back and had an air of tranquillity about her; even Marcia noticed. 'My, my, how good you look,' she observed as Capucine came into the kitchen where Marcia had an espresso ready for her. 'You must have slept well to look so good or have you finally a decent man in your life.'

'Yes indeed,' she said as she sat down. 'Doctor Dow has done wonders with me. You are right. I do have a new man in my life; he is Chinese and has the magic touch. He's revived my spirits as no other could.'

'Doctor Dow... you mean the acupuncturist you were on about the other week? Are you telling me you went ahead with it – that you let him stick needles in you and talk a load of mumbo jumbo, all that *gobbledegook*?'

'I certainly did, and oh, how good I feel, how relaxed and clear minded and yes, I understood his mumbo jumbo perfectly and his *gobbledegook* was a tonic.'

'Well, I can't argue with that, but that kind of practice is not my idea of fun – sticking needles all over the body and talking drivel... I'd rather be fried alive.'

'It's early days yet, but I have a feeling this ancient practice will change my life, not just how I live it, but how I look at it and the world about me.'

149

Marcia looked at Capucine over the rim of her glasses, and then looked down at the three of us, as we sat listening to them, nodding her head in a disapproving manner. 'Just be careful, my love,' she advised. 'Be very, very careful.'

Capucine didn't reply but looked sheepishly at her, knowing Marcia rarely approved of any alternative medicine. She was convinced that only medication prescribed by her doctor and psychiatrist was her only salvation. Capucine rarely started an argument with her because in general, she would lose but was aware Marcia always had her best interest at heart.

So, the Happy Chinaman and Sahoo arrived every week, each time giving her more confidence in his technique. We were very impressed and perhaps I was wrong to dismiss his treatment out of hand, as I did. It could be I was doing a disservice to this so-called doctor and his ancient practice. Perhaps he held the key to unlock the misery of Capucine's life. If he could, then we should welcome it. I was even warming to Sahoo. On every visit, she wore different shades of glasses, coat and shoes and hair rinse. These would range from light greens to soft pinks and gentle mauves. In her own way, she was quite a stylish woman.

Audrey had called around a few times, but Capucine never told her of the treatment. She swore Marcia to silence. Audrey noticed how relaxed and in good form she was but didn't probe any further.

After four weeks of treatment, Audrey happened to call and Capucine, feeling confident that the treatment was working told her of the acupuncture course, saying how well it was progressing. Audrey raised her eyebrows in disapproval and wondered why she hadn't mentioned this before as she had visited her and talked on the phone at least once a week, but she didn't remonstrate with her, well, that was until Capucine let slip that the Happy Chinaman said he could *cure* her.

'CURE!' she cried. 'Dear God, are you serious? Did he actually say that?'

'Yes! Well, it's working – I've never felt better. He makes me feel wonderful, and his technique is superb. It is so liberating. I can't fault his treatment. I should have tried it years ago – he's the best hands-on practitioner I've ever had. He has the gentlest of touches.'

'Codswallop! We need to have a good talk.'

And they did. The rest of the evening, Audrey was seething over her friend's reckless behaviour, but Capucine closed her ears to her protestations. Audrey, normally a naturally cool person could be driven to distraction and lose her calm and assured composure as she did that evening by Capucine's behaviour and her inability to understand that there was no cure – no magic potion, that medication was her only option. This at times caused Audrey to lose her normal cool and assured manner.

'Cap, what on earth possessed you to go on such a dangerous course? You should have talked this through with me or better still, your doctor or psychiatrist. For Christ's sake, this man, whatever his name is – he can't cure you. Did he really say he could, or do you just want to believe he did, that you wanted someone to agree with you, reassure you there is a cure?'

'Yes, he did, and I believe him. I've never felt better... the benefits from it are excellent, far beyond my expectations, so don't go spoiling this on me, Audrey, please.'

'Listen, Cap,' she said patting her hand. 'I don't want to spoil anything but this acupuncture; it's a myth – nothing more than a Chinese myth. You may get some release from stress, I'll grant you that but that's about all you will get and yes, it may make you feel well for a time, but that is it and there will be no long-term benefit from it and never will be. It's always best to leave myths where they belong, like this one, back in the mystical past. There will be no magical cure, and he is irresponsible to give you that impression. This will only bring you more discomfort and disappointment. Believe me, it will end in tears.'

'It's good for me and I will finish the course,' Capucine insisted.

Audrey just shook her head knowing whatever she said would make no difference. Capucine had her mind set and that was that. She gave her a hug and told her she loved her, kissed her goodnight and went home.

About two months into the treatment, Capucine had decided to refrain from taking her medication. She felt so good she thought she didn't need it after the Chinaman indirectly suggested it at one of the sessions; at least that is what she thought. It didn't take long until we noticed the changes in her demeanour as once more, she had allowed her demon to override her sensibilities. The battle had begun and there would be only one winner, unfortunately, it would not be Capucine. Tutalou as always was the first to detect any change in her. She noticed she was not taking her medication and warned us. We knew what was about to happen but could do little to stop it.

The doorbell buzzed and Capucine reacted by violently poking at the switch, allowing the main doors to open. It was the next visit of the Happy Chinaman. The moment the apartment door opened, she was at him and Sahoo, ranting and raving, her eyes ablaze. He stood rigid to the spot as she screamed at him then pushed the startled doctor against the wall. Sahoo, realizing immediately what was happening and being a moral coward, ran from the apartment leaving her boss to be savaged by a beauty in a rage. He tried to pacify her, but she clawed at him and realising he was unable to control her, departed sharply, leaving her in the doorway screaming at him as he made a dash for the staircase – not hanging about for the lift.

When Marcia arrived at her regular time, she found the door open and Capucine lying on the marble floor with the three of us trying to comfort her. She managed to get her into bed then called Audrey and the doctor and so ended Capucine's ill-fated acupuncture adventure and the beginning of another hard slog to get her back on medication and re-store some semblance of normality to her life. What had she gained through acupuncture, nothing but a few months of rel-ative calm? Good in its own way but the consequence of her listening to her heart instead of her head was a traumatic re-turn to the tortuous claws of the demon bipolar.

Regret of a Humanitarian

The funeral was over. Audrey was bereft and hapless. She had said goodbye to her friend, goodbye forever but could not shake off her sadness and despondency. It was difficult to think, to breathe – to exist. She felt as though part of her had been violently torn away, leaving her exposed, bleeding and in excruciating pain.

The ache of it would not ease as she sat in the beautiful garden at her home, La Paisible in the village of Tolochenaz not far from Capucine's home. She wanted to be alone amongst her roses and fruit trees, alone to try to settle her mind and emotions and come to terms with her loss.

In the last decade of Capucine's life, Audrey tried to involve her in projects to keep her from stagnating in her apartment, to keep her mind focused on the more positive elements of her life. She tried hard to get her to work as a goodwill ambassador for UNICEF as she had but Capucine said she would not do justice to it and the commitment needed; she could not give. Audrey regretted she was unable to coax her into it as she believed it would have saved her, that spending time helping others rather than dwelling on her condition and her past would have given purpose to her life. She was keen to get her involved in gardening as it proved very therapeutic for herself and was certain it would do the same for her friend, but this failed too.

As she sat in the shade of her garden, she recalled a sunny summer day six months before when Capucine visited La Paisible and brought Océane, Cheyenne and Tutalou with her. The cats liked the freedom of Audrey's garden and ran about chasing each other, then settled down under the shade of the trees to snooze for the afternoon as Audrey and Capucine sat and chatted under a white parasol.

'It might be worth trying, Cap. UNICEF, I'm sure will be delighted if you could be one of their ambassadors.'

'It sounds a good idea, but I can't see myself in that role. I couldn't possibly have the same effect as you do. My mind is too fragmented, too tired to give it the commitment it deserves. I would have loved to do it, but I'm only too aware of my limitations.'

'Nonsense – it will revive your spirits and give purpose to your life. I have never regretted a moment of my commitment to UNICEF. It has given me an inner peace and satisfaction that acting, and modelling could never do. Please, consider it.'

They sat for some time on that glorious summer day not saying a word. Audrey lay back, her eyes half-closed whilst Capucine smoked nervously as tears welled up in her heavy eyes.

'I'm tired of life, Audrey, tired of living,' she wearily confessed. 'I just want to end it.'

Audrey shot upright, her hat falling to the ground.

'I am tired, tired of the sadness in my life – tired of this emptiness inside. I have never felt as low as I do now. I need out of this life, Audrey. I need peace, a permanent peace.'

Audrey was startled and reached out and touched Capucine's trembling hands. She had experienced many of Capucine's traumas, but this was on a different level altogether.

'I don't see much future. My illness is emotionally and physically crippling me; my finances are depleting at an alarming rate, there is no man to share my life with, and I'm so lonely, so very lonely. There's nothing left for me, nothing.'

She held Capucine in her arms, and both wept on each other's shoulders. Audrey tried to pacify her and helped soothe her troubled mind. She realised danger lay ahead and how to avert it she had no idea.

Audrey spent the rest of that late summer evening reassuring Capucine that life is always worth living and she loved her and did not want to lose her. The cats realising something was amiss sat close to Capucine's feet to be near, to help soak up her pain.

Audrey accompanied her home. They talked into the early hours and finally fell asleep wrapped in each other's arms with the cats snuggled up to them. The next morning to Audrey's relief, Capucine was in good spirits. The sleep had done wonders. After she kissed her friend and the cat's goodbye, she called to see Marcia, bringing her up to speed about Capucine's condition. Marcia was not surprised.

***

Once home, Audrey sat alone amongst her roses and fruit trees with memories filling her mind until the sun went down over Mont Blanc. She would forever regret her failure to save the tortured and tormented beauty of Lausanne.

Mansion Villette

It was the tenth day, and the sparkling morning sun lit up the apartment as Tutalou gave a yawn as she stretched out on the sofa with Cheyenne softly snoring on the top of the book-case as I lay on the rug. I had a restless night. I was thinking about Capucine and worrying if Camille's claim was true or whether she was once more messing about with our emotions as she had a habit of doing. Camille was an expert at playing mind games and surpassed herself this time as she had us on tenterhooks.

My mind was full of memories and especially Capucine's visit to the Mansion Villette. This was another one of her efforts to seek relief, another so-called newfound remedy, destined as usual, never to work, just as the others had not.

Capucine was always open to any kind of new alternative medicine treatment that might help beat her illness. She would never be content with containing it through a mix of medication and meditation, as her mind was set in defeating the black dog and that meant indulging in alternative therapy such and mindfulness and an array of other extreme so-called remedies.

I remember Mansion Villette well. Capucine had so much faith in it – another madcap idea of hers. She was never short of them.

The first time she mentioned it I had a terrible sinking feeling. I was far from convinced of its possible value, especially its healing value. Mindfulness with its Technique Mood and Chart Psychotherapy sounded like more rubbish to me. It's amazing what some people dream up. That acupuncture non-sense was bad enough and there she was heading for another disaster. It was the whole set up that was annoying me; the idea of locking herself away in a place like Mansion Villette for three weeks to practice mindfulness didn't make any sense. Of course, she couldn't see the dangers of it, but I did. Mansion Delusion was more like it. Capucine was easily influenced when it came to alternative treatments for her condition. For a woman of intellect, she could be very naïve at times.

Christophe Moras her personal trainer put her up to it. I would have thought he had more sense, but no, he was daft as you could get. She told him in her younger days she once studied Buddhism and its relaxing techniques and had practised yoga off and on until recent years but was unable to get into a regular routine and drifted away from it. She told him everything, in turn, he wasn't shy about suggesting ideas, many off-the-wall and ludicrous, and this Mansion Villette was one of them and far from a remedy for her condition.

I remember that slimy creature, Monsieur, Sainte-Beuve, who came to explain to Capucine the therapeutic value of Mansion Villette, that in his oasis of tranquillity she would not only find her soul but be liberated from her illness. He did say 'liberated' and that was enough for me to feel uneasy. What a slick operator he was. He was as bad as the acupuncturist and his needles and that self-obsessed hypnotist and not forgetting the dervish from Kathmandu who developed an obsession about her and had her floating on air with his seductive talk. When Capucine opened the door, there he stood, dressed like a peacock. He pranced into the apartment, as

158

though he was the latest revelation. I had never seen such an overdressed individual in my life and his high-pitched voice, which I'm sure, was put on, added insult to injury. The whiff from him was so overpowering. He must have spent hours getting dressed, titillating and spraying himself with whatever perfume came to hand. The man was crass, with his fake eyelashes and puffed-up cheeks – even had his eyebrows plucked. That should have been enough for her to hightail away from him, but no, she was transfixed. He was more like a vaudeville performer than a serious alternative medicine practitioner. I had profound reservations about the Chinaman but this blow-in was just too much to take. Cheyenne and Tutalou were appalled by his appearance and thought, how can a man dressed like this be serious.

However, he captivated her just as the Happy Chinaman had; it was amazing how she fell for the likes of him and for such a sparkling and intelligent woman to believe all the trash this fellow was spouting was hard to fathom. We put this down to her burning desire to seek relief – to find a cure by any means available and if Sainte-Beuve could offer one then she would take it. She never even questioned him in any depth about the treatment, just accepted what he said as gospel. We, however, had this fellow summed up immediately he opened his mouth. His words of wisdom never washed with us wise felines.

'The mindfulness approach is ideal for you, my dear. Perfect!' Sainte-Beuve gushed, his teeth glittering with every smile. 'You may have looked at or tried other methods, but I can assure you, madame, my approach is second to none, as are my credentials,' he said theatrically handing her the papers.

She looked through them. 'Yes, very impressive indeed – I see you've been in practice for many years.'

'Twenty good years,' he replied. 'I've treated every kind of person and every sort of condition. I'm the ultimate professional.'

Worse still, she believed it. I remember Tutalou saying it was a load of crap. Cheyenne just laughed her head off as she observed his antics.

Capucine was desperate; so, I can understand her grasping at anything that could relieve her depression. She had faith in this fellow to deliver and no one would be able to talk her out of it, not even Audrey or Marcia.

He presented her with a book of photographs of the mansion, turning each page, giving a running commentary. 'This, my dear,' he said as he tapped the photo with his index finger with its purple nail, 'is the driveway to the mansion. As you can see it is lined with poplar trees and lush manicured lawns and behind them, our excellent rose gardens and for further relaxation, over there to the right, is the maze – a favorite retreat for our enlightened patients. He turned another page. 'Ah – this is the entrance hall. Isn't it… superb? Look at the sculptured pillars depicting the Workings of the Sub-Conscious Mind – a piece of artistic excellence if there ever was one.'

We looked at each other in amazement as to the nerve of this upstart.

'This,' he beamed, as he presented another page, 'is the hallway that leads to the Staircase of the Mind; decorated in pastel pink and green by the most respected of Parisian interior decorators, Mademoiselle Yvette.'

'Very nice indeed,' Capucine cooed as we cringed. Cheyenne felt like puking from his sickly demonstration.

'As you can see, madame, it is not a complex layout but quite simple and easy on the eye. Can you see the gradual changing and blending of the colours? It will be more clearly demonstrated as you ascend the stairs; all designed to soothe the most troubled of minds.'

He was succeeding by the look on Capucine's face. The more he went on the more concerned we became. He was playing mind games with her and no doubt with the minds of other patients unfortunate enough to take up his invitation to visit his so-called oasis of mindfulness.

'And these are your living quarters, painted in soft white with gentle yellow furnishings and fittings to give your surroundings an air of liberation,' he said as another page materialized. 'The colour scheme throughout the mansion follows the art of Feng Shui. Nothing left to chance. Colour is so important to manage the space in our lives – colour is food for the mind. You will sleep soundly as your mind is emptied of the troubles, tensions and burdens of everyday life.'

What a flash operator he was. There was no stopping him. I think he loved the sound of his own voice.

'And here we have the Six Doors of the Senses,' he said as a photo of six coloured doors appeared. 'Each door is painted in the colour of the sense it represents. Through each of these doors is the way to your salvation.'

'How wonderful,' she cooed again.

161

'This is the dining room,' he continued, revealing a well laid out room, 'What a delicious place it is. Part of the treatment is the correct diet to stimulate the mind and body. The cuisine here is second to none, prepared by our Cordon bleu chef, Raymond.'

Capucine smiled as she looked about her. 'Nice, very nice indeed.'

'Finally,' he gushed again, 'these are our treatment rooms.'

God! There was no stopping this fellow as he turned more glossy pages showing the mansion's layout.

'They are extremely luxurious for treatment rooms,' she observed.

'I only have the best. I make sure all my clients are as comfortable as possible. I am a stickler for detail – nothing escapes me. The mind will not rest if surrounded by clutter and untidiness. Mindfulness in this mansion is only of value if you are able to clean and clear your mind.'

He had her hooked.

'All that is needed now,' he continued, as he flicked his oily hair, 'is to agree a time for your admission to Mansion Villette and then your journey to normality will begin. The mansion is secure from the paparazzi and any other unwelcome interference.'

If this Mansion Villette was as good as it was cut out to be, a supposed haven for troubled minds – then there wasn't much of a waiting list. Any decent and self-respectable clinic would have a waiting list of at least a few months or so – to give it respectability – status, but not this one. This was lost on Capucine but not on us. She was so transfixed by him she didn't question it or anything about the treatment and without hesitation of any kind fixed a date for admission ten days hence, time enough to clear her diary for the three weeks period of treatment. We all agreed she was mistaken and being taken in by this fake and his Mansion of Deceit. The price he quoted for three weeks treatment was extraordinary. Another charlatan – unfortunately, the world is full of them. It is always difficult to know what is genuine or not in the human world – it's so full of pretence. But Capucine being Capucine would do exactly as she pleased and would pay dearly for it, not only financially, but mentally.

She had fallen, hook line and sinker to his approach. The sad thing about it, he was manipulating a theory that benefits so many with depression and doing so to his own ends. The only motivation of this man was money, nothing more, and certainly not the welfare of his patients. There was no way his treatment was going to work on someone like Capucine.

She didn't need to visit Mansion Villette to benefit from this mindfulness approach as we had been giving her treatment well in advance of what he was offering. For years, she had meditated, which is a form of mindfulness, and this gave her release and stability. For some reason, she gave up the practice. When she did meditate, it was always beneficial to her well-being but what Sainte-Beuve offered would relieve her condition to some degree but certainly not cure her. That's what was bugging the three of us was his assertion he could cure her. What he was indulging in was one of those many moneymaking rackets aimed at the most vulnerable of society, the mentally ill. If only we were able to speak, we would tell her straight that this Mansion Villette would be of no benefit and she should settle for our simple techniques, carried out for the best of motives and of more value to her and without any side effects unlike what Sainte-Beuve and other alternative practitioners were offering.

Just like the Happy Chinaman, he would be unable to cure her, unable to give her any meaningful relief. He used silken words to suggest he could, but it was all an illusion, a deception of the vulnerable – a deceiver of the worst kind. He knew there was no cure but gave her the impression there was which was a cruel stroke to pull. Many of these practitioners are dishonest in the extreme by manipulating the ill and giving them false hope. She already knew all about the mindfulness concept but something about Mansion Villette and Sainte-Beuve made her look at it in a different light, a light she was being blinded by.

So, off she went to Mansion Villette. Marcia was there when she was preparing to go and gave Capucine a bit of her mind, telling her to grow up and not be so stupid. Capucine pursed her lips, refusing to answer and continued to organize her wardrobe. Marcia argued with her, but it was a waste of time as Capucine was not for turning. She was heading off to Mansion Villette and that was that.

'Can you not see it's a load of nonsense,' Marcia said as Capucine busied herself packing, not listening to her at all. Capucine was up for it and Marcia's concerns wouldn't make any impact at all.

'OK, off you go then, but remember, I've warned you – I can do no more than that. Why do you have to stay there? What I know about mindfulness can be practiced in the comfort of home, not locked away in some over-the-top health resort and what about the downside to all this living in the moment? There is one, you know. Every time you come out of a mindfulness session; your underlining problem will still be there. It will not go away. It is only temporary release you'll get – nothing more and certainly not a cure. How can you believe him – that he can *cure* you – when you know darn well there is none?'

'There is! Yes, there is!' Capucine yelled. 'There *has* to be. There *has* to be.'

Marcia recoiled at her reaction. 'Please, Capucine, listen to me,' she softly said as she reached out to her. 'Please, don't go. Let's sit down and talk about it.'

'No. I'm going!' She said pushing Marcia away.

'He's like the Chinaman, and all the others, making money by playing with your mind and emotions. They are fully aware there is no cure and are taking you and others for a ride, not only a financial one – worse still – an emotional one that will surely come to no good. Talk to Audrey first. Ask her advice – it's always sound. Please, put it on hold for a while until you've had a chat with her – please.'

'Stop! Stop! Stop!' Capucine screamed as she clenched her fists and stamped her feet. 'you've said enough. I'm going, and that's *that*!' She grabbed her coat, gloves and case then dashed out of the apartment, for once not saying goodbye to us, then into the waiting taxi to take her to the station – then to Mansion Villette on the outskirts of Geneva.

Marcia was so upset. She sat at the table, holding her head in despair, and wept as she had on many occasions over Capucine and the consequences of her irrational decisions. She was fully aware of the Mindfulness Technique and

165

its positive and downside effects as her cousin indulged in its practice to resolve her depression. It did not. She could do nothing but wait for her return and pray there's no damage done.

Sainte-Beuve warmly welcomed Capucine on the steps of the mansion and showed her to her room. Once settled in he gave her and other patients a guided tour. She was overly impressed. The grounds were exactly, if not better than what he had described – beautiful, impressive with sculptured parkland and the mansion as its central point. Her first impression was a place of calm and tranquillity. She was confident that within this beautiful and relaxing mansion she would find salvation from her demons and looked forward to the treatment.

She was only at the Mansion for a week when Audrey called the apartment. Marcia took the call and when she explained Capucine's latest act of folly, she was fuming. Marcia could feel the heat of Audrey's rage radiating from the phone.

'What!' She cried. 'Why on earth did you let her go?'

'And since when did she ever listen to me when she had something fixed in her mind? Tell me – when? What was I supposed to do? Stop her – how – send her to her room, as if a naughty little girl – put her in a straitjacket? She'd made her mind up and that was that and insisted she didn't want to be disturbed by anyone, including you, by the way.'

'Well, we will see about that!' Audrey said, abruptly hanging up.

She was tied up with commitments abroad but caught the first available flight to Geneva and high-tailed it to the mansion to give Sainte-Beuve a piece of her mind.

The moment he caught sight of her he knew she meant business. She may have looked slight and skinny, but he could see she was a woman of steel, a woman on a mission. He also knew why she was there and determined not to be dictated to by her, but he didn't quite realise her determination.

'I insist on seeing Madame Capucine, immediately! I have come to take her home. Please bring her to me,' she insisted, not giving him time to introduce himself.

'I'm sorry, that's not possible – she is receiving treatment and should not be disturbed. A condition of admission states that the client can decline visitors until her treatment is complete. She does not wish to be disturbed.'

'Rubbish!' Audrey snapped, brushing him aside and storming off down the corridor. He shuffled after her. 'Please, madame, please, you must respect the client's wishes and the integrity of this clinic. She came here at her own free will and you must respect this. The treatment she is receiving is of value to her and her well-being and you must desist in causing a disturbance. This is a respectable establishment.'

Audrey stopped dead in her tracks and turning sharply, glared at him. 'DESIST! – RESPECTABLE! Listen to me, Monsieur, Sainte-Beuve, if you do not allow me to see Capucine, now, I will leave here and seek an emergency injunction compelling you to do so. I can assure you; you will be making a grave miscalculation in doing battle with me. I have had investigations carried out about you and your practice and if you believe you are running a credible programme then you can argue its merits in court. It's up to you, monsieur, but don't tangle with me – if you do, you'll surely live to regret it.'

He stood rigid to the spot, not knowing whether to believe her or not. He knew she was a formidable woman in every respect and one who kept her word and decided retreat in this situation was the better part of valour.

He turned to his nurse. 'Take *madame* to Capucine's room.'

'I'm glad you see sense, monsieur. Delicate minds need care, not manipulation. I'm here to take her home with me to give her the care she needs which your establishment cannot possibly provide. However good you believe your therapy to be it is not the kind she needs or desires. Of this I'm certain.'

He glared at her, his upper lip quivering with rage. 'You are being unreasonable as well as trespassing on my property. Taking her away from here will be detrimental to her mental health and well-being. What you are doing is irresponsible.'

'Rubbish!' She said and smartly followed the nurse.

Capucine was sitting on the bed with her head bowed. She looked up at Audrey with tears in her bloodshot eyes. They ran into each other's arms and wept. The nurse, realising she was trespassing on a tender moment, discreetly departed and re-joined Sainte-Beuve.

Quickly packing her bags, they left, ignoring Sainte-Beuve who stood in the foyer as they passed, still seething and quivering with rage with his fists clenched in indignation, showing the white of his knuckles and sweating profusely.'

'*Adieu, madame*,' he said through gritted teeth. He was oblivious to the presence of Capucine or the fact his client was clearly distressed. This wasn't lost on Audrey and confirmed in her mind that her instinct to come and rescue her friend was justified and timely.

Audrey held Capucine's hand as the taxi drove them home to Lausanne. They didn't say anything. Once home Capucine ran to her bedroom and threw herself on the bed and cried, soon becoming hysterical. We ran over to her, but this time Audrey shooed us away and drew Capucine into her arms. It was only in her friend's arms she felt secure, the arms that have held her through many of the traumas in life, a safe haven from the harsh realities of her life.

'The first day was wonderful,' Capucine uttered in a low voice after she recovered her composure. 'The mansion and grounds were beautiful, a kind of Paradise you could say, but I soon realised behind all that beauty, behind the intoxicating fragrance of the rose gardens lay nothing that could help me. Sainte-Beuve talked the talk and did so with authority as did his assistant, but I was soon to find there was nothing of substance in what they said. The first day was good. I settled into my room and then had a guided tour of the mansion and their extensive gardens, which were more impressive than the photos in the brochure. That evening he gave a talk about the merits of the therapeutic sessions, and I was quite happy with what he said and retired to bed in a positive frame of mind. But the next morning as I looked out across the magnificent, manicured gardens all of what he had said became muddled in my mind. I soon realised something fundamental was missing but couldn't quite fathom what. Throughout the day, I saw little of him or his assistant. The rest of the staff who supervised the sessions were very pleasant but there was no such radical approach to depression as he pontificated. The sessions were of no real value as all they consisted of was the theory of mindfulness, most of what I already knew and practised before. It gave the impression the therapeutic sessions would be on a one-to-one basis, instead it was all group sessions apart from my initial consultation. I was far from the only patient unhappy. It was a few days later that I managed to talk to Sainte-Beuve. I did challenge him on many of his ideas and treatments, but he suddenly became defensive and said in a shrill voice I should keep quiet, relax, and let him get on with his valuable work. I insisted that he listen to my concerns. He just glared at me and dismissed me with a wave of his hand. He was far from the man I had met at my apartment. His assistant tried again to explain to me the benefits of Sainte-Beuve's mindfulness approach and the benefits of the treatment within the mansion, but she failed miserably to convince me that it would work for me, especially through group therapy or in the surroundings of the mansion. In truth, the mansion was nothing more than an over-the-top health resort, just as Marcia had told me. A good place to be spoilt – a relaxing spa with essential oils, something you can find anywhere. As for a cure, well, it was clear by the programme and the treatments that none was to be found or any possibility of one. I once more let myself be misled. I did challenge him on his assertion that he could help cure my condition, but he aggressively turned on me again, saying he said no such thing. I reminded him of the fact that he did at our first meeting and two subsequent ones prior to my admittance to the clinic. Again, he became aggressive and told me quite tersely to just concentrate on the treatment and don't let my mind wander. I felt threatened and demeaned by his manner and tried to arrange to leave but they continuously put obstacles in my way and there was no access to a phone to contact you or Marcia.'

'Don't let it worry you. Forget it. Forget all about him and his mansion of deceit.'

Capucine smiled. 'How many times have I had to rely on you, Audrey, to get me out of a mess?'

'A lot,' she replied, laughing and giving Capucine a bear hug. 'Come now; let's cheer ourselves up with a meal and a good bottle of wine, or two. What better way is there to forget our troubles? We will send off a stiff letter to Sainte-Beuve, demanding your money back on the grounds of deception.'

'No, let's leave it as it is. I've had enough of him without getting into a slanging match over money. It's so vulgar a subject!'

'But we can't allow him to get away with it – he's deceiving vulnerable people for financial gain. We can't possibly let him away with it!'

'No, Audrey... Please, I'd prefer to let things lie.'

Audrey shrugged her shoulders. 'As you wish,' she replied then set about preparing the meal whilst Capucine sat on the sofa with us snuggled up to her. It was good to have her home. Audrey decided on one of her special pasta dishes that she was expert at and of which Capucine loved.

Over dinner, Audrey emphasized again that her current routine of medication was more beneficial than dishing out money to slick and sleight-of-hand operators such as Sainte-Beuve, the Travelling Hypnotist, the Happy Chinaman or the Dervish with their over-the-top nonsense and practices.

Capucine looked sheepishly at her, knowing she was right again. Once again, she had to rely on Audrey to rescue her from her latest folly.

If humans want to know what real relaxation is about, they can do no better than studying us felines. We have all the answers, and they would save a fortune in the process instead of dishing it out to dicey practitioners. Relaxation is second nature to us. It's in our genes – we have it in spades. We are the essence of relaxation and don't need mind-bending methods or drugs to keep us on our toes. If only humans could learn the art of relaxation, how less tense and stressed out they would be and a lot less irritating to us tranquil felines.

Carolien Junas

Fifteen years before the passing of Capucine an event occurred that would have a knock-on effect on the lives of others directly or indirectly connected with her. Just as Capucine was a stunningly beautiful woman there was another that lived on the outskirts of Toulouse who was not famous or well-known who suffered, not from bipolar but from that other unwelcome intruder in our lives, a broken heart. Her name was Carolien Junas, only daughter of an Italian property tycoon.

She was in a reflective mood as she arrived home to her luxury villa on the fashionable side of Toulouse after a short visit to her parents who lived on the shores of Lake Como in northern Italy. It had been five days of coming to terms with the end of her relationship. It hurt and it was to her parents she retreated to be comforted in her sorrow.

Shelia, the concierge was waiting to greet the young woman as she entered the villa. She looked nervous and ill at ease. Carolien was tired and dishevelled after the long journey and ready to shower and relax beside the pool for the rest of the evening with a long cool drink.

'Salut, Sheila. What a journey that was – I'm only dying for a shower. I need to chill out – you look rather distracted. Is there anything wrong?'

Sheila began fidgeting with her hands and walking back and forth across the pink tiled entrance hall. She was tense and out-of-sorts.

'My dear, whatever is it?' Carolien asked as she put an arm around Sheila's shoulders and giving a gentle squeeze. 'You look absolutely terrible.'

Sheila tried to talk but was unable to utter a word. She was shaking with her breathing becoming heavy. Carolien embraced her; she was shocked to see Sheila in such a state. Her usually calm and composed friend was falling apart. She sat her down. 'My dear, whatever has happened?'

She shook her head in despair, unable to answer.

'My God, tell me – are you ill?'

'No.'

'Then, my love, what is it?'

She looked at Carolien. 'Juliette – she's missing,' she managed to utter.

'Missing! What do you mean; missing – she is never missing? She's probably hiding away somewhere as she usually does,' she said, then called out for Juliette.

'No,' Sheila said, stopping her short. 'I'm afraid she has gone missing and has been so for five days now. I have searched high and low. She is nowhere to be found.'

'But she never wanders off. Are you sure?'

'Yes. I'm afraid there is more bad news.'

Carolien knew this was serious. She had never known Sheila to be so on edge; she was normally so good-humoured, laid-back and relaxed.

'What is it?'

'When I arrived the day after you left for Italy, Juliette was not there to meet me as she usually does, and for some reason, I had a feeling something was wrong as there was an air about the house I had never felt before that unnerved me. I searched everywhere for her, but she just seemed to have vanished. I first thought she had decided to hide on me, playing one of her games so I began cleaning the house and when tidying up your room I noticed the safe door slightly ajar and was surprised you hadn't locked it before you left.'

'But I didn't use the safe the day I left. It was never opened.'

'Well, it was open. As I was about to close it, I noticed the contents were dishevelled. Someone had been through it.'

Carolien was horrified. Her throat went dry at the realization a stranger had been rummaging about her bedroom.

'I tidied it up and nothing seemed to be missing apart from the silver cross you'd taken with you.'

The colour drained from her face. 'But, I hadn't!' Carolien cried as she dashed upstairs to the safe box with Sheila in close pursuit. She opened it and checked its contents. Everything was there except her silver cross. 'No, it can't be missing. It can't be,' she screamed as she sank to her knees, bursting into tears. 'No! No! Not my precious Tutalou.'

Sheila, after holding back her tears for so long, let them flow. Carolien held her close. 'It's not your fault,' she whispered to her distraught friend.

'I don't understand,' Shelia said as she wiped her eyes. 'If a thief had been in here, why did he not take the money and the rest of your jewellery? He is very selective. Nothing else is missing from the villa; nothing was disturbed but the safe box. It doesn't make sense, any sense at all.'

'But where is Juliette? She is missing too. We must call the police.'

'Are you sure you haven't mislaid the cross or worn it lately or even took it with you to Lake Como?'

'No! No! The last time was for my father's birthday a few months ago. I definitely put it away. We must call the police. That was my grandmother's favourite piece and my most precious possession. I must find it. And why is Juliette missing at the same time? I don't understand.'

Before calling the police, she checked with her parents to see if she had left it there although certain she had not taken it with her. Her father called back later to inform her he had searched the house and found no trace of it, insisting she did not bring it and advised her to call the police immediately.

The police arrived and checked out the safe, dusted it for fingerprints and remonstrated with Sheila for not calling them the moment she discovered the safe open. Then the delicate questions like, who had access to it.

'Only me, Shelia and my parents – they live at Lake Como. It's nearly four months since they were here.'

The officer looked strangely at her. 'You let your concierge have access to your personal safe box?'

Sheila's face creased. 'I beg your pardon,' she snapped.

'Sheila is utterly trusted, not only by me but also my parents. She is not just the concierge of this villa and the rest of the complex but also a close family friend. I have known her since I was a child. She is beyond reproach when it comes to honesty. You should apologize to her immediately,' demanded Carolien.

'I'm sorry mademoiselle but I must ask as it is unusual for someone outside the family to have access to a safe, containing valuable assets. Even a family solicitor wouldn't be given that kind of access.'

Sheila was far from impressed by him.

'Nobody else has access?' He asked.

Carolien face went ashen. 'Yes, yes, oh dear, yes, my boyfriend, my ex-boyfriend, Pablo.'

'You gave access to your safe… to the boyfriend and the concierge?'

'He was a long-time boyfriend.'

'Even so, it's strange to give him access. Along with the missing cross, the rest of the contents as you describe are very valuable. I'm just surprised there was such easy access to all and sundry.'

Carolien's face reddened at his remark. 'I don't like your tone, officer. It's most disturbing.'

He looked sheepishly at her. 'When did you split up with your boyfriend?'

'Not long ago – about five days before I left for Italy to be precise.'

'I suppose he had a key to the villa and the code, too,' he asked with a sarcastic edge to his words.

'Yes.'

'Did he not give the key back after you ended the relationship?'

'No.'

The officer raised his eyes to the heavens and gave a deep sigh.

'We had such a terrible row it never crossed my mind to ask, I was just glad to see the back of him. I was so upset. I left immediately to see my parents in Italy, leaving instructions with Sheila that I did not want to be contacted as I was so distressed at the breakup and needed space to breathe, to get my thoughts together.'

'Did you change the code?'

'No!'

The officer sighed again. 'I see. And you say your cat is missing too.'

'Yes. She is an extremely rare breed – an Egyptian Mau. She was a present from my boyfriend.   The whole thing is so bizarre. My boyfriend was so angry at our separation and the end of our engagement, but I can't see him having anything to do with this. He's not that kind of man.'

The police officer gave her a telling look. 'We'll see, mademoiselle. It is amazing what couples do when a relationship falls apart. Men never take rejection well.' He said this with some certainty, as though he had some experience of it.

'No, he might be silly at times, but he is not a thief and far from stupid.'

She gave the officers details about Paulo, but it was a waste of time as he had already returned to Italy. If he had taken them, it seemed little chance she would ever see Juliette or the silver cross again.

The Pleasures of Le Pigeonnier

The three of us spent most of day eleven deep in our own thoughts. I was once more up on the roof with Tutalou curled up on the bookshelf and Cheyenne resting on the pillow in Capucine's bedroom. We liked to be apart at times to gather our thoughts or just have our own space. Later we got together and once more considered out escape options but seeing we were getting nowhere, we recalled some of Capucine's treatments. She was never far from our minds.

'The hypnotist... we've forgotten about him. He was a bad egg,' I cried after Tutalou reminded us of another alternative treatment that went astray.

'I wouldn't mind being hypnotised – sounds cool, like another way of getting out of oneself.'

'My God, Cheyenne, you never fail to amaze me,' Tutalou laughed. 'It was bad enough with you wanting to experience being a human and now this. I must remind you these hypnotists rely on fellow humans, who think just as you do, to keep their deceptive practices on the go. After what Capucine went through with him, I'm surprised you can even mention his name.'

What a clown he was. He did a lot of damage to Capucine. He had no idea how to handle someone like her and didn't understand how brittle she was and how tender was her spirit. This putting her in a trance and getting her to retrace and regress her past was not a good path to take and worse still he maintained when she came out of each trance her depression and anxiety would be dramatically eased. The effect of her being hypnotized was traumatic. Of the many treatments she tried, this was, without doubt, the most disastrous, the most mind altering. She was more confused than ever after fifteen sessions with him.

She was so down after her experience that Dirk invited her to his home, *Le Pigeonnier*, a fifteenth-century farmhouse not far from Grasse, to recover her sensibilities and relax in his Provence retreat, an oasis to stimulate the senses. Better news still, he invited us along too. It was a surprise as he was an extremely organized and neat man with everything in its place and habitually tidy which was the complete opposite to us three bohemian cats. So, off we went after Marcia packed our bits and pieces for our sojourn in the sun. Capucine was in a hurry to get there, away from her apartment, to be comforted by Dirk and the tranquillity of *Le Pigeonnier*.

He had a dog. This canine was a large English mastiff and soft as putty and gentle in her manner, so we were delighted to go. Her name was Candida – odd, I thought, naming a dog after a yeast infection.

Tote collected us in Dirk's Silver Cloud Rolls-Royce. He was great fun. He entertained us on the journey and had Capucine laughing at his silly anecdotes. We arrived and there stood Dirk and Candida as we sprang out of the car. We were in for a long weekend of fun and devilment. Dirk welcomed Capucine with a lingering hug and Candida allowed us to run between her legs and run circles around her. Tote said goodbye, as he was going to Nice for the weekend. He waved and said he'd be back to collect us after our visit.

Although Dirk wanted Capucine there, he had however expected to have a difficult time as she was in a very disturbed state after her hypnotic experience. Since the end of her sessions with the hypnotist, she had been difficult to live with, so tense, irritable and distracted. She was like a highly wound coil, ready to spring loose at any moment. For hours, she sat on the balcony staring out over the lake. She was miles away. What she was thinking I had no idea and only snapped out of her stupor by Dirk's arrival and his insistence she comes to Grasse as soon as possible. When she had mentioned her intention of going to the hypnotist, he had told her to forget about it, but she was determined to go. Now that it was over, he was taking no nonsense from her and wanted her at *Le Pigeonnier* to rest and recover. He didn't have to cajole her this time. I remember her looking up at him, her eyes heavy and dark-rimmed with a slight smile on her sallow face. She didn't say anything, just nodded her head, relieved he had asked and that with him at *Le Pigeonnier* she would get some welcomed relief as well as the pleasure of being with him.

'Do you think she will finally marry him,' Tutalou asked as we rested on branches of an apple tree.

'Highly unlikely,' I sighed as we watched her and Dirk stretched out on sun loungers, chilling out under a colourful orange and white parasol amongst the many potted plants of geraniums and hollyhocks with butterflies fluttering about and Candida snoozing beside them on the stone cut patio in front of a statue of a drummer boy. Capucine was far from difficult to handle as Dirk first thought, for once in the surroundings of *Le Pigeonnier,* she was relaxed and as ease, smoking and blowing smoke rings and sipping a Martini at regular intervals. He lay next to her, twirling her hair with his fingers and whispering something to her that made her giggle. He always had a way with her and whenever they met, they would huddle together and chatter away. They were like two lovebirds tweeting away in a language known only to them. We had only been at *Le Pigeonnier* for a few hours and Dirk had her relaxed and laughing, her irritation and depression evaporating by the minute. Yes, we were in for a good time.

'She's being rather reluctant to say yes, isn't she?' How many more times does he have to ask her to marry him?'

'If she keeps him on a string any longer, Tutalou, he won't ask again. I'm sure she loves him, but something is holding her back. Perhaps it's her illness,' I suggested.

'I wouldn't say so. He has known about it for years so it can't be that' Tutalou reminded us.

'Don't forget he has his own inner demon to contend with so she might think that two carrying them is a mixture for disaster and best avoided.'

'But look at them, they are so good together. The chemistry between them is sizzling. They spark well together.'

'It has to be love,' declared Tutalou. 'It's written all over them. He has always been in love with her and intoxicated by her beauty. They are both looking for love and fulfilment in their lives. Do they not realise, it's there, staring them in the face.'

'Ah, the person to fulfil your life is the one who sees not only your outer beauty but your inner one too, one who understands the rhythm of your being, the tenderness of your soul and the beating of your heart,' Cheyenne said, imparting her divine wisdom. 'And Dirk is the one who fits the bill. He will fulfil her in every possible way and better still, he loves her

182

– What better recipe can there be? She should marry him and stop pussyfooting about.'

'There's a secret between these two that I can't get a grip of, and I don't think they will reveal it here,' I said, as I looked at them whispering to each other. 'I wonder what it is.'

Tutalou laughed. 'You can't keep many secrets in a garden as there are too many bees ready to take the honey out of the secret so if we hang around long enough, we should discover what it is.'

That first evening Dirk cooked a fantastic traditional Provence dish of Bouillabaisse. This brought back happy memories of their visit a few years back, to Marseilles and the restaurant *L'Epuisette* at Vallon des Auffes. This most enchanting of places that specialized in Bouillabaisse is perched on the rocks and a great gathering place for lovers.

As they wined and dined, we relaxed watching them from the splendour of the lounge with its terracotta tiled floor and plush white sofas, very much like Capucine's but unfortunately, we were not allowed to relax on them. Dirk had a lot of style about him by the look of the contents of his house. A fine collection of paintings adorned the white walls. Each room was full of flowers in colourful pots, some hanging or in cut glass vases. On the sofas in the lounge rested richly designed and multi-coloured cushions and, on the wall, an antique clock with its hypnotic rhythmic tick. In the centre of the room stood a one-legged round oak table, weighted down with volumes of large, illustrated books on the theatre, films and the arts in general and many on gardening. Even his light stands were far from ordinary. In one corner was a large glass one with a fancy shade. A stylish man was Dirk, in every possible way.

Dirk gave us free rein to wander about the farmhouse. It was a wonderful place full of nooks and crannies. We discovered Capucine's bedroom. It was decorated in a black and white theme with large floor tiles and in the centre a large white bed with a black frame. The walls were white in keeping with the rest of the house. The paintings on the walls were set off with black frames. It was a well-designed and chic room befitting its exotic guest.

The second day was glorious with clear blue skies and a gentle breeze. We ran about the olive groves with Candida joining in. She was great fun, even letting us ride on her back. After dashing about the place, she retired to the shade of a tree to recover. We returned to the terrace where Capucine and Dirk were finishing breakfast. Tutalou and I lay on the plinth of the Drummer Boy with Cheyenne stretched out on its arm. Capucine and Dirk were relaxed, smoking and chatting away, with regular bursts of laughter. How different things were now. It was hard to believe only a few days back she was strung-out and in a terrible state, full of agitation, with suicidal thoughts. Most of the day they lay there, only broken by a few half-hour strolls amongst the olive trees and a spell or two by the pool.

That evening was very much like the first with the two of them relaxing and enjoying a good meal. They settled down to another Provence dish, this time, Ratatouille, prepared and cooked by Dirk. Afterwards, they devoured a good helping of strawberry sorbet 'Garigette' washed down with a glass of *ni-*

gori sake. They sat there for the rest of the evening chatting away as we settled down for the night.

What a splendid stay it was. We had the time of our lives and Capucine was re-energised, relaxed and ready to face the world again. *Le Pigeonnier* worked wonders.

Tote arrived after breakfast the next day ready to drive us back to Lausanne.

'To think, if Capucine came here more often how much improved she would be, or better still if she married Dirk and moved in with him. She would be in safe arms, and he would help keep her inner demons at bay.'

'If only that could be so, Océane, if only,' Tutalou sighed as we snuggled up on the back seat of the Rolls-Royce as it left *Le Pigeonnier* and headed back to Lausanne.

The Young Lover

He was unable to move and stricken with grief; his once handsome features now creased with pain from the harrowing news from Lausanne. His mother tried to console him, tried to coax him to eat, to find something to give him strength to get him through the ordeal of his bereavement, but his despair and pain were so overwhelming they left him mentally and emotionally crippled.

'Take this,' she said as she handed her son a bowl of steaming hot soup. 'You need to get your strength back.'

He pushed it away. 'Go away, mother. Leave me alone,' he said in a weary, forlorn whisper.

He was as fragile as the beauty of Lausanne, living on the edge of sanity – always waiting for disaster to strike, giving his inner demons time to work their evil when he was in his most vulnerable state. It would not take much to push him over the edge, and the news from Lausanne was driving him nearer to the precipice. However hard his mother tried to console him she got no response apart from a stare of blankness. She knew deep inside he would not survive the loss of Capucine as he did not have the mental or physical stamina to do so. The effort of years trying to keep him sane, to control his moods and erratic behaviour was now taking its toll on her. She felt far older than her forty-seven years and was physically drained by the constant care afforded her son.

He and Capucine were less than a year together, still in the process of getting to know each other when she died. He was half her age but the only thing they had in common was *their depressive illness and their inability to deal with it. When they first met, her mother advised him not to become involved, as he was not emotionally strong to cope with a relationship, especially with someone who was suffering from the same condition. They were two troubled people seeking solace in their shared illness, and she knew it would end in heartache and tears. He was to become Capucine's last male friend. It was doubtful they were lovers.*

Marcia was in two minds whether the relationship was good for Capucine as he was too tense a man and extremely seriously minded and unable to talk about anything positive. All this did was compound her depression and reclusive isolation. Marcia did not like the atmosphere when he was around as it was detrimental to Capucine's now fragile state. The cats kept their distance. They did not trust him and resented how he bombarded her with his problems when what she needed in her vulnerable periods was reassurance and positive thinking, which he was unable to give. He was an emotional time bomb that needed to be neutralised, but she was unable to find his elusive fuse.

His presence in Capucine's life was unknown to most of her friends and associates so no invitation to the funeral was forthcoming which his mother thought a blessing in disguise as her son would not have coped with the stress of a funeral and its aftermath.

Walkies with Capucine

It was hard to believe we were now at the twelfth day of our captivity and to lift the gloom and despondency of our situation that was weighing us down, we decided to cheer ourselves up by having a good laugh at some of the capers Capucine used to get up to. She had a wacky sense of humour only matched by her even wackier ideas. To recall them all would run to a few volumes but here is one of our favourites.

Capucine's household was far from a conventional one. She prided herself in doing things differently and she certainly did when it came to us felines. Being unusual was second nature to her. In nearly every aspect of her life, she approached in a unique manner and sometimes in a chaotic and hilarious way, like taking us out for walkies was one of them. We know dog owners like to take them for walks, down to the park or around the block, well, what made us different was she'd take each of us for a walk on a leash – yes, cats on a leash. Sounds mad – it certainly was at times. There was already a handsome looking leash hanging near the front door she used when taking us out – it was good enough, but Capucine had other plans. Out of the blue one day, she had three leases spectacularly designed by Rubas, the famous designer she knew in Paris. More adept at putting her hand to *haute couture*, Capucine, somehow talked her into designing leashes for us. This was some achievement, as Rubas disliked people having domesticated animals, believing all animals should live in their natural environments and free from intrusive humans.

She presented these special leashes to us with great panache. Marcia was there along with Dirk and Tote to witness the performance. She called us out to the hall and there she stood as glamorous as ever in a light pink satin dress and matching wide-brim hat and hanging from her arm, the three leashes. 'Look what I have for you, my pretty ones,' she oozed as she showed us her latest acquisition. Mine was yellow with brown and green dots. Tutalou's, pink with thin blue lines and Cheyenne's, light blue with small black circles. Around the harness part of the leash were our names made of minute silver studs.

One day, not long after their delivery, Capucine decided to take us out for a walk – yes, the three of us. She always did individually but never together. We looked at her to see if she was serious… she was. Well, what a commotion it was. She dangled the fancy leashes in front of us, enthusiastically informing us we were going for walkies and weren't we lucky pussies to walk through Lausanne with such wonderful leashes. This was not a good idea – this was madness! I knew in my bones it had calamity stamped all over it. As we passed concierge Courcelles in the foyer, he scratched his baldhead in amazement.

'Capucine... What are you doing?'

'– taking this motley crew for a walk up to the market.'

'Are you sure,' he asked, once more scratching his head.

'Of course... A good healthy walk will do them good. They spend far too much time lazing about the apartment.'

Once she managed to get us out of the door it didn't take long until our leashes became tangled. Concierge Courcelles followed us outside and stood on the steps shrugging his shoulders and throwing his arms up in the air as he watched us being untangled then comically staggering down Chemin de Primerose. Every time she untangled us; it wasn't long until we were in a bind again. Don't know what possessed her to do this, taking the three of us together for walkies on leashes and expecting us to walk in an orderly and genteel fashion. It was pure madness. All the way down Chemin de Primerose, through Parc de Milan and up towards the town centre we managed to get tangled then released then tangled again.

'Whatever is wrong with you lot,' she cried. 'Can you not walk like ladies? Have you learnt nothing I have taught you? Let's try it again. It is quite easy. Just follow what I do.' Off she strolled with her sensuous walk, and we walked beside her but not to the same effect. We could see the hot-blooded males watching her every move and laughing at us trying to keep up with her.

'This is not a good idea,' Cheyenne said as she bumped into me again, then Tutalou, who hissed at her.'

'This will never work. What's got into her today?' I asked as we stumbled along. 'When she said she was having leashes designed I never imagined she wanted them to take all of us out together. This is not a very practical thing to do.'

'Just one of her odd days... it will pass.'

'I hope you are right, Tutalou, otherwise she'll have us strangled if she keeps this nonsense up any longer.'

We managed to get to the market but only after changing tact. She had me and Tutalou to her left and Cheyenne to the right and off we went but with all of the excitement of the bustle of the place and trying to look as sensuous and stylish as she, we soon ended snarled up again. She was getting annoyed with us so retired to Cafe Sue to refresh herself with a glass of wine and told us to lay still and give her a moment's peace. This we did. Once refreshed she led us off again. All was well for a few minutes then once again; we were in trouble.

'Right, that's it. I can't take you anywhere without you misbehaving.' She hailed a taxi and that was the end of our little excursion. She opened the door, and we dashed in, to the dismay of the driver.

'Get out! You can't bring them into a taxi,' he cried trying to shoo us out.

Capucine sat next to us. The driver was in rapture. 'Oh! It's you, Capucine... how good to see you again. How are you?'

'I'm fine, just fine, apart from this lot annoying me today. You will not believe how naughty they are – won't do anything that I ask. I went to all the trouble to have new leashes made for them and how do they repay me, by being naughty. They are in a disruptive mood today. You don't mind them taking a ride in your taxi?'

'No, no, not at all – it will be a pleasure,' he gushed, unable to hide his excitement of her presence, soon forgetting he didn't want cats or any other animals in his cab. That's what it was like when out with her, wherever we went men drooled over her, bending over backwards to be of service. Rather sad, these males, getting so hung up over women, the more beautiful, the more pathetic they get. Their first impression of women is how beautiful or attractive they look rather than who they really are.

As he drove us home, he talked non-stop, with his eyes glued to his mirror looking at her rather than the road ahead. We were glad to get home.

After the disaster of the communal walk, Capucine was wise and decided on individual walks again. This was after Dirk said she must be mad to have even considered taking three cats out for walkies never mind having them on leashes. Tote thought it a hoot. However, when it came to our outings, she was very disciplined and made sure we took turns and none of us received preferential treatment. She didn't think it odd or different by having a cat on a leash. The locals took no notice as we walked down Chemin de Primerose as they knew Capucine and her ways, but strangers would look curiously at her as she paraded each of us up and around town, her with her distinctive walk and a cat on a fancy leash.

I remember the first time she took me for a walk with my new leash. It wasn't long after our communal one. She dangled it in front of me. 'Time for walkies – Pierre and I will take you for your walk downtown.'

'What!' Pierre cried. 'Not on your life. Not me – I'm not walking down the street with a cat on a leash. Are you nuts altogether? I'd look a right pansy, wouldn't I? Do it yourself.'

'Don't be such a prig,' she snapped, 'and get your lazy bones up and come for a walk. A little exercise won't do you any harm.'

'Go on your own. Folk will laugh if I'm seen walking that bag of bones down the street. People will talk. I do have some pride and reputation to uphold.'

She looked at him and thought, who is he kidding? Pride was never an attribute of most of the men in her life and certainly not this one. As for reputation, she thought he was getting carried away with himself.

Pierre was her latest beau, well, not quite a lover but more an acquaintance she was toying with, to see if he was worth the trouble – a bit like a trinket she picked up somewhere and in two minds whether to keep it or dump it. He was like the last one, only smaller and less attractive and an absolute bore.

'Take no notice of him, Océane,' she said as she fastened the leash to my collar. 'He's just a spoilsport. Men are like that. They never grow up, you know – big kids all their lives. Don't worry, I'll take you for your walk and let this clown stew in his *pride*.' He just looked her up and down then resumed reading his comic.

'Off we went on our merry way along Chemin de Primerose, through the park, under the archway and up towards the market. I looked cute with my personalised leash as I walked step-in-step with one of the world's most desirable women – couldn't get better than that. Everyone looked and admired us, and why not? After all, we were both beauties – different kind but beauties all the same. On that sunny afternoon, we lit up Lausanne as we sauntered our way to town.

At first, I thought folk were looking at me because of my fabulous silky coat, sparkling eyes and my lady-like bearing but the truth be told, it was Capucine they couldn't take their eyes off – and who could blame them? I never did tire looking at her or listening to her laugh at her own jokes. If I'd suffered being a hot-blooded male of the species, I'd be hooked on her too.

Folk would stop, chat, and say how cute I was, stroke me, but it was her they were engrossed with and would rather stroke. She was always well turned out, whatever the occasion. You couldn't fault her choice of clothes or perfumes. She had such a bearing she would look fantastic in anything – even sackcloth would hang well on her. On reaching the market, she walked with a light step into the butchers introducing me to Denis de Buc, who the moment he saw her was in his element again but took one look at me and began to tremble. Denis was another man afraid of furry creatures, but his eyes soon drifted from me to Capucine who introduced me as her latest cute pet, and he began to tremble in a far different way altogether. He stuttered a few words, saying how good I looked – he was lying of course – the male's way out of awkward situations. He was dying to tell her how beautiful she looked, but as usual, didn't have the bottle to say it. The poor fellow spent most of his life in perpetual frustration and anxiety and would forever regret his inability to ask a woman for a date. As he chatted with Capucine, his heart was beating ninety-to-the-dozen, the poor soul. The excitement was just too much for him. After we left, he had to sit down and have a brandy to recover his equilibrium.

From there we visited Vaillant's greengrocer shop, where the proprietors' teenage son, Marc, was goggle-eyed when Capucine asked for carrots and onions. I was trying to get his attention, but he had eyes only for her. She made his day, but the imp never even noticed my fancy leash or me. Outside we came face to face with Lausanne's favourite police officer, Nathan Moreau, a jolly, well-built man of forty. He took one look at me and was in ecstasy. 'What a beauty you have there, Capucine,' he enthused. Unfortunately, he wasn't talking about me but my fancy leash. We continued our shopping expedition with me out front as though leading a goddess to her throne. It was great fun. We traversed the city, visiting boutiques and chatting with some of her friends we met on route then walked down the Market Stairs to Place de la Palud. There we sat on the rim of the Fontaine de la Justice and watched the world go by. We weren't there long when children came up and stroked or tickled me under the chin, and the men folk soon gathered around wanting to say hello to Capucine. You could smell their testosterone as they surrounded her like an animal ready to pounce. Then off we went again down the twisting cobbled roads towards home after a wonderful afternoon in the city.

When we arrived home, Pierre was still in his obnoxious mood. 'Uh, you managed to bring *it* back,' he sneered. A good pee on his lap would have soon put manners on him. I was tempted.

Once, when Tutalou went out for a walk with Capucine they stopped for coffee at Café Tressa, a fancy chic place on the rue Grand-Saint-Jean. As she relaxed with a magazine and drank her coffee, an elderly man sat opposite her. Capucine was always nervous about strangers getting too near her space or crowding in on her and this man was doing just that. He was too close for comfort. He was trying to chat her up, using every corny one-liner he could think of. She had heard them many times before, and at first ignored him, but was starting to get irritated by this would-like-to-be Casanova, who became very persistent with his seductive talk. She politely told him to leave as he was annoying her. Not being a gentleman, he took exception to this rebuff and became aggressive. His language was offensive. He grabbed her arm, in the process spilling the coffee over her Coco Chanel skirt. That was it – she'd had enough. She was about to strike out but Tutalou, who saw red sank her claws into his hand. He screamed blue murder and flung poor Tutalou across the floor, then grasping his bloody hand ran from the café to the consternation of the rest of the customers. This, unfortunately, was the downside of being a stunningly beautiful looking woman... men wanted to try their luck. This fellow was certainly out of luck as well as out of his depth with scars and bruised pride to prove it.

Cheyenne's first outing was when she was still a kitten and this, I believe was the beginning of her inflated vanity. When out, everyone was stopping Capucine and cooing at the little white creature and her cute black spot on her paw. They would pick her up and say wonderful things, tell her how beautiful she was, how exquisite were her eyes, that she was the prettiest thing they had ever seen; what a gorgeous coat she had and how well-manicured were her nails. They never mentioned her fancy leash. No wonder she turned out the most outrageously vain cat one could meet. Flattery, she loved, and her head was easily turned by well-placed words and a tickle under the chin.

So, as you can see, we were no ordinary cats in any shape or form and Capucine, no ordinary woman.

The Felines of Lausanne

Tutalou, standing on the highest point on the roof of the fashionable apartment block on Chemin de Primerose as dawn broke, looked out across the city of Lausanne and gave out a mournful cry that a lover of the feline fraternity had passed away and been cast to the wind over Lake Geneva. Her cry echoed across the city in the early morning stillness. Behind her stood Océane and Cheyenne and the other cats of the complex that joined in the sorrowful chorus and cried out their lament for the lost beauty of Lausanne, who was not just in tune with the feline mind but knew the very nature of their being. Early morning passers-by could hear their cries that included Ruffin, an American Bobtail, Wilma, a wispy Russian Blue and Delphi, a suave German Rex. Next to her, Suzanne, the green-eyed Chausie stray, then there was Laurent, a handsome Javanese. Behind them was Noémi, a petit Savannah, the albino, Tullie, the slim Siamese twins, Clemence and Éléonore and Fagan, a common tabby.

The felines of Lausanne responded and cried out their regret at the loss of a special human being whose inner pain they collectively felt.

Gossip Camille sat on her own near the lead flashing chute casting her eyes now and then at the others. Their cries made her isolation more profound. It was sad to behold as she sat alone. Deep inside she would have loved to be with them, but her nature never allowed her to be one of the crowd. She was an outsider and would always remain so. She tried to cry out and join the chorus of regret, but no sound came from within. She was as tortured and lost as the beauty of Lausanne.

The Visit of a Nasty Yorkshire Terrier

On day thirteen, I was up early as I couldn't sleep and the other two were in dreamland, so I went for a stroll up to the roof to get some fresh air and clear my troubled mind. To my surprise, Camille was there. She sat at the top of the chute and as I sauntered by gave me a sly and nasty look. We could never understand why she was so nasty, so anti-social. Her nastiness brought another creature to mind.

One day as we were lazing about the apartment, as we were apt to do, we were reminded how our lives had changed – all because of another unwelcomed four-legged creature. I was on my belly with my front paws dangling over the edge of the sofa daydreaming as there was nothing better to do. Cheyenne was up on top of the bookcase, softly snoring in between Victor Hugo, Sartre, and Tutalou sound asleep in front of a roaring fire that Capucine had lit to make the place cosy and warm for her visitor – a welcome one but not the devious creature she often brought with her. The doorbell gave a buzz.

'Allo!' Capucine cheerfully said as she answered.

'I've forgotten the key,' the voice replied.

'Come on up, Audrey… can't wait to see you.'

My ears pricked at the mention of Audrey. I stirred from my relaxed position and looked at my companions. 'Oh, no… here we go again – more trouble. She'll have him with her,' I sighed. 'Let's get to our stations and hope he's not and if he is, he'll behave himself.' This was our regular routine every time this obnoxious and nasty visitor arrived. It was like taking up battle positions.

'She doesn't always bring him along. Perhaps she's left him behind this time,' Tutalou said as she poked her head over the bookcase.

'I hope so. He's just too much. I can't stand him – he's an absolute pain. He's anti-social and rude… and we should not be exposed to him and his antics. Audrey knows he scares the life out of us, yet she always brings him – doesn't bother her at all. She thinks it's a joke and can be so insensitive at times. I think she's a tease, too,' I moaned as I sniffed the air searching out his scent.

'Audrey thinks it's a howl with him chasing us all over the place,' lamented Cheyenne.

'She knows we don't like dogs,' I continued, 'yet she lets that brute in. Dogs are dirty things, have no manners and etiquette is lost on them. Audrey is a great woman… a devoted friend to Capucine, her only flaw being, she owns that brute. Why she has him as a pet is beyond me – He is so different in manner to her. She is gentle and kind – he is rough, abrasive, nasty and a bad-tempered brute and worse still – smells. You would have thought she'd have a dog in line with her own personality rather than the complete opposite.'

The door opened and in dashed Mister, the yapping-like-mad Yorkshire Terrier, his tail wagging, eyes alight with mischief and making a dash for Tutalou who protected herself by leaping from her cosy fireside spot and up onto the window-sill, in between the pots of gladiola and busy-lizzies. Cheyenne hissed at the intruder from her safe bookcase perch. I glared at him from under the sofa where I had run for cover and safety. He poked his nose under the sofa, and I gave him a little nip with my claw just to let him know I'm far from a submissive pussy. He howled and ran about the place. He made a meal out of it – I only touched his nose with my paw, and he acted as though he was at death's door. He then noticed Tutalou as she sat on the mantelpiece with her claws at the ready. He was wise, just barked at her then dashed about the place growling, clearly enjoying dominance over us, letting us know who was boss. When he realised, we were out of his reach and had control over our domain, he lay down in front of the hearth and the warmth of the fire as though he owned the place. There was a look of satisfaction on his face as he made himself cosy on *our* rug. He licked his sore nose and wasn't long until he was sound asleep but always with one eye half-open, ready to pounce on us if we made a move.

Audrey and Capucine had welcomed each other with a peck on the cheeks and a lingering embrace. They clung together not saying a word, just swaying back and forth with their heads on each other's shoulders.

'How are you, Cap, my love?'

'I'm, *fine*, just *fine*.'

Audrey broke away from the embrace, looking hard at her friend. 'Tell me... what's wrong. Something is bothering you – it's written all over your face. What is it? You're still taking the medication?'

Capucine shrugged her shoulders in a way that her friend knew there was trouble ahead. 'It's difficult,' Capucine whispered.

Audrey's heart sank. 'Oh no, not again, don't say you're not taking them.'

Capucine turned away from her friend and lowered her head. 'I know what you're going to say, that the medication is essential, that it's the only solution, my only salvation, I've heard it all before, but I've lived with Lithium and those other concoctions for years and it's only had little, if any effect.'

Audrey sighed and cast her eyes to the heavens. She turned Capucine's head towards her. 'Not again... please tell me I'm wrong.' Audrey, although extremely sympathetic to Capucine's long-time suffering, sometimes would lose patience and despair at her erratic behaviour. For years she had to do battle with her about the value of medication, had to argue over and over every element of it repeatedly that it became wearisome.

'I'm not certain if medication is the answer – I've tried a multitude of concoctions and find little benefit from them. It causes me more anxiety than it's supposed to stop and compounds my insomnia. Perhaps I should be brave and try the more radical alternative therapies. I must be broadminded about it. So many other non-medicine options are open to me.'

Audrey nodded her head and pursed her lips. 'We've been through *this* before. Let's not agonise over it again. You know you must be disciplined, Cap. Forget about the other options and concentrate on your current medication programme. The medication is essential if you want to keep your life in order, to function, to feel normal. You know this already. Whatever you may like to believe, the truth is, your medication has worked very well over the years. If it were not for it, you would not have enjoyed the life you have. You know what I mean. There were long periods when you lived a good life and free from pain, when your life had structure. You seem to forget that. Your medication helped you do this, the medication you deride so much. It is only medication that keeps you stable – nothing else and certainly not those overrated alternative remedies you've tried, and no doubt will try more, like that Chinaman with his needles and smooth talk. I'm not saying they don't have any value, far from it, only they are not suitable for you. It's only your medication you benefit from. It's when you stop taking it you have trouble – like now – like last year and twice the year before. You know this. You had a four-year stretch once without any episodes and you know how well it felt. That was the result of your adhering to your medicinal programme. How many times have we discussed this over the years – how many times? I can tell you – umpteen and here we go once more through the same old rigmarole.'

'I don't just want periods of relief. I want to be free of it forever, don't you understand, Audrey, free from this inner pain, free from this everyday struggle, free from this darkness in my life. You are the only true light in my life, Audrey. Without its brilliance, I'd be lost.'

Audrey wrapped her friend in her arms and hugged her tightly, letting her cry away her sorrows. She cared so much for Capucine it hurt to the core to see her deteriorating once more.

'Have you missed many days?' She asked after Capucine calmed down.

'A few – I do try, but... it's so difficult.'

'A few – how many exactly – tell me, how many?'

Capucine pulled away from the embrace, hung her head and turned away. 'About… two weeks,' she whispered.

Audrey grabbed and hugged her again. She knew the consequence of this. Without doubt Capucine would have suffered a breakdown of some sort since they last met and probably another to follow. She was right. We had been through a hellish six days as she reacted from the deprivation of not taking her drugs. Some days she was subdued and would lay on her bed for hours, often in a comatose state, not eating or drinking and other days, was like a bat out of hell, screaming and shouting and running us from room to room, screaming like a banshee. On this particular day, she was in a reasonably good mood, and we mistakenly thought she was reaching the end of her episode.

Audrey had been down this road many times, far too many to mention. Medication was always Capucine's Achilles' heel. We three could write chapter and verse on Capucine and the effects of her medication and her fight against it. She was never comfortable with it and far from convinced as to its beneficial value. Every time she popped a pill, it was a constant reminder of her condition. Try as she could she was unable to stay on the medication for long periods that would keep her stable and subsequently suffered the after-effects with Audrey always there to pick up the pieces. It would be the same old routine. Audrey would gain her confidence and gradually talk her into resuming the medication after convincing her of its positive effects. Every time she let the medication lapse, she would be in a terrible state, erratic and antisocial and near on demented with suicidal tendencies. After each lapse, it would take up to three weeks to stabilise her.

204

This was common to most bipolar sufferers. Because of her continuous rejection of the medication, she was doing more damage to herself, compounding her symptoms, and making them more acute and therefore more difficult to treat.

So, Capucine would recommence her medication regime and life would return to some kind of normality. She would resume her acting commitments, social events then something would trigger doubts in her mind then she would gradually refrain from taking her medication and the downward spiral would start all over again. Audrey had become an expert on bipolar and all of the medication and their side effects and understood precisely what was required to keep her friend sane. She was Capucine's guardian angel and Capucine treasured the fact. However, at times she became worn-out by her vigilance care of the fragile soul.   She knew all the moods of Capucine, her highs and lows and was able to handle her with care, tenderness and understanding. Whenever an episode afflicted her, Capucine, after some argument would always listen to Audrey, and in general take her advice, but the issue of her medication always caused friction and fierce arguments. Audrey also knew when her friend was hiding something… could read her like a book; could always second-guess her which in turn would annoy Capucine to distraction. How it would normally work, was, after recovering from an episode, Audrey would set about a programme of recovery. She knew the process well. She would spend the rest of the day pacifying and reassuring Capucine of the necessity of resuming her medication and with the help of the doctor and an assessment from her psychiatrist, be put on another course of medication. Because she came off the medication suddenly, the same cocktails of drugs might not necessarily work so it was down to trial and error again. This could be a traumatic process and often necessitate a hospital stay. She would be giving a new cocktail of drugs and hopefully, they would work, but chances were she would suffer side effects. Some would dumb her down; make her passive or stupefy her; others caused hot flushes, palpitations, memory loss and spells of paranoia. This would last until her psychiatrist could regulate them, but by then the damage was already done, and after each lapse, her condition would become more severe. Once stabilised, she would again continue with her life until the next time when the demon inside would dictate otherwise.

Meanwhile, the three of us, with a sharp eye on Mister, listened to the friends sobbing as they clung to each other. I looked at Tutalou. 'Wish Audrey would move in. She would have Capucine taking her medication and better still, staying on it. She always listens to her – might argue the toss but in the end would listen and take her medication.'

Tutalou laughed. 'Not a chance – Audrey's a sensible woman and a wise one too. She's of better use to Capucine as she is. She might not be as effective if she moved in. If she did, we'd have to live with Mister, wouldn't we and our lives would be made a living hell. We can just about put up with him on his odd visits, but to live with him permanently – no, thank you. I'm fussy who I live with. We would need therapy if he lived with us – would need a psychiatrist. If he was a man, he wouldn't be the best catch in the world for a woman, would he and we don't need him, and his doggy ways inflicted on us.'

I laughed. 'I don't know about that. Some women like men who are snappy, rough around the edges, obnoxious, surly and bad tempered... just like Mister. They are not all like Capucine who prefers a more refined and good-mannered kind of man.'

'Pfff! Pity, she can't find one, then. They're probably thin on the ground or should I say, rare, judging by the ones who have so far who traipsed through her life. Anyway, Audrey has too busy a life, with her work with UNICIF that takes her around the world; she wouldn't have the time to care for Capucine, even if she lived with her. Then there's her family and acting commitments that takes up so much of her time,' Cheyenne reminded us. 'Yes, she's of better use as she is.'

As time passed with Capucine and Audrey chatting away with regular bursts of laughter, we decided to make our move to regain our patch. Mister was now sound asleep and Tu-talou moved gingerly towards him and our place on the rug. I crawled from under the sofa and made my way tentatively towards him, followed by Cheyenne. We lay near the brute. It was our rug, and we were determined not to allow him to hog it all. He growled in his sleep, his eyes rolling about, then once certain he was in a deep sleep we settled down, closed our eyes, and dozed off.

After a while, Mister started to stir, grunted a little and yawned. We opened our eyes and wondered whether we should be wise and scarper to our safe hideaways or stay put. This, believe or not was our exercise in psychology, trying to pacify Mister and show him we could be friends if he would let us. We were looking to have peace restored, as he was too active for us. We preferred a slower and more sedate way of living, not the erratic ways of the canine. This strategy didn't always work. Sometimes he would wake up, snarl, and send us scurrying for cover. In this mood, there was no pacifying him as he was like a demented lunatic. But this kind of disturbance was becoming rarer and rarer by each visit as we got to know him and when Mister was friendly, we'd enjoy a few hours of relative calm together, snoozing on the rug. It was a slow process of getting to know each other, seeing how far we could push each other in trying to get our own way. Seeing that he was to be part of the furniture, as they say, it was in our interest to come to some kind of arrangement with him. The more he got away from the puppy stage the easier he was to handle and for us to sleep on the rug, but it wasn't always like this, this sleeping with a nasty Yorkshire terrier. When first introduced to us, all hell broke loose. He was only a pup then but what a nuisance he was. He was wild and noisy and thought we cats were easy game, something he could toy with, but he was very much mistaken. As never been exposed to dogs before, the arrival of this scallywag was a jolt to the system, a real culture shock. How we managed to survive his first appearance I will never know. I remember Audrey arriving to introduce her new puppy. Capucine cuddled and kissed him then let him down and the moment he caught sight of us he ran us ragged around the apartment. Audrey and Capucine had a good laugh about it as we tried to escape from the nasty little brute as he snapped and snarled.

Cheyenne had only arrived six months earlier so was rather traumatized once exposed to Mister and his antics. It took us a while to accept him as part of the family. He didn't

208

always get his way. On one occasion, he cornered Cheyenne, and she duly left him with several lumps missing from his coat as a reminder of their encounter. After that, he was always wary and looked at her with a little more respect. However, Tutalou and I would rather make a dash for cover than confront the bully.

Audrey also owned a cat. Her name was Emily, who she rescued from the Geneva animal compound. She was attractive, black as the ace of spades, sparkling eyes with a dash of mystery about her. Audrey adored her, reserving most of her embraces for her to the annoyance of Mister. Mister, not a lover of the feline fraternity was always jealous because she always slept with Audrey, whereas he had to sleep under the stairs but somehow, they managed to coexist in complete harmony. When Audrey came to visit one day, she had both Mister and Emily with her. We were pleased to see her and got on well, far better than with Mister. The odd thing, he would run after us, making our lives a misery then the next moment he and Emily would play together then cuddle up to each other as if they were lifelong lovers.

So, Mister became part of our lives. Not the best of set-ups we thought but if we wanted the presence of Audrey then Mister was part of the deal.

Hiding Her Pain from the Three Feline Philosophers

Suicide always concentrates the mind and so it did for Lucie Plessis. Since the moment she looked from her balcony after hearing the harrowing cries from below and seeing Capucine's body lying crumpled at the foot of the building, she had found it hard to breathe without feeling Capucine's pain and the emptiness she must have felt to take her life in the way she did. She had not slept properly since that terrible day and was unable to work. Her employers at the model agency were pressurising her to strut the catwalks and smile when inside she was broken-hearted and an emotional mess. The frivolity of the fashion world seemed such an irrelevant thing to her as she prepared to feed the traumatised cats. Each morning, she would put on a brave face for Océane and her pals as she fed them – masking the pain she was feeling. She patted each of them, saying a few words of comfort then sat with them for a while. Her nervousness of cats began to ease the more she visited them. She would look at them eating and wonder what was going through their minds and how they were feeling. Were they numb with grief, were their hearts breaking as hers was? She was determined she would not cry in front of them and cause them any further distress but kept the tears for the privacy of her apartment.

Her parents were concerned about her health and asked her to come home to recover from the shock. She told them she could not leave the cats until she knew what was to happen to them as she had told Inspector Lewee she would.

They decided to come to her instead but all she wanted was to be alone, just her, her thoughts, and the orphaned cats.

She tried to clear her head by going for a long walk every day but there were always reminders of Capucine wherever she went. As she passed newsstands or places where they would often meet – memories of Capucine's kindness kept coming to mind – her advice about the fashion world, about the honesty of being yourself and not as others want you to be in the unreal world of the fashion industry. As for men, she was not short on advice on how to handle them and their peculiar ways, always best to let them know you are no pushover she said. She gave her such good solid advice on so many things without sounding like a matriarch. Even though there was a big age gap between them, it did not make any difference as they communicated well and understood each other perfectly.

The pain of suicide never goes away as Lucie was to find out, as many had before and unfortunately will continue to do so.

Cocktail of Hope

When it came to medication, Tutalou was in tune with Capucine's needs. She had something Cheyenne, and I lacked – intuition – she understood everything. Nothing escaped her. She always kept a sharp eye on Capucine and if late with her medication, she would walk in between her legs, meowing and annoying her until she took it. There would be no half measures with her, so if she wanted peace; she would only find it after taking her medication. Tutalou believed medication was Capucine's one and only hope. However, this strategy didn't always work. Capucine many a time would run her out of the room telling her to get lost, to hop it. We would have a good laugh at Tutalou's expense as she scurried for safety with Capucine in close pursuit. Not one to give up, she would try again when Capucine was in a more congenial mood. Tutalou was always the first to know when Capucine was going through her denial period. She was in tune with her and prepared for the drama and trauma that enviably followed each of these lapses.

The fact that Capucine had read everything about mental health and received the best of medical treatment she continued to believe there was a cure, although medical research, a lot of which she had read through and through, showed there was none. She would never accept the reality of her situation –would not accept that her condition was there for life – that it could be managed and contained to such a degree she could lead as near a normal existence as possible, apart from the side effects the medication caused. These too could be contained to some degree. She had been through the whole gambit of medication available: Lithium, Haloperidol, Quetiapine, Carbamazepine, Depakote, Eskalith, Lithane, Lithobid, and many more. A few of these were effective in many ways but could also cause her untold suffering. The side effects at times were severe and debilitating. They ranged from anxiety, which at times was chronic, to severe tiredness and insomnia. Nausea was so regular a visitor she just learned to live with it and problems with her menstrual cycle added to the misery of her condition. One side effect she managed to avoid was weight gain and throughout her illness managed to keep her trim figure intact. These side effects along with physiological ones made her stop taking her medication. Although she knew the consequences of not taking it, there was that demon within overruling her sensibility, sending her once more on a downward spiral. Once on this slippery course, she could do nothing to save herself but wait for rescue, either by Audrey, Marcia or through medical intervention. She understood well the nature of the drugs prescribed to her and how beneficial they could be, but instead fixed her mind on the damage they could do. We dreaded these lapses as she suffered so much. We were diligent and discreet in our care, just keeping a quiet eye on her – to be there when needed. When she slept, we would creep towards her taking our normal positions at her head, heart and feet. Sometimes when she was having a restless night, we would perform our skills and help her to relax and finally find sleep.

Marcia loved and adored Capucine and fretted over her continuously. However, she would take no nonsense from her and would scold her if she neglected her medication. Marcia was an angel but far from a soft touch and was able to handle the violent outbursts whenever they came, the tantrums and all the other manifestations of her condition. She could soothe Capucine's troubled mind with a warm embrace and a few words of comfort and was blessed with extraordinary patience, a requisite for anyone caring for bipolar sufferers.

Throughout her lapses she still managed to maintain her poise and never allowed her condition to interfere with her professional life and would always turn up on the film sets immaculately turned out and always very sociable with the cast and crew, masking the pain she was suffering. Everyone loved her. It was hard not to, but they never realised the agony she was suffering and how she was dying inside from the loneliness and sheer abjectness of her condition.

Headaches were a curse. They affected her mostly in the early morning, so intense that her vision was blurred. Tutalou was always on hand to massage her head with her caring paw as she lay on her bed. She had perfected her technique over the years, but even with all her skills she could not relieve her completely of them, only help ease their intensity. She even asked some of her lovers to massage her temples. Now, that was asking for trouble. Most had no idea how to do it while others were not interested in the least. A few did try but what a disaster, unlike us felines; men do not have the touch, that special touch that can ease pain and stimulate, not just of the body but also the mind and soul. Although these techniques were beneficial, the truth was, the medication was all-important to her, but she refused to accept this reality, instead, her mind was off down a path that was completely opposite to where she should have been heading.

Life Turns in the Most Peculiar of Ways

On the same day Capucine died, Carolien Junas received an unexpected letter. It was from Italy. She examined the familiar handwriting and had a terrible sinking feeling. She walked out onto the terrace and sat by the pool and looked forlornly at the blue-tinted envelope, then laid it on the table beside her. She sipped at some cool lemonade, deep in thought of things past, the thing's she would prefer to forget. She knew it was from Pablo. She could feel him radiating from the envelope. Should she read it, or throw it away in the same casual way he had done so with her love? She was unsure. It was a long time without a word so why now? Why did he wait so long? He could have written earlier, at any time over the last fifteen years but elected not to do so. It was painful for her even thinking about him and what he had done never mind opening a letter from him or even handling something he had touched. The pain of rejected love is heavy to bear – does he not realise that she said aloud as the tears welled up. If he did, he would not have sent the letter and opened old wounds, he would have let the past rest.

Her mind went back to when the cross and Juliette vanished those many years ago and the agony of it all. The police had contacted the authorities in Italy about the theft and whom they believed was the number one suspect, Pablo Arti, businessman and socialite. Pablo had left France not long after the event and returned to his hometown of Montecatini and tried to forget about Carolien until one day as he was about to leave Bogata airport on a business trip he was in for

215

a shock as he was arrested at the departure gates accused of the theft.   The French police were seeking his extradition. His first reaction was to laugh at the officers.

'This is no laughing matter, signor – A serious allegation has been made against you by a Carolien Junas of Toulouse and the extradition papers are before the court. First, we must ask you some questions.'

'He laughed out loud again. This time the officer slapped on a pair of handcuffs, swiftly wiping the smile from his face. To his shame, they manhandled him away in front of the startled passengers.

Pablo was questioned for hours, denying any involvement in the theft, saying his former girlfriend was out for revenge and for no other reason and there was no truth in her allegation. His parents secured the best lawyer they could find and the next day he appeared in court to answer the extradition summons.

The judge at first thought this was a simple extradition application but once he scanned the papers he was fuming and annoyed to distraction.

'Who presented this application?' he snapped.

'I did, your honour,' said a nervous young woman lawyer.

'Counsel,' he said in a slightly raised voice. 'As well as this being outside the scope of extradition, there is no prima facia case here or probable cause, no evidence whatsoever to support this application. Whatever possessed your client to consider presenting this? As I see it, a valuable antique silver cross and a cat of rare breeding went missing, when this young woman, Carolien Junas was here in Italy, at Lake Como, visiting her parents. Before she left Toulouse, she ended her relationship with her long-time boyfriend, the accused, Pablo Arti, after a fierce argument, which was, as these papers state, an irrevocable breakdown in their relationship. He had keys to her home, given by the applicant and the access code to her safe at her villa on the outskirts of Toulouse. On her return from Lake Coma, Ms Junas discovered the theft and called the police. They examined the scene and took fingerprint samples from the safe that included those of Pablo Arti, Carolien Junas and her concierge who also had access.

'The affidavit of Carolien Junas states she 'believes' Pablo Arti stole the silver cross and the cat, an Egyptian Mau, but produces absolutely no evidence whatsoever to support it. I cannot consider this application on the grounds that Carolien Junas and the police in Toulouse 'believe' he was responsible and without any shred of evidence or possible cause to support it. The fingerprint evidence is not credible as it is reasonable to expect the accused prints to be there as he had legal access to it. The motive produced is flaky at the best and frivolous in the extreme. This is not a serious enough an offence to be brought before the courts as an extradition application.

'I'm subsequently not allowing a full hearing of this application as what is produced does not remotely conform to the criteria laid down by the European Extradition Treaty. I also refuse leave to appeal.'

The judge, annoyed by the waste of the courts time would not even listen to any argument from any side in the proceedings and told the legal team in no uncertain terms to go away and study the European Extradition Treaty and stop wasting precious court time. He also criticized the Toulouse police for attempting extradition proceedings on an issue completely outside of the remit of the extradition treaties. He concluded by saying Pablo was free to leave.

When this news arrived in Toulouse, Carolien was astonished and outraged by the judge's attitude. She sought all the legal advice she could, but it looked as though her legal challenges were at an end unless she secured credible evidence to back up her claim and the French authorities make a fresh application in full compliance of the European extradition treaties.

She realised it was the end of the legal route and reluctantly had to accept the reality of the situation. She missed Juliette so much and was inconsolable at the loss of the family heirloom.

Over the years, she got on with her life and tried to forget Pablo but periodically memories would return to haunt her. The end of their relationship was bearable and in a way a blessing in disguise, but the loss of the cross hurt, hurt her to the core. She even lost out on the insurance, as there was no evidence of a break-in of her villa. As for Juliette, she often wondered what happened to her. It was the worst period of her life but being a stoical kind, she buckled down, got on with her work, and put her heartache behind her. There were new men in her life but nothing serious and never got emotionally close to any as she lost all faith in men, that none could be loyal enough to win her love and trust. She never did replace Juliette. She busied herself in running her parents' company and travelling a lot in the process. You could say she buried her head in work and gave men and romance little thought. She had no idea what happened to Pablo and cared less when unexpectedly she receives this letter from him. After looking at the bulky envelope, she picked it up and gingerly opened it. The engagement ring that she had last seen as she threw it at Pablo fell out of the envelope into her hand. It was indeed from Pablo, the deceiver, heartbreaker, two-timer and thief of Juliette and her precious silver cross. She was in two minds whether to read it or tear it to threads and cast them to the wind. It was fifteen years since they parted and the pain of what he did was still raw, the cuts of rejected love, still seeping. She nervously read the letter.

Salut Carolien,

I hope this letter finds you well.

I realise I am the last person you would like to hear from, but I hope you will read this.

Time has caught up on me. I will not see another summer and I need to make amends for the hurt I have caused you and others.

I did a terrible injustice to you, and I ask your forgiveness.

When you left for Italy, I took your cross and Juliette with me on my journey back to Montecatini. When the train stopped in Lausanne on route, I left Juliette, with the cross attached to her collar on platform two. To my shame, I did this out of spite and in one of my tempers, that you always warned would be the undoing of me. How right you were. I do not know what happened to them. It shames me to think about it. I always hoped Juliette would be found along with the cross and returned to you.

I recently contacted the police in Lausanne about what I had done, and they informed me they would check their records. I earnestly hope they have news of what happened to them and have them returned to you although Juliette will now be of advanced age and may have passed away.

Over the years, I wanted to contact you, but my shame always stopped me from doing so.

I knew how much the cross meant to you and your family and how attached you were to Juliette and my only motive in taking them was to hurt you and I can't forgive myself for doing this to the one I once shared my love with.

I have returned your engagement ring. I always kept it, as I could not bear to part with it.

I wish you love and happiness, Carolien, and beg your forgiveness for my grave sin.

Pablo

She sat for some time, stunned and shocked. He was dying and his lasts thoughts were of her. Tears began to trickle down her cheeks, quickly turning into a torrent. Her days of love, of the passion of her life, of the halcyon days of her youth came flooding back. It was all too much for her to take. She was one who loved and gave her all, only to lose out in a cruel and painful way. Why did he not write earlier – things could have been so different, she cried aloud as she slumped in her chair in despair.

Sheila arrived. She had retired recently as the concierge but always called in to see Carolien whenever she had time. She noticed Carolien sitting slumped in the chair and ran over to her. She still had the letter in her hand that was hanging *limply by her side and in the other, the ring grasped tightly, resting on her lap.*

'My dear, what is it?'

Carolien looked at Sheila, her eyes red and swollen. She handed her the letter. Sheila read it. 'Oh, dear God,' she cried then wrapped her arms about her sorrowful friend.

An Inventory

It was the fifteenth day of our captivity, and we were in for a bit of a surprise. The day started with Lucie arriving with our meal in a flood of tears. She was distressed and upset and as we ate, she knelt and placed a white rose petal in each of our collars. She left wiping her eyes. What was ailing her we had no idea. Perhaps she knew what was going to become of us.

We had just finished our meal and settled down for our morning snooze when two men, one tall, the other small, dressed in sombre, grey-striped suits, stood at the entrance of the apartment with clipboards and pens at the ready. They meant business and looked far too serious for my liking. The smaller one was breathing heavily.

'I'm knackered,' he moaned. 'You'd have thought a high-class joint like this would keep their lifts in operation.'

'Stop moaning. It's only eight stories,' the other laughed. 'If you kept yourself trim you wouldn't be out of breath.'

'I need time to recover before we begin,' he gasped as he leant against the doorpost, wiping his brow.'

The taller one had the bearing of a gentleman, the small one, that of a seedy back-street pimp. They looked about; the small one sniffed the air, like scenting his prey then walked into the sitting room as though he owned the place, plonking himself on the white leathered sofa to recover from his exertion, putting his size ten feet up on the sofa arm as though he was settling in for the day.

'Not a bad pad at all,' he observed, tapped the sofa with his stubby, nicotine-stained fingers. 'A new makeover and I'd fancy this place. Get rid of most of this feminine paraphernalia and it would have the making of a good bachelor's pad.'

'You are married.'

'So, what – a bachelor pad would add a little spice to my already exciting life. Just because you are married doesn't say you shouldn't have any fun and not sail close to the wind on occasions.'

The tall one laughed at the brassiness of his colleague then clicked his pen ready for business. 'Yes, very nice indeed – as I imagined her place to be. It is a good apartment. I disagree with you, though. It doesn't need altering at all. It's perfect as it is. This lady had style and a beautiful soul she was too.'

'She wasn't my cup of tea,' the other grumpily announced as he scanned the paintings on the wall.

'The problem with you... you have no taste, no finesse.'

The small one gave a dismissive wave.

They were from the legal and auctioneering firm, *Grimolens, Grimolens & Company* of Geneva, appointed to deal with Capucine's estate. Their job was simple; to list the apartment's contents, take note of all her worldly goods and tag them ready for probate. From the moment they were given their brief for the day, they realised this inventory would be somewhat different and no doubt far from a run-of-the-mill one. They both knew who Capucine was. The tall gentleman knew her as the well-known model, actress and patrician beauty who suffered in life and was loved and respected by the people of Lausanne. The other thought her estate was easy prey to extract money from and to bad-mouth her at every opportunity and this low life was an expert at demeaning others weaker than him.

The tall one looked down at his colleague as he stretched out on the sofa. 'What are you doing laying there? Get up and stop acting like a prick.'

The other sat up smartly. 'My, my, very touchy this morning – what's got under your skin?'

'You have, as usual. Up you get and stop messing about. We have a job to do and the quicker we do it the better, so we can get out of each other's sight.'

Dragging his slovenly body up he gave a look of contempt and thrust his index finger menacingly up in front of colleague's face.

Casting their eyes about they caught sight of the three of us who looked at the visitors through slit eyes as we snuggled up to each other on top of the bookcase, where we had run for cover when the key turned in the door.

'What will become of these cute ones, I wonder,' the tall man said, pointing at us with his pen.

'Cute ones – are your nuts? Cats – cute – rotten trash is more like it. Oh, but don't worry though, their fate is sealed,' replied the other, sneering at us. 'They'll be dispatched and disposed of this Friday, so I've heard. Once the paperwork is complete, it will be bye-bye for them and good riddance too. They deserve a good skinning, anyway, skinned alive if possible. That's what they'll get on Friday, hah-hah. Anyway, by the look of them, they have been spoilt rotten and chances are they wouldn't survive the streets so where they're going is the best solution, you could say the final solution,' he laughed.

We froze. That's not funny. I was overcome – my heart was beating hard, and a cold shiver went through me. Cheyenne was near apoplectic and Tutalou gave a long regretful sigh as though all hope was gone. Was gossip Camille right after all – that we were doomed to die – that we were simply surplus to requirements and to be disposed of? This was the first confirmation of Camille's assertion, and the cold facts hit us hard. We had a few days left to make our escape, but how. We looked into each other's terrified eyes as we huddled together, in hope of feeling secure amidst all of the uncertainty and the presence of these strangers in the apartment.

'I'm sure they'll be looked after by someone, perhaps by a member of her family or maybe a neighbour.'

'They will be *looked* after, OK. Don't worry about that. I never liked cats anyway,' the small one continued, rubbing it in, glaring at us with his bloodshot eyes. 'Too mysterious for my liking... devious little buggers – they give me the creeps. Yes, trash, that's what they are, nothing but stinking trash! Best rid of. I'd prefer a rat as a pet than them any day. Why anyone wants to have one, never mind three about the place is beyond me... couldn't think of anything worse. This Capucine had to be mad – any cat lover has to be – they must be a special breed of sadists to want the company of those devious four-legged creeps.'

Tutalou looked terribly angry. 'Trash indeed – at least we don't have pig-like features as he does.' We nodded our agreement.

They continued walking about the room casting their eyes over its contents as we stared at them.

'Who are they?' asked Tutalou.

'Rats on two legs,' Cheyenne sighed as she eyed up the two men as they poked around getting their bearings, ready to do their business.

'They're here to list all of Capucine's belongings, including us, I presume,' I informed them as the strangers looked at and touched some of the apartment's contents.

'They look like thieves to me,' observed Tutalou, 'well-dressed ones but thieves all the same. I don't like these strangers walking about Capucine's home, our home, touching her treasures – contaminating her personal possessions with their grubby hands. It's indecent and vulgar. Can't understand why they have to do this. I don't like the short one – something about him – something creepy.'

'It's what is called an inventory,' I informed them. 'All to do with red tape that humans seem stuck and addicted too. It's a law thing, you know. Humans have this thing called legality wrapped around them. We don't need legalities in our lives, but they do to keep them in order. They are not safe without rules, regulations and legality. Humans – they sure are a peculiar lot.'

'Odd, isn't it?'

'Indeed, Tutalou. They are here to list everything Capucine possessed – I mean everything, so they can say what her estate is worth.'

'Why?'

'Haven't a notion – another one of those human oddities. Can you imagine us felines worrying about what we are worth in material terms after we are dead? That's what makes us superior to them,' Tutalou reminded us. 'We don't tax our mind with such irrelevancies. They spend so much time worrying about anything and everything; about what others have or don't have, what others do or don't do, what others think or don't think and what others look or don't look like, that in the process they forget what life is about – like living. They worry about everything, where we, in general, don't worry about anything, apart from eating and sleeping. We don't worry about what others have apart from how cosy their cushions are and what they have in their larders. We certainly don't worry and fret over what others might think of us. How pathetic would that be – sounds like a terrible waste of mental energy. No wonder humans are always uptight, tetchy, and highly strung. Most need treatment of some sort or other.'

'How right you are,' Cheyenne laughed. 'What's the purpose of all this listing of things anyway? No logic to it at all.'

'They do so, so everything can be disposed of at what they call an auction, once those benefiting from her will have taken their share, the apartment will be sold off and the proceeds will be added together with any monies she acquired, if any, and that is what the value of her estate will be. Then the taxman gets his grubby hands on a good chunk of it. He's like a vulture hovering about ready to take the flesh off, not only the living but the dead – nothing socially decent about him. Has no conscience whatsoever – his only loyalty is to legality. Sometimes there can be bitter arguments and fights between relatives or friends claiming the deceased left them a certain item or other. Some swear they were promised money and argue the toss in court by contesting the will. Some spend years battling it out in court only for the inheritance to be frittered away and swallowed up by greedy legal eagles that always seem to swarm about when relatives quarrel, ready to sharpen their legal claws and swoop on their treasure troves. Legal eagles are nothing more than human vultures, no wonder the outer rims of hell are reserved for them and their kind. Greed is another unfortunate trait in humans that we felines are blessed not to suffer from, but their greed is never-ending – a kind of addiction; some even say it's in their genetic makeup.'

Cheyenne was flabbergasted at this revelation. 'Are you saying people will fight over Capucine's belongings, over her personal things and maybe, over us? How sick can that be?'

'It can happen,' I replied, 'but I don't think it will in Capucine's case... Well, I hope not. She doesn't have any relatives that I know of, to pick over her treasure or financial bones.'

'She must have. Everyone has a relative of some sort or other, maybe ones they can't stand and prefer never to see again, but relatives all the same,' Tutalou announced. 'And if there are treasures to be found I'm sure many a mysterious relative will emerge from the woodwork and make themselves heard – and loudly. Greed, after all, is part and parcel of the human condition.'

'Pfff... Seems they will dispose of all of her treasures as they will with us – cast to the wind without ceremony,' sighed Cheyenne.'

The two strangers, after a quick walk about the apartment to get their bearings began their task in the sitting room, diligently taking note of every item and sticking a number on each one. Capucine's apartment was a treasure trove. It was like her, stylish and elegant. She owned interesting and valuable works of art acquired by her, in many cases, unique pieces, including delicate wall hangings, paintings, such as Impressionism, Neo-classicism, Surreal and Abstract. Along with these were porcelain and a superb collection of books, many first editions, including a signed copy of Hugo's *Notre Dame de Paris*, Baudelaire's *Les Fleurs de Mal* and Simone de Beauvoir's *The Second Sex*. Other volumes she treasured were editions of the works of Scott Fitzgerald, George Sand, Voltaire, the Brontë sisters and many more that gave her a substantial library. She had good taste when it came to the arts, collecting many treasures on her journeys around the world. Our Capucine was the quintessential woman of good taste.

We jumped down from our perch and followed the interlopers and continued to keep an eye on them. The tall one bent down and stroked me. 'Hello there,' he said trying to tickle me under my chin. I was still unsure of him, so I sprinted towards the cedar cupboard to take cover. As I ran, the small one kicked out towards me. He missed. I glared and hissed at him before I vanished under the cupboard. There was something about this man that had an air of disaster about him. How right I was. The other two joined me and we nervously watched as they continued their unsavoury task.

'Have you seen this – take a look? It's strange, very strange indeed,' Benoit, the small one said as he picked up a silver locket. 'I don't understand it at all.'

'What is it?'

'The silly cow has strands of hair concocted into a design. It's weird! Look, the different strands intermingled into some design or other. Wonder what the hell that's about. What a strange cow she was.'

'How dare he call our Capucine a silly cow and strange,' cried Tutalou. 'Who does he think he is? The cheek of him – She has more sophistication in her little finger than this rat has in his whole body – silly cow indeed.'

'Let me have a look,' said Maurice, the taller of the inquisitors as he snatched the item out of Benoit's hand, showing his annoyance with his colleague's use of language. 'It's one of the signs of the Zodiac – scorpion to be precise. Don't you know that? I thought you were a know-all! She must have been into astrology. Not my kind of thing but each to their own.'

'What is astrology?' asked Cheyenne.

'It's to do with the stars, the universe and all that kind of thing,' I informed her. 'It's a kind of delusion. Humans love to delude themselves. Some believe your star sign dictates your fate – how your life will span out and how it will end – like telling your fortune of what will be.'

'Didn't I tell you humans are nuts,' Tutalou reminded us. 'There's no hope for them, is there. How can anyone tell the future? Crazy nonsense – as crazy as that religious dogma so many peddle and are bent on – yes, Océane, you're right, nothing but delusion?'

'Oh, yes, religion, that's weird OK, believing in a God, isn't it? They have some odd notions do these humans.'

Cheyenne was confused. 'Was Capucine *really* into this astrology, this looking at the stars? I can't remember her talking about it.'

'She may not have talked about it, but she certainly looked at her sign every day in the papers, before she tackled the crossword. Surely you must have noticed.'

'Can't say I did… So, do we have astrological signs, then? If so, we could have ours told and perhaps we might find out what fate has in store for us, see if Camille is right or if we've been fretting over something that will never happen – that after all, we will be saved, and Capucine had indeed planned for our future.'

'Don't be daft, Cheyenne,' I laughed. 'We don't need that nonsense to clog up our minds. We felines are on a higher level than that, as you well know. It's all more mumbo jumbo nonsense dreamt up by humans – they are full of it.'

'Look at the back; it has something written on it – real fancy engraving too,' Maurice said as he examined it, 'and stop calling her a cow, Benoit. The poor soul suffered enough in life without the likes of you demeaning her at every opportunity. Have you no respect.'

'Never mind *respect*… what does it say?'

Maurice looked at him with contempt. 'William, Dirk and Audrey,' he snapped, agitated at Benoit's tone.

'Who the hell are they?'

'Well. Audrey was the actress, I presume. She was a friend of Capucine – her closest friend – it would be fair to say, a kind of soul mate.'

'Audrey who?'

'For heaven's sake – Hepburn, you clown – Breakfast at Tiffany's…'

'That skinny one, you mean – the one who's a do-gooder and all that – the Moon River one who lives down the road at Tolchenza?'

Maurice gasped with indignation. 'What do you mean – *do-gooder*? Apart from being an outstanding actress and model, she is a humanitarian of the highest order – nothing 'do-gooder' about her. You are mixing up your metaphors again.'

'Well, she is always putting her nose into some cause or other, keeping her image on the go and her ego stimulated and in tip-top condition. She's always out and about, up to something or other. Only a few weeks back I was watching another item about her on the telly. There she was again, announcing to the world another of *her* projects, another of *her* good deeds another of *her* sad little tales. There's no stopping her! She's obsessive about it. She doesn't impress me at all – never did – never will.'

Maurice cast his eyes to the heavens in disgust at his partner's outburst. 'What an ignorant one you are at times. You have no idea about her; have you, not the foggiest. Why be so cynical about her motives and especially someone you don't even know? It's not decent to talk about her in the way you do. You obviously know little about her or her work for UNICEF, if you had, you wouldn't be talking such drivel. She is a sensitive and compassionate woman and a great friend to the unfortunate soul whose home we are now in – have some respect and a little decorum. Anyway, no decent soul will ever impress you.'

'All I know she's always parading herself on the telly or in glossy magazines letting everyone know of her new project and her next act of *goodness*. That's the impression she gives me – a professional do-gooder, full of self-praise.'

'Rubbish!' cried Maurice, his irritation showing at Benoit's derogatory remarks. 'Let's stop talking like this and get on with the job; we are wasting precious time. We have serious business to attend to.'

'God! You do go on, don't you? About time you jumped down from that high-principled pedestal of yours before someone knocks you off. Remember, those with pride always have a long way to fall.'

Maurice ignored him.

'Anyway, this Dirk chap, I suppose you know who he is too?' Benoit said out the side of his mouth.

'Yes, but seeing you are in one of your obnoxious moods today, I won't tell you who or what he was.'

Benoit laughed aloud. 'Well, smarty, I already know *who* and *what* Dirk *was* and what Dirk *did*.'

'Do you now. Then why ask? I'm glad you know some-thing. Sometimes I think the decent things of life have been wasted on you... kind of passed you by without even noticing you.'

Benoit was furious. He stood close to Maurice and eye-balled him. 'You underestimate me, Maurice Kilber, the trou-ble is, everyone does, but there's more to me than meets the eye, I can tell you. I don't just have hidden talents but also hidden depths.'

'Have you now? – how *very* interesting.'

'Yes... deep... *very* deep.'

Maurice chuckled away to himself. 'Well, lucky you.'

'Just you wait. One day you'll see how deep they are, and you'll regret ever laughing at me.'

Maurice had heard all of this before, and it was becoming wearisome. Every time they were together, there were always implied threats or smarmy remarks. Maurice had thought of

233

asking his boss to avoid putting them together for assignments but thought twice about it as it would cause questions to be asked, and his past would be discovered. This he thought, must be avoided otherwise he'd be done for.

'What will we list this silly piece of *art* as?' asked Benoit.

'There you go again. It's obviously a very personal and emotional item and shouldn't be laughed at. What's silly about it? It's a work of art with meaning behind it and there's nothing *ever* silly about art.'

'So, you're an art connoisseur as well. You are full of surprises. So that's art, is it? Uh, you could have fooled me.'

'Even a fly could fool you, Benoit. Don't act the prat. List it with the rest of the miscellaneous – no, on second thought add it on the silver list.'

Benoit labelled it and added it to the list. It seemed a terrible end to someone's time on earth when strangers mooch about, touch and disturb your belongings all for the sake of legality and stick labels on them. I began to wonder if we would be added to the inventory and which list, we would be on. No doubt Benoit would put us on the 'to be disposed of' list but I'd say Maurice would have us down as three of Capucine's treasures and add us to the jewellery one. I wished they would go quickly, but no, it looked like we would have to put up with them for some time to come.

'Look at this. Did you ever see such a fine specimen of a walking stick? What a beauty! This is superb! Look at its handle, so well crafted. Wonderful! It must be around the 1880's.'

'My, my, Benoit, you do surprise me,' Maurice said as he examined it. 'Yes, a fine piece of work. I'm glad you have some regard for perfection. I'd say French, Parisian to be precise.'

'I'd say English. London, to be more precise,' Benoit retorted, confident in his knowledge of walking sticks.

'No, look at the hallmark, very Parisian indeed.'

Benoit snatched back the cane, rubbing the silver handle and examined it carefully. 'Uh! Right again – can't be easy being such a know-all and high principled, too,' he grunted, throwing the stick back to Maurice.

Maurice ignored him and pencilled in the walking stick on his never-ending list.

'The stick belonged to Capucine's grandfather. Wish they'd not touch her things, it's wrong, so indecent.'

'Take no notice, Cheyenne!   Let them get on with their dirty work and leave. The quicker they depart the better. We have better things to do, like trying to finalise our escape plan. We will have to think harder as to how, as time is our enemy,' I reminded them.

'I agree,' Tutalou sighed. 'Escape is the only option we have.'

'Wait a moment,' I cried. 'Surely this is the time to try and escape – now, when these two invaders leave. A quick dash should do it. When they open the door, we'll skedaddle – as easy as that. It might be worth a try – nothing to lose. Let's prepare for it. This might be the only opportunity we may have.'

'I don't know if it will work,' Tutalou replied. 'I can't see them allowing us to get anywhere near the door.'

'They can't stop us – we're faster than they are. They'll be no match for us, especially that stump of a fellow. The door will be open enough as they prepare to leave to allow us to make our escape. Let's do it.'

The other two looked at me and nodded their assent.

Beinot and Maurice continued their work, with Maurice being very thorough about it, meticulously taking notes. He didn't miss a thing, even added knives, forks, cups and any knick-knacks they could find to the list. However, Benoit was not as meticulous as Maurice was. He seemed to have his eye and mind on something else. The signed books caught his attention, as did some rare editions. He took down Hugo's *Notre Dame de Paris* from the top shelf and putting it to his stubby nose, sniffed it and sighed.

'Look at this, Maurice! I wouldn't mind owning it.'

Maurice took the book and leafed through it. 'Yes, a fine volume indeed. This is valuable,' he stated as he replaced it and scanned the shelves. 'What a fantastic collection. Make sure you log all of them, everyone – no mistakes. It will take you a while, so let's have our first break of the day before we go any further.'

This they did. Maurice departed for the kitchen to make the coffee expecting Benoit to follow. Alas, he was having none of it. He picked up his bag he had left in the entrance hall, brought it into the lounge, and settled once more on the sofa, opening his bag and spreading its contents on the coffee table. He opened the tin foil to reveal a delicious and tasty looking quiche Lorraine. He licked his lips then called to Maurice. 'Bring the coffees in here and don't forget the sugar.'

Maurice arrived with the coffees on a silver tray.

236

'It's not right, Beinot, for us to eat in here. The kitchen is good enough,' he said as he placed the tray on the table. Benoit gulped as he looked at the exquisite tray before him.

'God, look at that.'

'Yes, a superb piece of antiquity. We shouldn't be using it but there was no other tray.' Maurice explained.

Benoit put his quiche aside and examined the tray in detail. 'What a beauty you are,' he said as he turned it over to examine its hallmark and engraving. Maurice opened his lunch box, took out a small ham and cheese salad, and looked at his colleague. He could read Benoit's mind as he caressed the tray as though he was in a passionate embrace with a lover. Maurice sighed then finished his salad in silence as Beinot whispered words of endearment to a cold but beautiful piece of art.

As they continued their break, we put our heads together to hatch our escape plan. Cheyenne reminded us of what Benoit had said when he arrived, that the lift wasn't working, that meant the staircase doors would be open as a security precaution, so we planned to dash out of the door and down the stairs to freedom. This invasion of our home may be a blessing in disguise as it gave us our most likely avenue of escape.

After their break, Benoit started to catalogue the books. Capucine was well-read. Her library covered a wide range of subjects and interests. Many of the classics adorned the library along with books on physiology, the natural world, fashion and works of art. When nearing the end Benoit took a large volume from the bottom shelf that had no title on its cover or binding. It was heavy – a box book. He opened it to discover it was a manuscript. His eyes widened as he read the opening pages.

'Did you know she had written a book?'

Maurice looked at it in astonishment. Taking the book from Benoit, he read the synopsis and soon realised that what he was holding was Capucine's unpublished manuscript of her biography of the Brontë sisters. 'Well, how about that,' he said as he flicked through its pages. 'This is very interesting. This will have to be listed separately. There will be a lot of interest in it, I would say. The Brontë's are a highly bankable commodity. Unlikely it will be up for auction. I would say her family will claim and possibly publish it.'

'Who the hell are the Brontë's?'

Maurice looked at Benoit and laughed. 'I thought you said you were well-read.'

'I am.'

'Well, not as much as you think. They were three English sisters from Yorkshire who were literature's *crème de la crème* in the 19th century. The elder, Charlotte wrote Jane Eyre, Anne, Agnes Grey and Emily, Wuthering Heights. They published their works under male pseudonyms because of the strict moral code of their time that didn't allow women to have work published.'

'Are you showing off, with all this literary knowledge?'

Maurice gave a chuckle. 'No, just saying what all 'well-read' people know.'

Benoit told him to get lost.

'Make a special listing of it. We will have to bring this to the attention of the probate manager. Let's get on with the rest of the rooms.'

238

They headed for Capucine's bedroom and so did we. They entered what was her haven, the place of her dreams and schemes, of her sorrows and pleasures. Benoit walked in with a swagger, followed by Maurice who was more respectful. We popped our heads around the door to keep a sharp eye on them. The first item to catch Benoit's eye was the patchwork quilt. Capucine's mother made it years ago, that was neatly spread on the bed that Capucine had made up the day she left. Benoit jumped on it and bounced up and down like a kid. 'This will be worth a few bob – unusual design – well- stitched too,' he said as he felt its texture with his grubby fingers.

'What are you doing? Get off for heaven's sake and keep your thieving hands off it,' Maurice warned him.

'Get knotted, will you?' came Benoit's snarly reply. 'Bet there's been a lot of action in this little love-nest if we believe all the tittle-tattle about her many lovers. She didn't seem too particular either by who she invited into her bed – seemed like a loose woman to me.'

Maurice's reaction to this crass remark was to stare hard at Benoit, his face creased as anger grew inside. It looked like he was about to lash out but refrained from doing so. We soon realised there was no love lost between these two. There was an edginess that was quite palpable.

'Just shut up, Benoit and keep your dirty remarks to yourself.'

Once Maurice calmed down and regained his composure his eyes caught the sight of a watercolour by the English artist, Russell Flint, hanging above the bed of a semi-nude woman leaning against a stonewall. He examined it, studying each brushstroke, each delicate shade. He was a dedicated art lover and as he said, 'a kind of expert' on watercolours and pastels. He was being modest as he was a connoisseur of fine art, especially paintings and his companies' expert in assessing artwork for the auctioneering side of the business and was a keen collector of art too. 'I like this,' he announced, not that his colleague would be impressed.

'Well, live dangerously and take it,' Benoit smirked. 'Who'd notice?'

Maurice ignored the remark as he continued to admire the painting.

'This room is full of goodies. I'll say this for her, she had good taste,' Beinot said, giving a rare compliment as he gazed about the room, still lying on the bed, his hands behind his head and his feet crossed.

Benoit was a stocky-built individual and as ugly as sin. His only redeeming feature was his mesmerizing blue eyes. His face was pot-holed, a legacy of his teenage acne days. His lacquered short black hair was stuck to his Germanic looking head. He had an excuse of a moustache above his flabby protruding upper lip. Maurice was the opposite, a tall handsome and elegant looking man with sharp Roman nose, hazel eyes, well-cut hair and immaculately groomed with an air of sophistication about him. He came across as a man of style, a man who appreciated the finer things, and a man who valued the beauty of life. Watching how he handled and looked after Capucine's possessions confirmed this. He had finesse, unlike his companion who I would say preferred the cheap thrills in life, the seedier the better – he'd be happy and at home in the back alleys of any city.

Next in line for Benoit to violate with his touch was the dressing table containing Capucine's *lingerie*. It was sickening to watch him handle them. He didn't say anything as he went through each item, just waved them in the direction of Maurice who was sickened by the clown he had the misfortune to spend the day with. It was clear Benoit was getting some kind of warped thrill as he handled them. I felt like jumping on his shoulders and digging my claws into his hard neck.

'He's sick,' stated Cheyenne.

'Sick!' replied Tutalou. 'More like evil.'

Maurice, in the meantime, began to list her clothes, coats, shoes, hats, chokers and scarves. There was a sadness about him as he registered each item, conscious of the history behind them. He knew he should do as his job required and not think of the deceased, but he couldn't. He was too sensitive a soul to be indifferent, unlike Benoit, who we watched in despair as he handled Capucine's intimate clothing, accompanied by his crass remarks and sniggering laugh.

Once finished in the bedroom they started on the study. Benoit gave a gasp as he caught sight of Capucine's most treasured antique. It was an 18th century Louis XV1 writing desk and this, one of the best. He was in ecstasy as he touched it. His harsh features softened as he guided his hands over its shapely contours, seductively licking his lips. He had a thing about writing desks and this one set his passion alight. Desks and tables were the few areas he specialised in and quite an authority on them. Capucine had inherited this valuable piece of work. She used this well-crafted desk regularly. It was one place out of bounds to us to snooze on. It may have been a delicate piece of antiquity, but she used it and used it well. She would sit there writing letters, often with perfumed candles flickering away in Indian candlestick holders, which sat on either side of the top of the desk. These where elongated copper tempered pieces given to her by Dirk Bogarde that he picked up in India. Benoit continued running his hands all over the desk. He sighed with every touch. He had little respect for most of her property, but he did for this well-preserved antique. He made us cringe as he fondled something so emotionally part of Capucine, but we could do nothing about it but wait for him to leave the apartment.

'This has to be the most valuable of the items we have come across so far. Wish I could get it out of here. I hate to think how much this would fetch at auction or better still through a private deal.'

Maurice laughed. 'Don't even think about it as it's listed in her will, here, look, in bold letters,' he said waving a copy of the will in Benoit's face.

'Pity – I wouldn't mind owning it myself.'

Thank God there was no chance of that. Benoit was vulgar in every possible sense of the word and the thought of him owning something of Capucine's was enough to make us throw up. There was little to redeem this man. The quicker we saw the back of him the better!

The next item that caught his attention was a turtle shell fountain pen resting on the desk. Capucine used this when writing the biography of the Brontë sisters. Dirk had read the manuscript and thought it an excellent read, as did a few of her friends. For some reason, it was never published. This pen was a collector's piece, and Benoit knew it the moment he cast eyes on it. He examined it in detail then looked at the office listings and a copy of the will to see if it was there. It wasn't. He looked to see where Maurice was and once distracted, slid the pen into his pocket.

'Did you see that?' cried Tutalou.

'The thief – that's Capucine's,' Cheyenne squealed.

The three of us ran about Benoit's feet, hissing and scowling, our tail raised in anger.

Maurice turned around, alarmed at the commotion. 'What's up with them?'

'They're cats – that's what's *up* with them.' Benoit replied as he kicked out at us. 'Get away you scumbags. Off with you, you skin-full of bones. Cats are strange creatures, aren't they just? They always look at you as though they had something on their minds – something sinister. Off with you.' He kicked out at us again, but we managed to avoid his menacing shoe.

'Well, kicking out won't endear you to them. Just get on with your work and leave them alone – we have a lot to get through and have to complete this inventory today so stop messing about and leave the poor creatures alone.'

'I will if they'd keep their distance – creeps! Poor creatures indeed,' he snarled at us – we hissed back. He finally retreated but still had the pen in his pocket.

'I knew the man would be trouble the moment he walked in,' I said as Benoit shuffled through the contents of the desk in a clumsy fashion, which annoyed me even more as I knew how neat and tidy Capucine always kept her desk as she did with everything about her. He found a bundle of letters, tied up with a gold ribbon, tucked away in a small alcove in the desk. Untying them roughly, he had a quick look, then sniggered and headed for the lounge. He lay down on the sofa with his feet resting again on the Tibetan patchwork on the arm of the sofa. He began to read, smiling at some of the contents, unconcerned he was delving into private correspondence. He was a man of little decency and had little respect for others or their feelings. Maurice, wondering where Benoit had vanished to, rushed quickly into the lounge. He noticed what his colleague was doing and snatched the letter he was reading.

'What on earth is wrong with you? Reading the personal letters of the deceased is a total invasion of privacy. Have you no shame! Our job is not to humiliate or belittle the memory of this unfortunate woman, only to list her belongings and to do so with care and quiet propriety.'

'Give me that back, your smart arse,' Benoit shouted as he grabbed the letter. 'Quiet propriety indeed – I was busy reading it if you don't mind! You should chill out a little and enjoy the moment instead of being a nauseating and conscientious *bore*. This Capucine was well known and mysterious with lots of secrets about her, secrets that could financially benefit us if we find out what they are, so let's milk it for all it's worth. The shrouded mystery that was Capucine could be worth a fortune if we could strip away the shroud and reveal her secrets. By all accounts, if you believe the title-tattle about her, she got through quite a few men – no hanging about with this sassy one. There are a few questions about her sexuality too...'

Maurice sighed and shook his head.

'I bet there's a lot of saucy correspondence amongst this bundle – came across a few revealing ones already – *very* revealing, explosive ones too. The press will certainly be interested in these. I know a few people in the press who would pay good money for some juicy and salacious revelation and would love to have their hands on these letters.'

My fur was up on end by this man's vulgarity. Tutalou's palpitations returned, and Cheyenne's claws extended towards Benoit as I showed my teeth.

'No, Benoit! We can't! That's stealing as well as being indecent and in breach of our employment contract. You'd not only lose your job if it were ever traced back to you but a good chance of ending up before the courts and a lengthy stretch behind bars. Just take note of her possessions. That is all you have to do and leave it to the executor of the estate and the probate office to decide what has to be done with them.'

'Ah!' he groaned, dismissing Maurice's concern. He continued reading as Maurice, agitated by Benoit's continuous bad behaviour stood glaring at him, wondering what he could do to get his colleague to behave with a little bit of decorum. He was impossible and Maurice had no option but to just put up with him. They were well behind schedule with a lot to get through. It was going to be a long day and the thought of being with him longer than needed filled him with dread.

'Look at this one. Should get some ready cash for it, I'm sure. Listen! This is from the actor, Dirk Bogarde, the one you wouldn't tell me who he was. I know more now, a lot more. He's replying after she rejected his offer of marriage for the second time – very descriptive indeed, although a little flowery – a very feminine letter – for a man.'

Maurice took notice of him and continued his task.

'Why did he want to marry her? He wasn't supposed to be into women so why did he want to marry *her* – doesn't make any sense at all.'

'Don't go there, Benoit, you'll only confuse yourself.' Maurice pleaded. 'Put it away! It's a personal letter and not for the likes of your eyes. You're a fool if you think you'd get away with selling it or any other of her effects.'

'I could make a copy. I'm sure a tabloid paper will pay even to see a copy. Maybe she wasn't as squeaky clean as the world thought. I say hidden away in these letters is a different Capucine, a secret one, not the one we've been led to believe, but one a lot of people would like to read about. She always looked mysterious and where there's mystery there's always intrigue and seeing she was a 'star', I'm sure there is some dirt attached to her too.'

Maurice shrugged his shoulders. 'You can be a low life at times; you know that a real low life. Even if she wasn't 'squeaky-clean', as you call it, it's still no concern of yours or anyone else. Your only interest is money – that's vulgar to start with. That's the kind of sod you are, a grubby little money grabber, a leech on the soul of decency.'

'Get lost!' replied Benoit, as he settled down on the sofa, surprised by Maurice's use of words. He gave a little chuckle to himself, chuffed at his ability to make Maurice lose his calm.

Maurice returned to the study to resume his task. He was unlucky at times having Benoit appointed as his assistant. Thank God it wasn't a permanent arrangement, he thought, otherwise he'd end up throttling him. Maurice worked at the Geneva office not far from where he lived whilst Benoit at the

Lausanne one; thankfully, they didn't see as much of each other. Maurice had an office in both cities but only came across his unsavoury colleague when an inventory had to be conducted in Lausanne.

It was clear to us that Maurice was the most sensitive of the two. We could see he admired Capucine greatly and was saddened by her passing, unlike Benoit, who didn't have a caring bone in him. His only interest was finding ways of extracting money from the deceased's estate. He was not too fussy how he achieved it and took pleasure in demeaning Capucine at every opportunity. The job by its very nature demanded honesty and decorum, which he did not possess in any measure. They were handling items – in this case, many not recorded and easy pickings for someone dishonest like Benoit. This was far from the first case where Maurice had to do battle with his colleague over missing items from estates. When jobs like this came along there was always an opportunity for the dishonest to pilfer the estate. He knew Beinot did this at every available opportunity but had never actually witnessed him doing it and thankfully, he only had him as his partner on the rare occasion. His company for some reason kept Benoit employed even though they must have been aware of the rumours of his thieving habits. What that reason was he could not fathom.

Benoit lay on the sofa reading the letters and left Maurice to do most of the donkeywork. Occasionally, he would get up and do some listing to keep the inventory on schedule but returned throughout the day to continue reading the letters with Maurice reminding him they were behind schedule and must get a move on.

They had listed everything, along with the autumn-coloured batik curtains that adored the entire apartment and the light fittings and the numerous potted plants and hanging baskets. After labelling these and all the miscellaneous items, it was time for their second break.

Benoit made the coffee this time. Maurice walked over to the library and returned with the Brontë manuscript. He sat on the sofa and read the opening pages as his wayward colleague rummaged about in the kitchen.

'You give out to me for reading her letters and there you are reading through her book. You bloody hypocrite,' Benoit chuckled as placed the tray on the table.

'This is different – it's part of the job. By the look of this, it's laid out ready to be published. Wonder why she never submitted it.'

'Probably, because it's a load of old rubbish.'

He was at it again. There was no stopping him and his nastiness.

'You're fully aware that unusual items like this have to be scrutinized and listed separately. The letters you're reading are personal and should have been listed as letters in a bundle and not read.'

'Rubbish!'

Capucine spent a lot of time working on the manuscript and found writing therapeutic. She didn't tell many about her writing venture. It was a small circle: Marcia, Audrey, Dirk, and Cécile. She was very secretive about it.

After the break, they returned to their tasks. Beinot headed for the guest bedroom whilst Maurice to the bathroom, then all the nooks and crannies such as the cupboards and alcoves where items like umbrellas and memorabilia were stored. Benoit, after checking the bathroom had resumed reading the letters. Time was getting on as Maurice made a final check of his list, before getting down to the last task of the day.

'That's everything done apart from the safe. We better open it now, that's if you're finished reading private correspondence.'

Benoit's eyes lit up. 'I'd forgotten about that. Sure to be some goodies in there.' He jumped to his feet throwing the letter aside. 'Let's get down to it, then.'

'Not before you return the letters to the desk.'

Benoit gave Maurice a cold stare then gathered up the letters strewn across the sofa and floor and returned them back to their rightful place. He was gone for a long time.

'Will you hurry up?' Maurice called after him.

'Well. Let's get on with it, then,' he said on his return.

Maurice took from his pocket a small black book. He sifted through a few pages then tapped in a series of numbers and turned the knob. The click of the safe made Benoit's eyes widen and sparkle. When the door opened, he was in ecstasy at the sight of its contents.

The safe box was a treasure trove. Most of Capucine's jewellery was there. She had many admirers, male and female, many who bestowed this collection upon her, now gloated at by Benoit like a vulture with its talons ready to strike. One piece was a gold necklace given by an Arabian sheikh who because of his wealth thought he could buy whatever he fancied, including Capucine's favours. He was out of luck. She spurned his advances, kept the necklace and kicked the suitor into touch. There is no beating the style of women when it comes to diamonds and other sparkling things. One of her favourite pieces she often wore was a tiara, a love token from William Holden given to her after their two-year relationship ran its course. They remained friends until his premature death. He continued to visit her and set the place alight every time he appeared. We liked him or should I say, we adored him. One of her few male friends we did. He was a real gentleman, apart from his drink addiction that at times was not pretty. She cried oceans of tears at his tragic, alcoholic induced end, not long after his visit to her last soirée.

Also, part of her collection was her engagement ring given to her by her former husband, Pierre Trabaud in a marriage that lasted a mere year. After the divorce, she did what any self-respecting woman would and should do, kept the ring and said goodbye to the man.

The next piece Benoit had his grubby hands on was a single pearl necklace, given by a young businessman Capucine met when making the romantic movie, *North to Alaska*, in 1962, set in the outback of Alaska at the turn of the twentieth century. He was transfixed by her and wined and dined her on many occasions, but she let him down gently. She didn't want to accept the necklace but did so as she didn't want to hurt his feelings. She treasured it, as it reminded her of the happy times whilst making the movie.

'I thought she was broke,' Benoit said as he looked at the necklace. 'One of the obituaries stated she was stony broke amongst other things. If she sold a fraction of these, she would have had a small fortune.'

'No one will know how her finances are until her estate is sorted out. Don't believe all you read in the papers, even in an obituary.'

'Jesus, look at this? Benoit cried as he held up Tutalou's diamond-encrusted silver cross, shining and glittering as it twirled around. As he looked at it, wide-eyed, he didn't notice a piece of paper falling from the safe and fluttering to the floor.

'Wow! What a beauty – it must be worth a small fortune. I'd sell my mother for this. Do you think anyone knows it's here, that it *even* exists?'

'They do, stupid, 'snapped Maurice, knowing what was going through his colleague's mind.

'Yes, this is worth a fortune! We could have a handy little nest egg if we manage this well and flog it to the highest bidder. I know a jeweller in Marseilles who would pay handsomely for this with no questions asked.'

We recoiled at the brat's blatant cheek. Every minute that passed, we disliked this unsavoury individual more and more and resented his invasion of Capucine's space.

'Is it mentioned in the will?' asked Benoit. 'It's not on the official list.'

Maurice scanned his copy; then double-checked. 'No, but don't go believing others aren't aware of it. She was a diligent individual so I'm sure she'd had it registered somewhere or other. It's not the kind of thing you'd forget to insure.'

'Why don't you live dangerously for a change, instead of being the careful and conscientious sod you are? Taking a few things that won't be missed, will do no harm. As long as we cover our tracks all will be fine – chill out, won't you!'

251

'Won't be missed... an expensive piece of jewellery and it won't be missed? You must be mad to think you can get away with it.'

'Taking a few things, including this, is a perk of the job as you know damn well. All auctioneers do it. Everyone does. If there is no record of it, then no one can prove if it's missing or ever existed. The will is the most important document and there is no mention of it and no insurance documents to prove its insured. On the list from the office, there is no reference to it so why not take it and cash in on it. Who will notice?'

Maurice looked at him in despair. 'Well, I will!' He snatched the cross out of Beniot's hand and gazed at it in wonder. He hadn't seen or held such a fabulous piece before. No wonder Beinot had his thieving eyes on it. He registered it and tied a tag to it. 'Here, put it back in the safe and act your age.'

'You are too cautious for your own good, Maurice. Taking a few items is harmless if no one knows they are missing – perks, perks, Maurice, nothing but perks. That's what it's all about.'

'Not with me it's not,' Maurice replied as he began a final check.

'Please yourself!' Benoit said, shrugging his shoulders.

They compared their lists to see all was in order. Putting his pen in his pocket he closed the safe and made sure it was locked. He gave his colleague a cautious look as though to say, 'keep your grubby hands off'.

'That's everything done. Don't think we've missed anything. Let's be on our way.'

'Not quite,' Benoit said as he tapped his pen repeatedly on his clipboard.

'What do you mean?'

Benoit pointed to the balcony door.

'Oh, yes – how could it have slipped my mind? Let's get it done with and be on our way,' Maurice said as he made for the French doors. He opened them and his heart sank as he gazed about.

'This must be the place of destiny, ha-ha,' Benoit laughed, as he pushed passed Maurice and leant over the rail. 'So, this is where she did it, eh! It's a long way down. She must have hit the deck like a stone – poor sod!'

'For God's sake, that's enough of that kind of talk. Is there no end to it?' Maurice cried, angry with Benoit and his insensitive manner. 'Just take the notes and shut up.'

'I feel sick. Must he gloat?'

'Take no notice, Cheyenne. He'll be gone soon.'

'He's a wicked bastard,' added Tutalou.

The creep sat in Capucine's wicker chair between the pots of lavender and gazed around, adding everything he could see to his list: the ceramic plaques, hanging baskets, reading lamp and even her marble worry stone that rested on one of pots. The sight of him sitting in her chair gnawed at our nerves. This was her meditation chair – her place of peace, her little paradise in this mad, mad world and there he was, sitting in her space and gloating. God, I could have clawed his eyes out.

'Why do you think she did it?'

Maurice turned and frowned. 'You really want to know or are you just being a smart arse as usual?'

'Only curious – you must admit it's a brutal way to go. The silly cow could have done it in a far better way, a cleaner, more civilised way, like swallowing barbiturates, that's *all* I'm saying.'

'What!' Tutalou screamed. 'There he goes again, is there no stopping his nasty tongue?'

'Right, I've had enough! Any more nasty insinuations and I'll report you to the boss.'

Beinot shrugged his shoulders again then they finished the inventory in silence. 'Let's go,' he said. This place gives me the creeps anyway, along with those scrawny sods,' he snarled, pointing at us with his pen.

Maurice had had a bellyful of him and couldn't wait to leave to get out of his sight. He thrust his lists at Benoit. 'Here, take these. Have them typed up and cross-referenced. Leave them in my Geneva office when you have them ready so I can authenticate them and don't take forever – Wednesday afternoon at the latest.'

Benoit sneered at him then placed them along with his own lists into his leather attaché case.

'Let's get out of each other's sight,' Maurice said as he turned and headed for the door.

It was time for our escape. 'Are you ready,' I whispered. 'The moment the door is open, and their backs are turned we'll make a dash for it.'

Tutalou and Cheyenne nodded their approval.

Maurice made for the door with Benoit lingering suspiciously behind but stopped before getting there. 'What's that in your coat?' Maurice cried, grabbing at Benoit. 'Not the letters – are you mad altogether?'

We were ready to dash out of the apartment but halted dead in our tracks as they began to argue. Maurice tried to get the letters back, but Benoit pushed him away, laughing at his protestations. 'I've only taken a few, that's all. Nobody will miss them. As I said before, I know a few contacts that will pay good money for them. Give you a cut if you want – can't be fairer than that, can I?' he laughed.

'I want nothing to do with it. What you are taking could have an emotional attachment to a member of the poor soul's family. Have you no shame? Are you really that low? You don't even realise what you're doing is wrong – that what you are contemplating is theft?'

'Poor soul – what do you mean, 'poor soul'. She had a great life... had it all: fame, fortune, the lot, and travelled the world having a ball. There was never anything poor about her. As for shame... that's for suckers!'

'Only you could come out with that kind of remark! You obviously know little about her and care even less. She may have had everything material in her life, had success and wealth but this woman suffered, believe me, she suffered. I know that won't mean anything to you or your likes, but that doesn't mean you have to steal from her estate. Put the letters back, and let's be on our way.'

'I will not, and you can do nothing about it. Remember Maurice Kilber, I know your secret, so don't even think of doing anything – you understand?'

Maurice gave a resigned look, knowing Benoit had him in a corner, all because of a rush of blood to the head in his early twenties that turned his normally tranquil world into a living hell. He wished he had the courage to stand up to him and let his employers know exactly what he was up to with their client's possessions, but he thought it best not to look at what his dishonest partner was up to or what he wanted to steal. Deep inside, he knew that by ignoring Benoit's stealing, not only from Capucine's estate but from other clients too, he was all but condoning it by his inaction. He felt a helpless ass.

Maurice, shrugging his shoulders turned to leave. 'Let's get out of here.' He opened the door and bent down to pick up his briefcase. This was the cue for us to make our dash for freedom.

'Ready!' I cried. 'Let's get the hell out of here.'

Tutalou dashed through Maurice's legs. Cheyenne leapt past him. Benoit was blocking my way. He cursed and kicked out at me. 'Where the hell do you think you are going you little shit?' he cried as he caught me on the hip with his steel-tipped shoes. I squealed and dashed out of the door followed by Benoit who was screaming expletives at me with venom and murder in his eyes. Once on the landing, to our dismay, we discovered the doors to the stairs shut. We were cornered. Our grand escape plan came to a sudden dead end – there was no way out.

Benoit reached to grab me, and I dug my claws into his hand. He screamed blue murder but finally managing to grab me by the neck, throwing me violently back into the apartment, landing heavily on the marble floor.

Maurice was fuming. 'You sadistic, smarmy creep,' he cried as he gently lifted up Tutalou and returned her to the apartment with Cheyenne, her tail between her legs, following behind.

Maurice knelt and checked I had no broken bones then turned and glared at Benoit. 'Why have you to be so cruel to them. These cats have lost their carer and are suffering enough without your cruel antics.'

'Oh, give it a rest, will you. Look, the slime ball has taken a lump out of my hand. Go on! Off with you,' he snarled as he turned on Cheyenne and Tutalou who had run to my aid. 'Someone will be coming for you lot on Friday. That'll put paid to you once and for all, you scumbags... Grrr,' he screeched, kicking out towards us. Cheyenne hightailed into Capucine's bedroom, away from the madman but I stood my ground and hissed and reached out with my claws at the ready to take another lump out of him if need be. Benoit backed off. He spat at me, leaving his spit dripping from my left ear. He followed Maurice out of the apartment, slamming the door behind him, locking us in again.

'Well, we made a right mess of it, didn't we?' I groaned. 'So much for our escape plan... our great strategy. What a disaster. What have we achieved – absolutely nothing, nothing but bruised ribs, spit on the ear and dented pride. What will we do now?'

'Cheer up, Océane. We'll try again,' Tutalou said as Cheyenne re-joined us after sticking her head out of the bedroom door, looking around to see if they were gone. 'What a nasty piece of work Benoit is. His mother must have been scared witless when he arrived. As for Maurice, well, he seems a decent and kind sort of fellow. He did come to our rescue and was respectful and conscientious while handling Capucine's possessions. I think she would have approved of him. As for Benoit, I don't think she'd have let him put a foot in her door never mind touching any of her personal belongings.'

Once more, we lay on the rug in front of the hearth, a little sore for our efforts, still unsure how to escape. We went over the options again, but our hearts weren't in it. We had had lost faith in our ability to save ourselves.

Best to Keep the Past in the Past

The best you can do with past indiscretions or failures is to leave them exactly where they belong, in the past and let them rot, but there will always be someone who wants to rake over old coals, stir things up and cause untold misery in the process. We have all come across them sometime in our lives and so it transpired one morning in the offices of Grimolens and Grimolens & Company of the city of Geneva that one of these muckrakers raised his head, determined not to let the past rest but to bring a soul to ruin as an act of revenge.

Over the last few days, Benoit Monte had been hawking letters to a large selection of prominent editors of daily and Sunday papers. First, he waylaid the editors of La Monde, La Figaro, La Martin, and La Presse. They gave him short shrift when they realised, they were the property of Capucine. Not deterred, he tried his luck with the London papers, the Times, the Guardian and even the tabloid press turned him down flat. Benoit's confidence was waning at every turn, and it wasn't going to be as simple as he thought to earn his 'easy money,' but things turned for him when he contacted a downtown New York paper of low repute. They said yes but needed clarification they were genuine letters. Once confirmed they would buy them at a price to be negotiated. He was delighted by the minimum amount quoted – all depended on the quality of the letters and their revelations.

In the offices of Grimolens and Grimolens & Company, they were cataloguing Capucine's effects from the inventory lists provided by Maurice Kilber and Benoit Monte, ready for the Probate Court. For some reason, there was an alarming hurry to instigate probate of her estate, as she had only been dead a relatively short time. The office was an efficient machine, processing cases with all legal propriety and Capucine's case was no different. Next step was to organize the removal of her effects from the apartment and stored ready for auction if that was to be the direction of the Probate Court or through the provisions of her will.

Meanwhile, probate manager, Christophe Arnold received a phone call from the editor of a local paper. He wasted no time in stating the source of these letters being hawked about the place had to be from a member of staff at their offices as they were the nominated probate auctioneers to carry out the inventory and the only ones able to get access to the apartment. The probate manager was flabbergasted and unaware of any missing letters. He was also unaware of the missing silver cross until a report from the police noting Capucine had registered the item as found and details were with the police, and she had signed a document stating she would keep it safe and have the item insured in the hope the ownership might be proven. It also stated the true owner has made herself known. A letter from Capucine's solicitor also arrived that morning including a receipt from a Parisian auctioneer for a 19th-century tortoiseshell pen. This was not however included in Capucine's will, the list for the safe or in any of the insurance certificates.

Maurice Kilber, the most senior of the company's probate officers received a call to report immediately to head office. He had no notion of what had transpired and stood rigid as details of the missing items were read out. He was at a loss to know what to say. He knew who the culprit was, but should he come clean that he had remonstrated with his sidekick not to take the letters, as for the silver cross, he had no idea it was missing. He was certain he had seen it replaced in the safe before he left the apartment and he himself had added it to the list, as for the pen, he never knew it existed. As he stood pondering what to say, he was thrown a lifeline, well, only a temporary one. The manager wiped his brow and said, 'Listen here, Maurice, you've been with us a long time now and we don't want to lose you as you're one of our finest operatives and furthermore, we don't want the police involved as we have a reputation to maintain which is second-to-none and must be protected. Our business is grounded on honesty and discretion. You understand?'

Maurice took a deep breath. 'Yes, monsieur, whatever has to be done; I will do, if it's in my power...'

'It will have to be in your power, Maurice, as these items went missing on your watch. You were the senior officer responsible for the job. I see you had Benoit with you from the Lausanne office. You two don't get on, do you? Is there something you want to tell me?'

Maurice was uncertain as to what to say. As he was about to speak the manager said. 'This is what I want you to do. Replace all of the items to their rightful places in the apartment.' The manager pushed the keys across the desk towards him. 'I don't want to know whether Benoit or anyone else are the culprits, all I'm interested in at the moment is their safe return. I want this sorted out, now, before someone calls in the police. When replaced make sure the inventory is corrected before it is presented to the probate office. You understand?'

'Yes, I'll attend to it immediately,' Maurice said as he nervously picked up the keys and a copy of the inventory.

'Make sure you do. Remember, Maurice, you signed the inventory as complete and it's your responsibility to have the items returned and a new one drawn up and signed, and when you see, Benoit, tell him there'll be some explaining to be done.'

Maurice, closing the door behind him, felt faint. He could see nothing but disaster ahead of him. Benoit was always going to be his downfall. What would he do? How could he retrieve the stolen items? He had no idea where they were. For all he knew, Benoit could have sold the letters on, as for the cross, the chances are he has already cashed in on it. He had a terrible sinking feeling as he took a stroll in the park adjacent to the office to try to clear his head. He had to think and think carefully and fast. Sitting in the shade of a chestnut tree as dusk descended, he began to shake with rage at the antics of Benoit, placing him in this impossible position. He had put up with his antics for years; now look where it's got him, on the verge of being sacked or even worse, being accused of something he did not do. Every time Benoit was appointed as his partner, he had an overwhelming feeling of doom and despondency.

Maurice looked at the inventory list Benoit had compiled, and it was clear it was a forgery. He managed to do a good copy of Maurice's signature that would have fooled even him at a quick glance. When Benoit had brought in the list, he carefully read it and remembered looking for the letters and the cross. He found them listed as a bundle of thirty-four personal letters. This was incorrect but what could he do, all he could do was grin and bear it and pray it does not come back to haunt him. On the original list, he read the description of the cross and thought no more about it. He did not know about the pen so had no reason to check. He authenticated and signed them and then instructed Benoit to print four copies and put the original on the Probate Manager's desk. He thought no more about until called into the office.

He sat there for some time not knowing what to do, and then suddenly it came to him. He knew what had to be done and would waste no time in doing it.

It was late when he arrived at Beniot's house, on the outskirts of Lausanne. He tried to keep calm but the thought of Beniot's stupid behaviour was getting to him. He must keep cool; he thought, otherwise all hell might break loose, but he was raging inside and scared at how intense it was.

'Who is it?' Benoit shouted, reacting to the thumping of the door. There was no reply. The door rattled again but this time with so much power, it shook on its hinges. 'For heaven's sake, who the hell is it?' Benoit shouted as he opened it. Maurice let fly with his fist catching him full in the face. Benoit fell backwards and landed heavily clutching his chin.

'You little shit-bag,' Maurice screamed at his colleague then grabbed and dragged him to his feet. 'Do you realise what you've done? We'll lose our jobs over this, you silly, selfish, irritating little sod!'

'Are you mad?' Benoit screamed as he tried to get out of Maurice's grip. 'Let me go! You'll pay for this. Mark my words you'll pay for this. No one's going to get away with assaulting me. You are done for. You hear, Kilber – done for!'

'What on earth is going on here?' Benoit's wife, Isabella shouted as she came running into the hallway. "Get off him. Have you gone mad, Maurice?'

He let go and Benoit collapsed to the floor as blood gushed from his nose. Isabella knelt down and cradled her husband's bloody face as he whined like a wimp.

'The management know about the letters, the silver cross and the pen, you idiot, you bloody idiot. They know the lot – everything! We'll be sacked over this.'

'What! They can't know. You're winding me up – I was very discreet.'

'Discreet! You don't know the meaning of it. You're not as smart as you think. The police filed a report with the Probate Office stating the cross was in Capucine's possession, like in the safe, you blundering idiot. I sent the report to head office. Arnold knows all about it and he is angry, terribly angry! If we don't return everything we are done for.'

'I don't have it,' Benoit lied, hoping to divert Maurice.

'You listen to me,' Maurice cried, as he dragged him out of Isabella's embrace, pushing him against the wall. 'Arnold says the police are not involved yet and won't be if everything is returned to the apartment. We may lose our jobs over this, but the police will not be called in and we won't be prosecuted and face prison.'

'Police! Prison!' Benoit cried as his face turned ashen. 'Who mentioned the police? There's no need for them. Shit, I can't go to prison. I won't survive,' he sniffled and began to tremble, his normal pugnacious nature evaporating by the second.

Isabella face creased with anger. She clawed at her husband. 'You bastard, you are lying little bastard – you promised me you'd give up your thieving ways – you swore to me you were going straight.' pushing Maurice aside she waylaid into her husband, slapping him continuously about the head until Maurice intervened. She fled from the hallway in a flood of tears.

'Give them to me and they'll be returned,' Maurice demanded. 'If no damage is done and with a bit of luck, we might save our jobs and you might avoid prison.'

Benoit was now in a terrible state of flux, trembling uncontrollably – The mention of prison sent him into free fall and only helped increase his fear and anxiety. He ran into the sitting room where Isabella sat and began pleading with her for forgiveness. He needed her – he needed help. She was having none of it and spat in his face then pushed him towards Maurice who grabbed him by the scruff of the neck then flung him to the floor. 'Have you got them?'

Benoit was in a stupor. He was stricken. Maurice bent down, slapped his face, and threatened damnation on him if he didn't cooperate. He soon regained his senses. 'Where are they? Where are they? We must act fast.'

Meanwhile, Isabella sat slumped in a chair, staring at her husband as he squirmed in his infamy. She had suffered years of his stupidity and lying ways and as she looked at him, it dawned on her that enough was enough, and the time had come to kick him into touch and out of her life for good.

Benoit crawled over to a cupboard and rummaged through it. He brought out a shoebox, placing it on the table. Maurice frantically opened it and gasped as he took out Capucine's letters. He counted them. There were not just two, three, or a handful as Benoit claimed, but eighteen. He felt his stomach churn.

'You stupid fool. Did you think you'd get away with it?'

Benoit said nothing as he breathed heavily and dabbed his bloody nose as he slumped against the cupboard.

Maurice held up the silver cross, sighing with relief, but he was raging. 'You sniffling little toe-rag – how many more assignments have you stolen from? How could you have left me exposed like this? Your thieving will blacken my name and that of the company if this becomes public if the police and courts are involved – where is the pen?'

'What pen?'

'Don't start getting smart. It's too late for that now. Where is it?' Maurice went to grab him again but Benoit backed-off.

'Here,' he shouted, taking the pen from his shirt pocket and throwing it at him. 'Now get lost. This is your fault. You must have grassed on me. If you'd kept your mouth shut, we wouldn't be in this mess. I will get you for this. You wait and see. Anyway, how can I blacken your name, you fool? It already is. It couldn't get any blacker if you tried. I know your little grubby secret, Maurice Kilber, every smutty little detail of it and I'll get you good and proper for this!'

Maurice knew what he was alluding to but ignored him and gathered the items together. The quicker they were returned the better – at least all the items where there. The police must not be involved, he kept repeating to himself as he prepared to leave. If they were involved, his past record will help send him down to a long stretch in prison. Once replaced and a new inventory listing produced there will be no case to answer, no reason for anyone to be suspicious.

'These will be put back to their rightful place and that will be the end of it, hopefully, but remember, Benoit, the office will be wanting an explanation from you about your attempt at selling the letters and forging the inventory listings and my signature.'

'Huh! I'll survive,' he smirked. 'But you won't, I can assure you of that.'

He looked hard at Benoit, who was still sweating like a pig and knew he was deadly serious. Maurice could see it in his eyes that a plan of action was already formulating in his petit criminal mind. If Benoit were to be sacked, one thing was certain; he would get his revenge and take Maurice down with him. He had revenge stamped all over him. It is always in the fibre of any habitual crook.

Isabella, although crestfallen at the revelations, accompanied Maurice as he left. 'I'm sorry, Maurice, I'm so sorry he's done this to you,' she said as she opened the door.

'I'm sorry for you, Isabella, that he treats you with such contempt.' He kissed her on the cheek then stepped out into the cool evening air, holding tightly to Benoit's ill-gotten gains.

It was only a few miles to Capucine's apartment but to him, it seemed like a marathon. His mind was racing with all of the events of the day and wondering what the end game would be, would he be out of work or worse still, charged and face prison. He knew what was going to happen, knew exactly what lay ahead. They will have no option but to fire him. No company wants someone like him on their books. He knew that to lose his position by a company of such a high standing he would find it hard to find another job in the auctioneering business. He had managed to work for Grimolens and Grimolens & Company for twelve years without them knowing his secret and held in high regard, but Benoit had put all this at risk by his compulsive thieving. He did not know Benoit until nominated as one of his assistants but not long into their association he indirectly referred to a scandal in a company similar to theirs where Maurice once worked. He freaked out and had to take time off work to recover his sensibilities. He was not certain whether Benoit knew the truth or not or if he was just winding him up, just probing or worse still... he knew and was turning the screw. Benoit never mentioned it again until a year later when he was in an argument with Maurice over a minor discrepancy with an inventory. Benoit said if he did not stop pestering him, he would tell the boss all he knew. From then on, he lived in fear Benoit would blabber, and his good name and reputation with the company would be gone forever.

Every time Maurice had Benoit as his assistant, he had a feeling of impending doom. He never liked him. The dislike was mutual. This was a partnership from hell... one of equal loathing.

An Unexpected Visitor

On the penultimate day of our captivity, we had an unexpected visitor. It was late in the evening. A full moon lit up the apartment as we sprawled out in different parts of the living room ready to relax for the night when we heard movement on the landing. Next moment the door opened and in walked someone casting a dark, brooding shadow over the black and white marble tiles. We ran for cover to our favourite hideaway on the top of the bookcase. Once safe we looked to see who the trespasser was. To our surprise there stood Maurice, not in his smart suit but dressed casually and carrying a box. He looked pale and drawn and only a shadow of what he was when here with that rat-faced Benoit doing the inventory.

'What's is he doing here, I wonder.'

'Don't know, Cheyenne, but he looks rather sad and distracted as though he's been given a dose of bad news. As we know, humans don't take bad news well, not well at all. We had better be on our guard.'

'Let's just wait and see what he does,' I suggested.

'It's rather late to do another inventory. Surely one is enough.'

'No, it's not that he has on his mind, Tutalou, but something more serious,' I replied as we watched him as he nervously stood on the steps leading down into the living room, holding tightly whatever it was he had in the box. He looked extremely agitated, and it was clear he had something on his mind that was bothering him as he walked down the steps with leaden feet and sat on the sofa. He was perched on its edge, clutching the box, his head low and eyes shut as though in prayer.

We were at a loss to know why he was there. Then suddenly, he slumped back and gave out an almighty sigh.

'My God!' exclaimed Cheyenne. 'He's weeping.'

'Whatever for...?'

'Don't know, Tutalou,' I replied, 'but it's something serious as men in general don't cry. It's only the rare sensitive and caring ones that do and Maurice seems to be one of them.'

Maurice sobbed as he grasped the box, the moonlight illuminating his tears as they freely flowed down his sad face.

'Whatever can it be that's making him cry and look so sad,' I said, alarmed by his demeanour.

'I have a feeling this is something to do with his last visit. I can't think of any other reason,' replied Cheyenne. 'He's very distressed.'

He took something from his pocket.

'Look! Look what he has in his hand,' gasped Tutalou.

'What is it?'

'It's my silver cross,' she gasped in disbelief. 'Why does he have it?'

'He must have taken it when he was here before when he was checking the contents of the safe,' I replied.

'But why, why would he take it, then return it? It's rather puzzling,' Tutalou mused. 'It is strange. I would have thought it would have been Benoit who had taken it, not Maurice, as he seems like an honest kind of man.'

Maurice held the chain of the cross between his thumb and index finger and held it up and a smile enveloped his sad face as it twirled around and glittered in the moonlight. He looked up at us on the bookcase and beckoned us towards him. We did and sat around his feet. He bent down and attaching the cross to Tutalou's collar. Her eyes glazed over as she felt the cross dangling from her collar once more as memories flooded back of her happy days as a kitten with Carolien and the time she followed Capucine home from Lausanne market with the cross dangling from her neck.

'What a fool Beinot is,' Maurice sighed as he gently stroked Tutalou who arched her back at his caring touch. 'What a damn fool to steal the cross and Capucine's letters, and look here, he had taken her turtle shell pen, too. What a fool he is. He has always been like that. I'm afraid there is no hope for him – he can't help it, but he'll get his comeuppance one day as thieves always do.

'I did a foolish thing in my younger days and will now have to pay dearly for it. Beinot, I'm afraid is vindictive and will have his revenge for being found out as a thief. He will reveal my secret to my employers and that will be that. I'll lose my job, but I have no regrets as all the stolen items are safely returned to their rightful places. The loss of my job is better than to continue living a lie.'

We sighed at this bad news. We were right about Benoit – from the moment we cast eyes on him we knew he was trouble. Whatever Maurice did in his past, we had no idea, but he did return the items and was for certain, a good man.

He took the cross off Tutalou's collar, returning it to the safe. He was about to close it when his eye caught sight of a piece of paper lying on the floor. He read it, to discover it was Capucine's note about the finding of Tutalou at Lausanne market and the registering of the cross with the police. If Be-

noit had only noticed the note perhaps, he would have refrained from stealing the cross knowing there was a record of
its existence and maybe he might have had the sense not to
take the other items too and this sorry state of affairs would
not have happened. Once he replaced the letters and turtle
pen to their rightful places he returned to the sofa and called
Tutalou over to him. 'Here, you keep it until they sort things
out,' he said attaching the cross once more around her neck,
'and I'll add to this note that you have it.' Tutalou lovingly
brushed her head against his leg. He placed the note in the
safe, and as he reached the door to leave, he turned and
spoke. 'I'm sorry, but you will be leaving here tomorrow. Sorry
too that I can't help you, but your future has been decided by
others and is out of my hands. Adieu...'

We looked at each other and wistfully sighed as the door
shut behind him, leaving us once more to contemplate our
fate.

A Soft Spot for a Romantic

'You're sacked!'

Benoit gritted his teeth and clenched his fists – the veins in his neck beginning to bulge as his temper rose – his eyeballs about to pop.

'Be thankful we haven't called in the police,' Christophe Arnold, the probate manager said as he tossed Benoit's employment cards and last wage packet at him. 'We have been too lenient with you in the past but this time you've overstepped the mark. You are not only a very silly man but a stupid one too. You had yourself a good job, a job reluctantly given to you but done so because of our regard for your late father, a well-respected member of this firm and you, Benoit, you haven't only let him down but yourself and recklessly thrown away a good job, and, as it seems, your marriage and your long-suffering wife.'

Beniot's nostrils flared at the mention of his wife who had finally found the courage to give him his marching orders. She had put up with him and his nonsense over many years but finally had enough of his wayward ways.

'I don't know what possesses you at times,' Arnold continued. 'You're an authority of 18th-century furniture but instead of using it to your advantage to make honest money and enhance your reputation, you decide crime a more lucrative avenue. You must be mad.'

'It's that Kilber, who blabbered, isn't it. Well, he won't get away with it.'

'Be careful what you're saying,' the manager cautioned, stopping Benoit in full flow. 'Best to keep your mouth shut and your temper even. You've done enough damage; cut your losses, take your cards and get out of my sight and be thankful you're not facing court proceedings and prison.'

'But it's unfair! You sack me as a thief, yet you have another on your staff, one who, as well as being a thief, is a liar. You are very selective when it comes to your workforce and your standard of ethics.'

'Again, Benoit, be careful what you are saying. Just do as I say, for the first time in your life, be sensible, take good advice, pick up your cards and wages and leave.'

'I'll have my say come what may; I will. I'll have my revenge,' he barked as he thrust his fist into the desk.

Arnold sighed. 'Will you now? Just the thing I'd expect you to say.'

'You'll be grateful to me after what I have to say. No real damage was done when I took those items. I have returned them, yet you keep a self-confessed thief as a trusted employee and sack me. I know everything about him – I know his dirty little secret.'

The manager gave a half-smile. 'You do? Well, tell me – this big secret. What is it? Who is this thief you're on about? You have me curious. Out with it.'

This was Benoit big moment. Revenge is always sweet to some, and he was one of them. He was intent on bringing Maurice down and this was his big moment to put the knife in.

'Maurice Kilber, your so-called 'excellent' employee, that high principled twat you think is so good – so honest, so upstanding, well, he was sacked in Zurich for embezzlement, twelve years ago when he worked for Zurich and Bern Finance,' he said spitting it out with venom. 'He's a bigger thief than I am. I'm just a novice compared with him. At least I accept what I am, unlike that deceiving sod.'

The manager burst out laughing, as he twirled his pen around his fingers.

The manager's response took Benoit by surprise.

'If you don't believe me, check it out yourself. He pulled the wool over your eyes when you interviewed him for the position – he lied through his teeth. He's as much a thief as I am. The difference between us, I'm a thief telling the truth and he's one, lying.'

The manager gave a sardonic smile. 'You are telling me something I already know as do the other directors of Grimolens and it's not quite as you imagine, you silly, silly, foolish man.'

Benoit's mouth fell open. He was speechless, sweating profusely and shaking with rage. 'What!'

'You are not in the same league as Maurice. You are miles apart in every possible way. He is worth a million of you. Yes, he was sacked, as you say, but he didn't steal anything, you fool. You have only half of the story. It was the woman he loved who was responsible, not Maurice. He sacrificed his job for her by taking the blame for the theft.'

'Rubbish!' Benoit screamed.

'It's true. Not many men would do that. Any man capable of doing so for love, I would trust with my life, unlike you, who I would never trust. Now, do the decent thing, take your cards and payment and leave and do not show your face anywhere near this company or its staff again.'

Benoit was fuming. 'I don't believe you and don't give me that mushy, lovey-dovey stuff. He lied to you, didn't he, to get the job?' he said as he wiped his sodden face.

'No, he didn't. At the interview, he was upfront and said he worked for a company in Zurich and had to leave because of a personal issue. He preferred not to talk about it. Even though he was unable to produce a current reference, I contacted the company in Zurich. His honesty impressed me. There is a word for you, Benoit – honesty. You should try it sometime.'

Benoit baulked at the remark.

'I soon discovered the truth behind his sacking and it's not as you thought. His company discovered the truth a few weeks after they sacked him. His girlfriend was the real culprit. The only thing you have right, Maurice did once work for a finance company in Zurich where he met Ethel Doriss. The management was threatening holy murder unless the culprit owned up and the monies returned. Ethel, who was very much a trusted employee, confessed to Maurice she had stolen the money and had done so on a regular basis over a few years. Why she did it, he could not understand as she came from a well-heeled family. He was crestfallen and at a loss to know what to do or say. He loved her and feared he'd lose her if she were found out and prosecuted.'

'It's not true, it's not true,' Benoit violently interrupted, his fists tightly clenched with rage. 'You are trying to protect him, that's what this is all about... protection! I don't believe a word of it.'

'I don't care if you don't – I'm giving you the facts. Yes, Maurice did a foolish thing for love, a very foolish thing but an honourable one all the same – he owned up that he was the culprit and after finding how much was unaccounted for, withdrew the amount from his bank and gave it to the company along with a grovelling apology. They suspended him for a week to allow them to make their decision whether to have him prosecuted or not. They did not, they sacked him instead. He lost not just his well-paid job but Ethel too. His good deed for love only served to show that he was a man with little sense – that he let his heart rule his head. Maurice thought his job was a worthwhile sacrifice for the sake of love but love at times can be a foolish thing as he, unfortunately, found out to his cost. He left Zurich immediately after she ended their relationship. It was a sad period in his life but your behaviour, Benoit, brought it vividly back to life. Ethel was subsequently convicted and showed no remorse for her crime, nor why she allowed Maurice to take the blame. He was well rid of her as we are of you. You and Ethel are of the same vein of villainy.

'Not long after being sacked and rejected by Ethel, he moved to Geneva to live. I interviewed him for the position not long after. Later, after discovering the truth, we immediately hired him against the wishes of his old company who wanted to reinstate him but being the wise man Maurice is; he decided to sign for us. We never did reveal to him that we knew the truth – he still doesn't. Their loss was our gain. The moral of this, Benoit, is that love and honesty saved Maurice and your lack of it and other human necessities has been the ruination of you. Now, for once in your life, do the decent thing and just go.'

Benoit looked crestfallen. He didn't pick up his cards or wages, just turned and left and never looked back and vanished into obscurity.

Footsteps of Fate

It was Friday; the day Maurice said our fate would be sealed – the day Benoit said we'd be disposed of, when we would leave our home for good. The day had been uneventful, and we thought they were mistaken until that evening when heavy ponderous footsteps made their way up the marble staircase to the apartment. As they neared the door, we could hear the wrangling of keys. I looked at my two pals and froze on the spot. Was this it? Was this the day, the day of reckoning? We were terrified as the heavy footsteps came nearer. Was this the end for us – was Camille, right? Was that nasty, malicious gossip right after all – Were we done for – doomed to exter- mination at the end of a syringe or worse still, our necks wrung, just for being kind and caring? Had Capucine left us to a horrible fate, as horrible as hers – not our lovely Capucine – surely not? This can't be happening – this is not how she would have wanted our lives to end. She adored and loved us. She would never leave us to the whims of others – she must have provided for our care, she must have.

The key rattled in the lock. We clung together, our hearts beating fast as the key rattled again and then finally turned the lock. We didn't dash to our safe place on the bookcase this time but slumped to the floor, covering our eyes and let- ting out mournful cries as we resigned ourselves to our fate. The door creaked as it slowly opened. I looked up and a tall man, wearing a black beret and a heavy grey overcoat, with a ruddy face and bitty moustache, stepped into the foyer, carry- ing a large leather bag with big gold lettering on it, spelling out the initials: K.I. He looked mean and was unshaven which gave him a sinister appearance. He cast his eyes about the room and catching sight of Capucine's photo on the oak table, gently touched it and stood for a moment as though in prayer. He turned and caught sight of us, and his eyes gleefully widened.

'Here they are! I'll take care of them,' the man said in a deep baritone voice to the person standing outside the door who seemed reluctant to enter. 'Let's get this over with as soon as possible. The quicker we get them out of here to another world the better. It's cruel, very cruel to have left them so long to suffer in this state.'

Another world, I thought. Oh no, this is it! Cheyenne was crying with Tutalou gulping for air.

'They have suffered enough. Why we allowed this to drag on, I don't know. We should have ended it a long time ago,' he continued. 'They should have been put out of their misery earlier. It's cruel, the way they have been left not knowing what is to become of them. It is over for them now. It's no good prolonging their agony; it's time for them to go.'

Go! We nervously gulped at the word.

'They are entitled to closure, to be relieved of their burden. We'll take good care of them, won't we? We'll take *very* good care of them. Let's get this over with as quickly as we can without any unnecessary fuss. Let's take them from their home and make it as painless as possible.'

'*Painless*!' I cried as the other two shook with fear. I had a vision of a syringe. We snuggled up to each other, closing our eyes, waiting in terror as the man walked towards us, his

280

highly polished shoes squeaking as they neared us. A cold shiver went through me as the shoes came to a sudden halt.

He towered over us. We could hear his heavy breathing as he put down the bag with a thud. I nervously looked up. 'I've got them!' the man announced, his shadow enveloping us.

The bag, what was in the bag – the syringe – oblivion? Were we to be carried out in it after he did his dirty deed? It was big enough to carry the three of us.

The other two didn't dare look up, just hoping he'd go away. We began to cry as we clung to each other. We didn't have the will to fight. He stood quietly over us for what seemed like an eternity, the silence suddenly broken by a woman's voice.

'Oh, my darlings – my poor, poor darlings,' a voice cried.

Untangling ourselves, we raised our heads to the familiar voice. 'Could it be true?' cried Cheyenne. We looked at each other in surprise. 'It can't be,' I cried, but it was. There she was. It was Marcia, materialising before our eyes. She came running towards us with tears streaming down her round face as she shook with emotion and her arms wide open to welcome us.

'Oh, here you are, my poor little darlings. Come here! Come here!'

We sprang to our feet, ran towards her, and leapt into her arms. She hugged and tenderly ruffled our coats as we licked her face and nuzzled up to her. To be once more in her warm embrace was sheer heaven.

'Did you think I'd forgotten you, my little ones,' she cried as she sat down on the sofa with us clinging onto her for dear life, afraid of letting go in case she vanished again.

'I'm sorry, I'm so sorry to have left you so long. How terrible it must have been. You must have thought I had deserted you. But I'm here now.'

The relief, oh the relief of it all – saved at last. This unexpected turnabout was overwhelming. No destruction, no injection, no incineration and no being *cast to the wind*, only liberation in the arms of Marcia, our only direct link with our lost Capucine. We were saved – saved at last.

'I'll get their bits and pieces – then we'll be off,' the man said as he gave Marcia a hug.

'Well, my darlings, this is Karl, my other half. You have never met before. He doesn't look it but he's as cute as they come, and you'll love him. We have come to take you home with us. I promised Capucine if anything were to happen to her, I would take care of you and that is exactly what I am doing. Sorry, it has taken so long but I became very ill after hearing the terrible news. I thought I would die from the shock of it, but I am feeling better now. I hadn't forgotten you. I knew Lucie was looking after you, as Inspector Lewee told me when he visited me in hospital. Lucie kept me well informed about you. She never stops talking about you. I think she has fallen for you scallywags.

'Oh, our lovely Capucine – she will always be with us. I hope she has found peace at last... that her soul is at rest. She will never be out of our thoughts. I see her in my mind's eye all the time, her smile and her beautiful face.' She wiped a tear away. 'You are coming home with us to start a new life, and we will take our memories of her with us. Isn't that so, Karl?'

'Yes, my dear – we have a cosy home waiting for them. It may not be as grand as this pad, but they will enjoy our happy lived-in home with all its nooks and crannies.' He stroked us. He was a large man, but his touch was soft. 'We have a garden too, so you will have the time of your lives.'

'Look what I have for you,' she said digging enthusiastically into her pocket. Out came a bag of 'Kitty Kavier'. 'Here,' she said giving each of us a tasty treat then emptied the bag on to the floor. They sat together on the sofa watching us as we scoffed down every one of them.

'What is this?' cried Marcia, as she noticed the silver cross around Tutalou's neck. 'Oh my God, here it is. You won't believe the consternation this has caused. Look, Karl, here is the missing cross everyone has been up in arms over. Oh my God, everyone thought it stolen. The owner has turned up too, would you believe, after all of these years. She will be delighted to have it returned. They were mystified as to where it had gone and here it is, safe and sound and hanging around your neck.'

Karl knelt to examine it. 'Umm... what a lucky cat you are to have this jewel dangling from your neck. Don't go losing it again.'

'I think we ought to leave it in the safe.' Marcia said. Tutalou sighed as she removed the cross for the last time.

Karl gathered up our bits and pieces. There was quite a lot: three porcelain eating bowls, balls, rag dolls and three colourful rugs along with our comfort blankets. As he gathered our things together, Marcia cast her eyes about the apartment she knew every corner of and sighed. She could feel the tears whelming up again. It had good memories even if some of them tinged with sadness, especially the agony of Capucine's illness, her traumas and the many tears shed. She looked towards the balcony doors and the tears flowed. Her heart was breaking at the thought of Capucine's final moments. She would miss her beautiful and tortured friend and would love her forever. She wiped her eyes as she continued looking towards the balcony.

Karl came into the room with his bag full and other soft toys in his arms and noticed Marcia sobbing. He put them down and gave her a tender hug. 'Now, now, my love – let it out – let it out.' We rubbed ourselves against her legs, letting her know we shared her sorrow, shared the pain of her loss, of our loss. Karl guided her to Capucine's wicker chair on the balcony and she breathed in the lavender that was so much part of Capucine's life. Karl hugged her, kissing her head as she continued to cry. We left them together then retreated to the rug in front of the hearth and sat there for the very last time.

I gave Tutalou a tug. 'Didn't I tell you Camille was a no-good gossip, full of devilment and resentment? She had us frantic with worry with her nasty insinuations. How could we have doubted Capucine? How could we ever have thought she'd abandoned us to a horrible fate? Goes to show you should never listen to gossips. They are nothing more than vexatious souls, hell-bent on stirring it and causing as much upset and damage as possible. Always best to avoid their likes.'

'Do you think she's taking some kind of pleasure seeing us in such a state?' asked Cheyenne.

'Certainly... that's how gossips get their kicks. They are sad souls and need pitied.'

Karl and Marcia returned and made ready to depart. Marcia had taken a sprig of lavender and pinned it in her hair.

She called us over. It was time to go, time to leave our cosy home forever. We reached the threshold of the apartment then turned for one last look at Capucine's home... our home, her sanctuary, so full of memories, so full of love. We looked sadly at each other.

'Ah,' I sighed, 'if only humans could show love and understanding of Capucine's illness as we have. If only they could show compassion to those in mental pain, those near the edge, how better life would be. If only they could ease their pain and try to understand the agony they go through, how much more civilised this world would be? Alas, they are only human and don't have the understanding or the caring faculty we felines are blessed with.'

'How right you are, Océane,' Cheyenne sighed. 'But human's, unlike us felines are flawed and will always remain so, and most are incapable of caring for or understanding the pain of the mentally ill. That's the sad reality of the human condition.'

'Indeed,' Tutalou agreed. 'But there is some hope for them after all because there will always be the exceptions to the rule, like, Audrey, Cécile, Dirk, Philippe and Marcia. They showed so much love for Capucine and understood her condition.'

As Marcia closed the door for the last time, she leant her head against it and whispered a prayer. Karl laid his hand on her shoulder in solidarity. We were at her feet as we said a final farewell to our well-loved home.

As we turned to leave, Lucie was standing there in a flood of tears. She ran into Marcia's arms. They didn't say anything but just held onto each other. Lucie then picked each of us up in turn and tenderly kissed us.

'Goodbye my lovely ones,' she said as she waved us goodbye.

Turning, we left the apartment then skipped down the marble staircase and out into the open air. We didn't look back, but ahead, and into the sunset of our lives.

Tutalou's Cross

Maurice Kilder was a little nervous as he waited for his visitor at his Lausanne office. He had sent her letters about the cross and how it came to be in the possession of Capucine and how the legal formalities had to be gone through before she could have it returned. Many more letters and phone calls passed between them before all the legal necessities were completed. The letters soon turned from the formal to a more relaxed tone as did the many phone calls. It was time to meet.

The secretary guided the guest towards the office, pushing open the large oak panelled doors.

'Mademoiselle Junas,' the secretary announced as Carolien walked into the room.

Maurice stood looking at the revelation before him. She was not what he expected. For some reason he had an image of her as an older looking woman but before him was a relatively young and tall woman dressed in a saffron two-piece suit with long blonde hair that hung loosely over her shoulders. She wore little makeup on her fresh- looking oval face. He noticed she wore no rings on her long sleek fingers or any jewellery apart from small stud gold earrings.

'Bonjour, Carolien, how pleased to meet you at last,' he nervously said as he offered her his hand.

She looked at him with her light blue eyes and something about him appealed to her as they shook hands. He seemed rather familiar as though they had met before. Although she had talked to him on the phone many times, physically seeing him made her heart skip a beat.

'You too – it is a pleasure,' she replied as she held his hand tightly.

'Take a seat,' he nervously said as he let go of her hand but with his eyes well and truly fixed on her.

'I'm delighted to finally meet you, Maurice. I have looked forward to this day since you first contacted me. You are just as I imagined and perhaps a little more.'

Maurice smiled and after some small talk took out a petite red box from his pocket and handed it to her. She looked at it then at Maurice and for a fleeting moment, he thought she would not open it. At the sight of the cross, she was overwhelmed. Her eyes misted over as she touched it. She sat looking at it, her mind filled with memories of her family and the lost love that cause her so much sorrow. She kissed it then held it up to the bright light streaming through the windows. As it twirled around and sparkled in all its splendour, she let her tears flow freely.

'Oh Tutalou,' she sighed.

He smiled as he watched her and at the same time offered her a tissue.

'Thank you,' she said and wiped her eyes.

'It is beautiful.'

'Yes indeed. You will not believe how precious this is. It has been so much part of my life, my family's life. It reminds me of special people, my grandmother, and my mother who both owned it at some time. I, in turn, would have liked it for my daughter for her 21st but sadly, time is running out for me in that department. Isn't it strange how life turns?'

'Indeed.'

'I honestly believed I had lost it forever and out of a sad and tragic event, I'm reunited with it. I remember the day Capucine died and how sad I was at her tragic loss but how was I to know that from that dreadful news would bring happiness back into my life. Did you ever meet her?'

'No, but I wish I had. I knew a lot about her but as I carried out the inventory of her apartment and cataloguing her property, I got to know her better. Just being in her apartment and handling her personal things I felt her presence and also the sadness in her life.'

'And Tutalou, my Juliette.'

'Yes, she and her two pals were there too keeping a wary eye on my partner and me as we carried out the inventory.'

'How touching Capucine called her Tutalou.'

'Do you want to meet her? She and her pals are now cared for by Capucine's housekeeper, Marcia d'Orsay.'

'No, no. That would be unfair. You tell me she is well and in a new home with her pals. That is good enough for me – maybe that is how it should be, how it's meant to be. I have her pedigree papers and would be obliged if you can give them to Marcia.' She took out an envelope, handing it to Maurice. He looked through the papers and smiled.

'You know, Carolien, Marcia informed me Capucine often wondered where Tutalou came from and what kind of pedigree she had as she was certain she was a feline of the highest breed and here it is, the evidence in black and white. What a pity she never knew the truth about Tutalou.'

'Yes, a highly prized one. It is about the only good thing my ex- boyfriend did was buying her.'

After she signed all of the legal documents and was ready to leave, she asked Maurice if he would be kind enough to fasten the cross around her neck for her. He obliged. As he held it to her neck, her perfume filled his senses. He felt an inner beauty radiating from her, a feeling he had never experienced before. He had kept his distance from women since his humiliation at the hands of Ethel, but Carolien had awoken his sleeping passion.

'It feels so good to wear it once more.'

'Yes, it's back where it rightfully belongs and looks good, too.'

She smiled at his kind words as she touched the cross. 'Thank you, Maurice, for all you have done. Having this returned to me, you have brought happiness back into my life. Thank you.'

'My pleasure.'

'Goodbye,' she said as they shook hands.

'Goodbye, Carolien.'

She turned to leave but only managed a few steps then stopped and turned towards him. 'Maurice, are your free this evening?'

'Yes,' he stuttered, rather taken aback by the question.

'I'll be staying in Lausanne for a few days. It is a long time since I was here and intend to enjoy the pleasures of this fine city. I would like to take you for a meal, if you don't mind, as a thank you for your help.'

His heart skipped a beat. 'I don't need thanks. I was only doing my job.'

'Then, your company will do.'

'How can I say no?'

'You can't,' she smiled. 'Then, it's a date.'

'Indeed,' he said as his eyes sparkled at the expectation.

'I'm staying at the Hotel de la Paix – How about eight?'

'That will be fine.'

'Goodbye until then, Maurice,' she said, leaving him standing mesmerized by her departing wink.

The Final Farewell

Our new home with Marcia and Karl has been a happy one, full of love and devotion and lots of fun with special visits by Lucie and on occasions from Inspector Lewee to see how we were getting along.

Only three years after we lost Capucine, we suffered another loss, when news came that her beautiful soul mate Audrey had died of cancer. We cried for days, and Marcia was inconsolable. Audrey was such a caring and loving friend to Capucine.

Tutalou was the first to pass away. It was sudden, but thankfully, she didn't suffer. She enjoyed five years in her new home and the beautiful Cheyenne quietly passed away not too long afterwards. She survived much longer than anyone thought she would after her operations as a kitten. They were cremated and their ashes cast to the wind over Lake Geneva, just as Capucine had been and joined her in the celestial world. I miss them terribly as I do Capucine. I'm now on my own but comforted by all the happy memories of our time together and the loving care I receive from Marcia and Karl.

I'm very frail now, and to conclude this tale I have to add this chapter I wished I never had to recall, but it has to be told, to complete the story of Capucine and her Three Feline Philosophers.

The day of her departure was a fine and sunny one. She arose at six, her normal time, opened the widows wide as she did every day, winter or summer, breathing in the fresh lake air, then greeted each of us by name. I was always first, then

Tutalou and finally Cheyenne, in the order we arrived in her life. It was the same procedure as she fed and watered us. She called several friends, including Audrey who was in Miami as part of her *Anne Frank Tour* and Cécile, who she had not seen since the Christmas Fair, inviting her for dinner that evening. We had been mulling around her feet as she talked on the phone, meowing for our meal, and generally making a nuisance of ourselves. She told us to behave, or she would not feed us. Finally, she relented, and we hungrily tucked into our meal. We ate away as she sat by the window sipping an espresso and looking out over the lake. She was in a very relaxed state of mind, calmer than we had seen her for a long time, and we looked forward to a relaxing day.

She read the newspapers from cover to cover, often laughing or sniggering as she scanned the political columns. One of her pleasures was political satire. She adored it, always looking at politicians with a jaundiced and cynical eye and had little patience with them and enjoyed any article that ridiculed or lampooned them. In the past when she was obliged to attend receptions, politicians always seemed to be hovering around, trying to get a photo-shoot opportunity with her. She hated being used and no way would she be by the likes of dreary and dishonest politicians which she held in utter contempt, so she declined any further invitations.

Then, after a good read of the papers, it was down to looking at her horoscope and then her favourite pastime, doing and completing the crosswords. She was very adept at them or any mind-stretching solutions, always one to keep her grey cells stimulated and in peak condition.

After eating every morsel of our food, we retired to the so-fa for our morning stretch and snooze. The turning on of the hi-fi awoke us from our slumber and her favourite classical piece, *Ashokan Farewell* filled the air. She discovered this haunting piece of music a few years back when in the US. When she was thinking about her mother, she would often play it.

She sat in the wicker chair reading for the rest of the morning then returned to the kitchen and made a snack. Lat-er, I heard the music being repeated and woke the others. Suddenly, Capucine let out a piercing cry that echoed throughout the apartment and through the open window, traumatising the brightness of the day. We sprang out of our stupor and saw her run towards the balcony, clutching her hair, her eyes ablaze and shaking violently. We dashed after her. She turned and looked at us with wild, staring eyes; then struggled to climb onto the balcony rail. She stood looking out over the lake. We pleadingly meowed at her to get down. 'Why, why me, why me, dear God, why me?' she cried out re-peatedly as she clung onto the balcony post. 'Dear God, why must I suffer? Help me! Help me! Free me, free me from my pain – free me from this darkness in my life.' For a few mo-ments, there was silence, and we thought she had calmed down enough to come back from the edge, but once more, she cried out aloud, cried out to God, this time cursing Him, cursing her fate. She was violently shaking and sobbing un-controllably, literally falling apart mentally and physically be-fore our eyes. Suddenly, she jumped down and ran into the apartment clutching her hair, again screaming at God to set her free. He didn't hear her. We ran after her, but she was out of control. We could do nothing. She slumped to the floor and rolled around in agony then coiled up in the foetal position, crying for her mother to rescue her. 'Mamma, Mamma, take me home,' she whispered, 'Mamma, Mamma, help me, help me. Take me home, Mamma.' We ran to her aid, but she didn't see us as she was blinded by pain. Cheyenne tried to touch her toes with Tutalou reaching out her paw towards her head hoping their touch might calm her down, but she violently threw her arms about scattering us in the process. She staggered to her feet and once more ran to the balcony and climbed the rail. This time there was no Audrey or Inspector Lewee to save her, just us, her devoted cats and we could do little. We tried with our plaintive cries to coax her down again and get her to sit in her wicker chair and breathe in the lavender that always calmed her down, but it was all in vain. We tried once more to jump onto the rail to be with her, but she pushed us away with her foot. We stretched up to her, hoping our pleas would get her to see sense and come down. She ignored us, then turned around and faced the apartment, clinging tightly to the balcony post. On her previous attempts, she stood facing the lake, threatening to jump but never did. She looked at us as the tears streamed down her cheeks. We could see the pain in her sad eyes, the fear and trepidation and feel her abject loneliness. Her face was contorted, ashen and haunted. Her shaking suddenly ceased, and calm descended on her, the haunting look disappeared, and softness returned to her face. She let go of the pole and made her way to the centre of the rail. She looked down at us and then with her arms outstretched, cast her eyes to the heavens and cried 'Mamma, Mamma,' then threw herself backwards into the abyss. Our hearts stopped. For a moment, the only sound was the dying strains of a violin, and then the cries from below as Capucine crashed to the ground. Cheyenne leapt onto the rail and looking down gave out an agonizing cry. Tutalou and I followed. We looked in horror at the scene below. Huddling together, we cried out as the horrible reality hit us. Capucine was gone. This time she did what she always threatened. After years of eating away at her soul, ravishing and tearing it apart, the demon within finally got its deadly way, robbing another innocent soul of the beauty of life. We had lost our lovely Capucine, the beauty of Lausanne, in a moment of absolute madness.

***

As I live out my final days I see her beautiful face before me, her sparkling eyes light up the darkness that is now slowly descending. Her smile will see me through to the end of my days when I will join her, Tutalou and Cheyenne as I'm cast to the wind and follow them to the other side of Time, where there will be no grief, no mental pain, sorrow, or loneliness, only peace, tranquillity of the mind and the union of kindred spirits.

And so, they cast her to the wind
This beauty of Lausanne.
Out on the lake
They carried her urn
On board the Daughter of Toulon.
The sun was high
The wind set fair
As friends gathered to say adieu,
To one who suffered her mortal coil
In the depths of mental pain.
A violin played Ashokan Farewell
As they cast her to the wind
Her ashes hovering above the lake
In a dance of heavenly grace.
On the crest of a breeze, her ashes rose
Above the Daughter of Toulon
And way above the mountain tops
Till they kissed the face of God –
And there, to stardust made.
The sparkling form lit up the sphere
As another soul set free,
Then the Breath of God
Blew them earthward bound
On a mission of relief,
To seek out other souls in pain
And rest upon their brows
To let them know
They are not alone
In their world of mental pain.

If one precious speck
Upon on a worried brow
Can ease that soul in pain,
Pray, let this be the legacy,
Of the lovely Capucine –
The beauty of Lausanne.

www.ingramcontent.com/pod-product-compliance
Lightning Source LLC
Chambersburg PA
CBHW062122170626
46813CB00002B/546